Jet B

Sherryl D. Hancock

VULPINE
PRESS

Copyright © Sherryl D. Hancock 2016

All rights reserved. No part of this publication may be reproduced, stored in or introduced into a retrieval system or transmitted in any form or by any means, electronic, mechanical, photocopying, recording or otherwise without prior written permission from the publisher.

This is a work of fiction. Names, characters, places and incidents are either the product of the author's imagination or are used fictitiously, and any resemblance to any person or persons, living or dead, events or locales is entirely coincidental.

Originally self-published by Sherryl D. Hancock in 2017

Published by Vulpine Press in the United Kingdom in 2017

ISBN 978-1-910780-42-8

Cover by Armend Meha

Cover photo credit: Tirzah D. Hancock

www.vulpine-press.com

Acknowledgements

The covers to these novels are for the most part arranged by me and my wife Tirzah. We choose things that we feel represents the story I've written and try to arrange them in a fashion befitting the story as well. We hope you like them!

For our fighting men and women who not only put their lives on the line, but their hearts and souls out there too. Thank you for everything you do for this country and others as well!

Chapter 1

"This is Jet," answered a rich mellifluous voice, one Ashley remembered well.

"Jet, hi," Ashley said, suddenly feeling tongue tied. "Um, I don't know if you remember me… Ashley Simm… Foster, from Meadowdale High School…"

"I remember you," Jet said, smiling at her end of the line. "Or I wouldn't have given you my number to call."

"Oh," Ashley said, feeling dumb suddenly.

The Facebook page Ashely had found had the name "Jet Blue" and at first Ashley Simmons hadn't been sure that was right. The profile picture wasn't much more help; it was a picture of a jet. She was looking for Jet Mathews to invite her to the fifteen year high school reunion for Meadowdale High School. At least that's what she was telling herself.

The truth was she remembered Jet Mathews very fondly. Jet had been extremely popular in high school. So much so that even after almost thirteen years, the people on the reunion committee had basically told her that if Jet Mathews didn't plan to come to the reunion this time, they might as well cancel it. Ashely thought that was probably a bit over the top, but all the same, she had a definite desire to get ahold of this elusive high school friend.

In high school, Jet had been both popular and an over-achiever. She'd graduated at the top of their class, although she'd refused to be a valedictorian. That had not been Jet's style. A natural 'bad girl,' Jet was constantly in trouble, but always found her way out of it, usually using her charm and wit. Many of the teachers in the school remembered Jet fondly; others had always been flabbergasted by her antics. Jet was a natural student, and that made teachers crave the opportunity to fill her head with their particular area of expertise. Sometimes that happened, other times it didn't. She did exactly what she wanted to, when she wanted to and not a thing more. It was something Ashley remembered well.

Finally, Ashley had decided to go ahead and send a message to this Jet Blue person to see if it might be that Jet. She'd been through this a bunch of times already; it was amazing how many people were named "Jet" on Facebook. Ashley had hoped it would be easier to find her, but she persevered all the same.

She'd received a message back a few days later saying, "Yes, this is Jet Mathews, call me," with her phone number.

Ashley had picked up the phone immediately, but now that she was on the line with Jet, she was feeling like she was back in high school again. The dumpy fat girl everyone picked on, everyone but Jet Mathews. Ashley steeled herself, bound and determined to talk to this woman.

"Ash?" Jet queried from her end, taking a cigarette out of her pack and lighting the end.

"Still here, sorry," Ashley said, remembering that Jet had always shortened everyone's name, unless she didn't like you.

"So, to what do I owe this honor?" Jet asked then, her tone warm.

Ashley smiled; Jet hadn't changed much, always knowing what to say and when to say it.

"Well, ostensibly I contacted you about the fifteen year reunion coming up in about a year and a half…"

"However?" Jet replied, grinning.

"Well, I admit, I'd love to catch up with you too," Ashley said.

"Alright…" Jet said, moving to settle more comfortably against the wall she was leaning against.

Jet was sitting on the patio of the building where she worked, usually used as a smoking area. Jet was seated on a bench, leaning against a wall, her legs stretched out in front of her and crossed at the ankles.

"So, how have you been?" Ashley asked.

"I've been alright," Jet said. "You?"

"Oh, I'm good," Ashley said, smiling. "Got my dream job, married, house, no kids."

"So, you're writing then?" Jet asked.

Ashley widened her eyes on her end of the line. "You remembered that I write?"

Jet chuckled. "I remember things, yeah," she said, her tone friendly.

"Wow," Ashley said, shaking her head. "Where are you living these days?"

"Down in LA," Jet said. "I see you're still in Lynnwood."

"How?" Ashley asked, surprised.

"The area code you're calling from."

"Oh, yeah, duh!" Ashley said, shaking her head. Was there no end to how stupid she could sound on this phone call? "So, LA huh? I'm actually headed down there in a couple of weeks to do a story, I'd love to see you if you have time."

"Sure," Jet said, her smile evident in her voice. "Just let me know when you'll be here, I'll even pick you up if you need a ride."

"Wow, that would be great!" Ashley said. "I've never gotten very good at driving in crazy traffic."

"Well, LA's about as crazy as it gets."

"Well, great, I'll send you the details." Ashley smiled again. "It was good talking to you."

"You too," Jet said. "I'll see you soon."

"Okay."

After she hung up the phone, Ashley rolled her eyes, she wasn't sure she could pull off being cool in front of Jet Mathews. It had been thirteen years and a lot of gym hours and yet Jet still made her feel silly. How was that possible?

It was the high school senior camping trip; two weeks at Cama State Beach on Camano Island in the Saratoga Passage. Ashley had dreaded it since she'd heard about it sophomore year. She'd hoped to talk her parents out of making her go, but that hadn't happened. Two weeks with people who treated her like dirt, so much fun... NOT!

No sooner had the bus dropped them off, than the insults had started. "Did you pack extra food?" "At least the bears'll eat you first!" Then someone 'accidentally' tripped her up. They are so original, Ashley thought to herself as she got up.

Then there was a hand out to her, she looked up and saw Jet Mathews standing in front of her, with her hand extended to help her up. Jet had never been mean to her, she'd smiled at her a few times, never really saying anything, but at least being human. Jet waited patiently with her hand out while Ashley wiped her hand off on her jeans, then reached out to her. She felt how strong the deceptively lean girl was, when she was easily pulled to her feet.

"You okay?" Jet asked, leaning down to brush off the dirt on the leg of Ashley's jeans.

"I'm," Ashley stammered, "yes, I'm okay." She nodded, her eyes downcast, waiting for the insult that was sure to come.

"Good," Jet said, nodding.

Jet surprised her then, by taking her arm companionably. "Let's go find out where we're stuck for this trip, huh?" she said, grinning, her light green eyes sparkling in amusement.

"Oh, okay…" Ashley stammered, not sure why Jet Mathews was being so nice to her. Every bad eighties movie she'd ever seen said there'd be some kind of crazy Carrie moment any time now.

Jet walked her over to where they were posting the cabin assignments, looking around to pinpoint where the person was who'd tripped Ashley. When Jet's eyes met the other girl's, she narrowed hers, shaking her head slightly. The girl's eyes widened, then she looked away.

"Okay," Jet said, reaching up to run her finger down the list of names. "Ash, it looks like you're in B six… and look at that, so am I…" she said, grinning.

Ashley saw that the assignment clearly said B five next to Jet Mathews' name. As Ashley watched, Jet pulled out a black pen, took the cap off with her teeth and changed the five to a six deftly. Then she scanned the list and changed someone who was supposed to be in B six to B five. Turning, Jet's eyes met Ashley's and she'd quirked a grin, giving her a cavalier wink.

"Let's go get our stuff," Jet said, once again taking Ashley's arm and steering her over to where the bags had been left.

"Why…" Ashley stammered. "Why did you do that?" she asked, needing to know.

Jet looked at her for a long minute, then shrugged. "I don't know what you're talking about."

Ashley stared at her openmouthed, blinking a couple of times. Jet handed Ashley the small pink case her mother had given her to use as an overnight bag, and then picked up the other green larger suitcase. Ashley reached for that suitcase.

"I got it," Jet said, grinning. "You pack light."

Ashley noted that Jet had a black leather duffle that looked like it cost a fortune slung over her shoulder. Apparently Jet packed even lighter. Jet nodded toward the cabins.

"Lead the way, Ash," Jet told her, smiling.

It was surreal to Ashley that this girl was being so nice to her. It quickly influenced the way the rest of the group treated her during those two weeks. Jet never had to say a word to anyone, and if she did, she never did it within earshot of Ashley. People were both afraid and in awe of Jet Mathews. It was a lethal combination, especially in high school.

Sitting in her tiny office in Seattle, Ashley remembered that day at camp, and the days that followed. She'd never forgotten what Jet Mathews had done for her on that trip. It had made a world of difference in the last six months of her high school career. Even after they all got back to school, people didn't pick on her anymore. Many of them simply left her alone, others actually talked to her. She'd even made a few friends before she graduated. Jet had continued to say hi to her in the hallways, and would randomly come sit next to her on the lawn at lunchtimes. It was like she was keeping her influence around her, at least that's how Ashley had always seen it. Yes, she wanted to see Jet Mathews. If nothing else but to thank her for being the person she was in high school. Ashley knew it was stupid, but it was the rounding out of her journey.

Jet and Ashley communicated a few times via Facebook messenger before Ashley's trip to LA. Ashley found that Jet had a really great sense of humor. They hadn't talked about anything important, but Ashley always found herself laughing at many points in the conversation. It was easy to see why Jet had been so popular. She had a way of communicating that always had a bit of an edge to it, but never to the point of being rude, or nasty, always more ironic and funny. Ashley had also realized why Jet had been at the top of their class; Jet Mathews was very smart.

To her surprise, Jet had offered to let Ashley stay with her while she was in Los Angles during one of their messenger conversations.

You know, you could stay with me if you want to – Jet

I wouldn't want to be a pain, you're already picking me up at the airport, right? – Ash

Are you asking me if I'm picking you up? – Jet

I'm confirming that you're still picking me up, brat – Ash

I am still picking you up, yes – Jet

Then I don't want to put you out further – Ash

As opposed to fighting LA traffic all the way into the city to drop you off at some smelly run down hotel? – Jet

How do you know it's smelly and run down? – Ash

All hotels are – Jet

I'm sure the Waldorf would have something to say about that <wink> – Ash

So you like bed bugs… so be it. – Jet

Ew! Don't say that! – Ash

LOL I didn't, I typed it – Jet

Smart ass… – Ash

You know it! – Jet

Sigh… would it really be okay? – Ash

It would really be okay – Jet

You're sure? – Ash

OMG you are a pain… – Jet

LOL! Thanks! So sweet of you! – Ash

Then just say yes so we can stop talking about this – Jet

FINE you win! – Ash

I usually do – Jet

It had been an amusing conversation.

When her plane landed, Ashley texted Jet to let her know she was there. Jet texted back and said she was out front at the curb.

Walking out into the Los Angeles sunshine, Ashley couldn't have missed Jet if she tried. She was stood leaning against a very expensive looking black sports car. She wore jeans, black tennis shoes, and a black t-shirt that said "Pro" on it in blue letters. She was smoking a cigarette and looking exactly like the Jet that Ashley remembered.

When Jet's eyes connected with Ashley's, her mouth dropped open.

"Ash?" Jet queried. She dropped her cigarette and stubbed it out with her foot, then walked forward, her look stunned.

It was exactly the look Ashley had been hoping for. She'd changed drastically over the years. No longer overweight, she was trim, with medium length brown hair shot through with blond highlights. The three inch heels she wore put her at the same height as Jet at five eight.

"Is that really you?" Jet asked, smiling brightly at Ashley.

"Yes, it's me," Ashley said, smiling too.

"Wow," Jet said again, leaning in to take Ashley in her arms, hugging her.

Ashley smelled musk as she hugged Jet back. It felt really good to know that she'd impressed Jet. She'd worked hard to change her look for years now. The fact that someone she admired greatly had been impressed by that hard work was important to her.

Jet stepped back, her light green eyes staring directly down into Ashley's blue ones, her smile wide.

"You look absolutely amazing," Jet said in awe.

"Thank you," Ashley said, smiling too.

Jet leaned down to pick up Ashley's suitcase. "Come on," she said, winking at her.

As they walked up to the car, Ashley whistled.

"Is this really your car?" she asked, her eyes taking in the sleek black car, then seeing the trident style emblem. "This is a Maserati?" she asked, eyes wide.

"Yeah," Jet said, as she pulled out her badge to show the officer who was walking over with an intent look on his face. He grinned, nodding as he walked away.

"What did you just show him?" Ashley asked, as Jet opened the rear hatch and put her suitcase in.

Jet handed the badge to her as she moved to open the passenger door for her.

Ashley stared down at the badge. "Los Angeles Police Department?" she asked, as she climbed into the car.

Then she looked around the car. "Holy crap…" she muttered, as she took in the lavishly appointed vehicle.

The car sported leather racing seats with blue trim, carbon fiber accents, navigation system, the works! It smelled like leather and the same musk she'd smelled on Jet a few minutes before. She breathed in deeply; it was a heady smell.

Jet grinned at her, enjoying Ashley's reaction to her car. She knew her car was over the top, but she loved it and it had been worth every penny she'd paid for it. It was a pleasure to drive every time she got behind the wheel.

"This is an incredible car," Ashley said, smiling.

"Yeah, it is," Jet said as she put the key in the ignition. The car started with a rumble of power. A smile of pure pleasure crossed Jet's face.

Ashley saw the smile, and grinned, it was obvious that Jet was very connected to her vehicle. She remembered the classic Mustang Jet had driven in high school. The stereo started immediately; the sound system was crisp and clear and quite loud as it blasted out an upbeat song that sounded distinctly like Spanish.

As she put the car into gear and looked over shoulder before pulling out, Jet sang the words to the song with relish, her hands tapping out the beat on the steering wheel. Ashley also remembered that Jet had been very music oriented in school, even at the campsite. She'd had the only CD player there, and played music in the cabin constantly. The other girls in the cabin hadn't had the nerve to say anything. Ashley had enjoyed the music.

As the first song ended, Jet turned the stereo down, glancing over at Ashley again.

"You really do look incredible," she told her again.

Ashley bit her lip, never tired of hearing that from anyone, least of all Jet Mathews. "Thank you. You haven't changed a bit."

"Oh, trust me, honey, there are a lot more miles on these tires," Jet said, grinning.

Ashley shook her head. "If anything, you look better than you did in high school, and I wouldn't have thought that was possible."

Jet raised a black eyebrow, her light green eyes sparkling mischievously as her lips curved into a smile.

Jet Mathews was definitely a stunning looking woman, with her black hair worn shaggy and just long enough to touch the base of her neck. She had long, thick black eyelashes that framed impossibly light green eyes. Her skin was now more tanned than it had been in the gloomy weather of Seattle, Washington. Her face was smooth and flawless and the tan made her eyes glow. She wore no makeup, but didn't need it at all.

"It's disgusting, you know," Ashley said when Jet didn't say anything for a bit.

"What is?" Jet asked.

"The fact that you don't need makeup at all," Ashley said. "It's just not fair."

Jet grinned. "Wouldn't know what to do with makeup anyway. I have been known to put on eyeliner if the whimsy takes me," she said, her tone wry.

"Really?" Ashley asked. "Do you know how long it takes to get my makeup to look like this?"

"But it looks really good," Jet said, winking at her.

"Oh shut up," Ashley said, laughing.

Jet laughed too.

After a few more minutes, Jet pulled onto the freeway. Zipping between cars, the Maserati's engine purred with leashed power.

"So," Jet said, glancing over at her, "what are the stories you're running down while you're here?"

"Some law enforcement pieces," Ashley said.

"What department?" Jet asked, grinning as she saw that Ashley still held her badge.

"Oh!" Ashley exclaimed, seeing Jet's eyes on the badge in her hand. She handed it back to Jet who pocketed it. "Sorry," she said, smiling.

"S'okay," Jet said. "So what department?"

"Oh, the State DOJ," Ashley said. "I'm hoping I can score an interview with a couple of fairly high-level people."

Jet grinned. "Like who?"

Ashley had no idea what Jet's grin meant. "Well, if I get really lucky, the State Attorney General herself, but I'm also hoping to talk to one of her newest directors, Jericho... Te... damn I can never remember her name!"

"Jericho Tehrani?" Jet said, her tone amused.

"Yeah," Ashley said, nodding. "How did you know that?"

"Well, I work for her, indirectly," Jet said.

"How?" Ashley said, surprised.

"I work for a DOJ task force, called LA IMPACT."

"I thought you worked for the LAPD..."

"I do," Jet said, "but about six months ago I got asked to join LA IMPACT."

"And what do you do for them?"

"The same thing I did for the Army; I develop informants to feed us intel," Jet said, her tone so casual that Ashley had to stop and think for a minute about what she'd just said.

"Wait, you were in the Army?" Ashley asked, and then nodded. "Wait, I think I did hear that somewhere along the way you joined the Army."

"Not too long after high school," Jet said nodding.

"And you did that for the Army?" Ashley asked.

"Yeah, I was Military Intelligence," Jet said.

"And what did that involve?" Ashley asked, curious.

"Basically I developed and analyzed intelligence on targets and groups," Jet said. "I kind of had a thing for languages, so I ended up working in a lot of different areas."

"Languages?" Ashley asked, gesturing at the stereo, another Spanish song was playing. "Like Spanish?"

Jet grinned. "Spanish, French, German, some Farsi and some Arabic."

"Wow!" Ashley exclaimed.

Jet shrugged. "No big deal."

"Maybe not to you," Ashley said, shaking her head.

"So you're still in Lynwood, huh?" Jet said, changing the subject suddenly.

Ashley blinked at the sudden change in topics. "I, yeah, I am."

Jet nodded. "So married?"

"Yes," Ashley said.

"House, but no kids, right?"

"Right," Ashley said, grinning.

"Oh, speaking of houses," Jet said, as she smoothly exited the freeway, "don't be too impressed with the one I live in," she said, her tone wry. "It's not mine, it belongs to my parents."

"Is this Brentwood?" Ashley asked, looking around her.

"Yeah," Jet said her look unimpressed.

"Your parents don't live in Edmonds anymore?" Ashley asked.

"They do. This is like their winter home type thing," Jet said, her tone sounding disgusted with what she perceived as her parents' excess.

"Oh…" Ashley said, nodding.

Over the years in high school she'd heard a few times that Jet Mathews' parents were rich, but she'd never really known what to believe. Jet had never acted like the rich kids at the school. She'd always been down to earth. In fact, she knew that Jet had worked on her own vehicle, instead of taking it to a mechanic. She'd seen Jet working under the hood of her own car once after school.

The hood to the flat black '67 Mustang Fastback was up. Jet was under the hood, her jeans filthy with grease, one black combat booted foot stuck out from the side of the hood, as she reached across the engine for a tool.

"Car trouble?" Ashley asked, as she walked up.

Light green eyes, made lighter by the fact that she had black grease on her face, sparkled humorously at her.

"No, I heard engine grease was great for the skin," Jet replied winking at her and smiling, showing a set of very white, very perfect teeth.

Ashley laughed, shaking her head at the other girl.

"Anything I can do?" Ashley asked.

"Know anything about Mustang engines?" Jet asked, her tone wry.

"Um, no," Ashley responded with a shake of her head.

"Then you can sit there, look pretty and keep me company," Jet said, chuckling.

"Well, I can definitely sit here and keep you company," Ashley said, setting her backpack down.

Jet raised an eyebrow at the elimination of 'look pretty' but said nothing.

Ashely moved to sit on the ground.

"Whoa, wait!" Jet said, holding up hand to forestall Ashley's movement.

Straightening from the car, Jet reached into the car window, and pulled out her jacket. She turned to lay it down on the ground next to Ashley's backpack. Ashley looked surprised.

"The pavement's still wet," Jet said in explanation. She stepped back over to the car and began working on it again.

Ashely smiled, as she sat down, thinking that Jet Mathews had some seriously old world manners, but they were kind of cool all the same.

"So what's wrong with it?" Ashley asked.

Jet craned her neck to look back at Ashley. "Her," she said simply.

"Huh?" Ashley replied.

"Her," Jet repeated. "What's wrong with her?"

"Oh..." Ashley said, widening her eyes. "What's wrong with her?"

Jet grinned, nodding her head. "Oh, she's just being temperamental, looking for some extra attention, like most girls."

Ashley laughed. It was an interesting hour, listening to Jet talk to her car, cajoling, sweet talking, even cussing. In the end, Jet gave her a ride home.

"You were an excellent assistant," Jet told her, grinning, still a smudge of grease on her left cheek.

"Not really," Ashley said, reaching her hand up to rub at the grease on Jet's cheek. "We didn't get it all off."

Their eyes connected for a second, and Ashley would swear that her heart stopped for a moment. Later, she was sure she'd imagined the heated look in Jet's eyes, but the moment passed and Jet simply grinned at her, as she reached up rubbing at the grease on her cheek herself. Ashley chided herself that whole night, Idiot! Jet Mathews the most popular girl in school isn't gay!

Jet turned onto a tree-lined street. She reached up to touch a button on the rearview mirror, and Ashley noted a garage door start to open. As the door opened and Jet pulled into the driveway, Ashley saw the black Mustang in the garage.

"Oh my God you still have her!" she exclaimed happily.

"Of course," Jet said. "Couldn't get rid of my first, best girl."

Well, that's true, that would have been wrong," Ashley agreed, smiling.

It was a three car garage; Ashley noticed there was a motorcycle in the open area, near the work bench. It was a nicely appointed garage, with coated floors and finished walls. Tools hung neatly on racks and hooks.

"I see your working conditions have improved," Ashley said, smiling.

"Oh yeah, don't have to stand out in the rain anymore," Jet said, grinning as she turned the car off and got out.

She immediately walked around to open Ashley's door, and then pulled the suitcase out of the trunk. She gestured forward for Ashley to precede her. Inside she had to brush past Ashley to get to the alarm to turn it off.

"Sorry, forget the damned thing is on half the time," she said..

"No problem," Ashley said, smiling.

"Okay," Jet said, walking into the foyer of the house, "follow me. I'll show you the guest rooms, you can pick from five of them," she said, winking at Ashley.

"Oh my," Ashley said, smiling as she widened her eyes melodramatically.

"Yeah, big house. It's kind of a pain in the ass," Jet said.

Jet showed Ashley to one guest bedroom and told her where the others were in case she wanted to check them out.

"I'm going to go take a quick shower and change," Jet said. "Make yourself at home."

"Thanks," Ashley said, smiling.

An hour later, Ashley wandered out into the backyard and found Jet watering plants with a hose and smoking. Ashley noted that Jet had changed into black shorts and a black tank top and was now barefoot. There was music playing loudly, which Ashley would come to find was a regular thing with Jet.

"I was beginning to wonder if you'd disappeared," Ashley said, grinning.

Jet looked over at her, reaching over to pick up the remote for the stereo so she could turn the music down.

She took a long drag on her cigarette and shook her head.

"Nope. Just back here payin' my rent."

"Huh?" Ashley queried.

Jet gestured to the yard that had various bricks, yard tools and pots lying around. It looked like it was under construction.

"I'm re-doing my parents backyard to pay for the privilege of staying here," Jet explained. Seeing Ashley's look around the yard she added, "It's not done yet."

"I certainly hope not," Ashley said, with a raised eyebrow.

Jet narrowed her light green eyes at her. "I'm holding a hose, woman… you might want to be careful."

Ashley laughed. "It actually looks pretty great so far."

"Eh, we'll see, I'm no gardener," Jet said, shrugging.

Ashley sat down in one of the chairs near a table that had an umbrella. A few minutes later, Jet turned off the hose and walked over to her.

"Want a drink?" Jet asked.

"Sure," Ashley said. "Whatever you're having."

"Okay," Jet said and she stepped into the house.

A couple of minutes later she walked back outside, handing Ashley a bottle of Shock Top. Ashley glanced up at her.

Jet shrugged. "It's light, most people like it."

"Thank you," Ashley said, taking a drink and nodding her approval.

Jet sat down, lighting another cigarette and setting down her lighter. Ashley picked up the lighter, it was a classic Zippo with a black cross on it.

"Where's this from?" Ashley asked.

"Germany," Jet answered. "I was stationed in K-town."

"K-town?"

"Kaiserslautern," Jet clarified.

"Oh," Ashley said, nodding. "This is an Iron Cross, right?"

"A true Iron Cross, yes," Jet said nodding.

"True?"

"Yeah, before the Nazi's perverted it with a Swastika in the middle," Jet said distastefully.

"Oh," Ashley said, nodding.

They were both silent for a few minutes. Jet pulled one foot up to rest on the chair she sat in, resting her arm on her knee as she smoked, looking completely relaxed. Ashley was looking over at her when something on Jet's ankle caught her eye.

"What's that?" Ashley asked.

Jet looked over at her, and then down at where she was looking. "It's a tattoo…"

"No shit," Ashley said, narrowing her eyes at Jet. "Can I see it?"

Jet obliged by putting her foot on the arm of the chair Ashley sat in, canting her leg so Ashley could clearly see the tattoo. It was two horizontal lightning bolts in the colors of a rainbow, between which was the word "Pride" in black script lettering. Ashley looked over at Jet, her look shocked.

Jet looked back at Ashley for a long minute, a slow grin starting on her face. "You didn't know I'm gay."

"I..." Ashley stammered. "Well, no, I didn't."

Jet nodded her grin still in place.

"Stop it!" Ashley said, starting to grin too. "It's no big deal, I just didn't know, that's all."

"Okay," Jet said, her tone unconvincing.

"It's fine if you're gay, it really is," Ashley said.

"Good thing, 'cause I am," Jet said, smiling now.

Ashley gave her a dirty look. "Stop it."

"What am I doing?"

"You're being a brat, that's what you're doing," Ashley said.

Jet chuckled, leaning back in her chair, and setting her foot on the ground again. They were both silent for a few minutes.

"I really should have known..." Ashley said.

"That I'm gay? Why?" Jet asked, her look curious.

"Because you were always so chivalrous," Ashley said, smiling softly.

Jet looked back at her cynically. "How?"

"Like that time at camp."

Jet sat up a little straighter, taking a drag off her cigarette, her look considering.

"Are you going to try to say you don't remember camp?" Ashley asked her.

"I remember it," Jet said, nodding. "But for some reason, I'm not sure I remember it the way you do."

"Do you remember saving my ass there?" Ashley asked.

"I remember some stupid chick being a bitch. It wasn't cool."

"And do you remember being the one to help me up?" Ashley asked.

"Was I supposed to let you lie there on the ground?" Jet asked, her eyebrow raised.

"Other people would have," Ashley said.

"Other people are assholes," Jet countered.

"And you never were," Ashley said, "No matter how incredibly popular you were."

Jet made a face at that phrase.

"What?" Ashley asked, seeing the expression.

"Popular," Jet repeated. "That doesn't mean squat in the real world."

"Well, it meant a damned lot in high school," Ashley said, "and that's where we were."

Jet nodded, seeing that this was important to Ashley.

"I don't think you realize how much that time at camp changed my life," Ashley said, her eyes shining.

"Ash, I didn't really do anything," Jet said, shaking her head.

"Oh my God, yes you did," Ashley said. "You were nice to me," she said, her look serious, "when all those other people weren't. They looked up to you, they followed your lead."

Jet looked back at Ashley, honestly shocked by what she was hearing.

"Tell me," Jet said softly, her look searching.

"When you were nice to me at camp, even changing your cabin to stick with me, people saw that," Ashley said, knowing she probably sounded like a crazy person just then, but needing to get out what she'd wanted to tell Jet for so long. "After camp they stopped making fun of me, they stopped picking on me. I even made friends after that. And you were always around, saying hi, or eating lunch with me... People saw that Jet, and they figured if you liked me, I must be worth something."

"Ash..." Jet said, her voice affected, "you were always worth something. You were great. You were funny and sweet; you were smarter than most of those people put together. Why do you think I had anything to do with that?"

Ashley blew her breath out, shaking her head. "Because you did, Jet, you did."

Jet shook her head. "It doesn't matter now anyway. Look at you, what you've done; you're a writer now, just like you wanted. On top of that, you're beautiful as all get out, so fuck them."

Ashley smiled softly. "You'd never understand..." she said quietly.

"Ash, it doesn't matter, that was high school," Jet said.

"But it did matter."

"But it doesn't now," Jet said. "You can be whoever the hell you want to be now. You don't need anyone's permission for that."

Ashley looked back at Jet. The woman had self-assurance coming out of every pore, but she didn't think she could ever be like that.

"Did you know you were gay in high school?" Ashley asked.

Jet hesitated, narrowing her eyes, and then nodded. "Yeah, I was figuring it out then."

Ashley nodded, biting her lip.

"What?" Jet asked, grinning at the hesitant gesture.

"There was this one time… I thought… well…" Ashley started to say, but then shook her head.

Jet chuckled softly. "I know exactly when you're talking about," she said, taking a long swig of beer. "It was the day you kept me company while I fixed my car."

Ashley nodded, smiling.

"And then I drove you home," Jet said.

"And for a second I could have sworn you were going to kiss me," Ashley said.

Jet grinned. "That's because for a second I was going to kiss you."

Ashley looked shocked by that admission and Jet laughed.

"That surprises you," Jet said.

"Yeah," Ashley said, nodding. "I thought that I must have been delusional."

"See?" Jet said, her look warm. "What you thought wasn't always right, was it?"

"No, I guess not," Ashley said, then she looked back at Jet. "So what stopped you from kissing me?'

Jet smiled, shrugging. "I liked that we were friends, I didn't want to fuck that up."

"Oh," Ashley said, nodding.

Jet looked back at her for a long moment, saying nothing, her light green eyes searching.

"So," Jet said then, her tone informational. "Tomorrow is Friday, and if you really want to meet Jericho, you should come out with us tomorrow night."

"Okay," Ashley said. "Who's us?"

"The women I hang out with these days, they're pretty cool. Jericho's usually there…" She said the last with a sardonic grin.

"What's that look about?" she asked, seeing Jet's grin.

"Well, it's a gay club, and you know she's gay, right?" Jet said.

"Ah," Ashley stammered. "Well, no, I didn't know that, but it doesn't matter, everyone seems to be gay these days," she said, winking at Jet.

Jet laughed at that, nodding her head. "Oh honey, everyone is only straight, till they're not."

Ashley looked back at her openmouthed. "Oh my God!" she said and laughed at the comment.

Jet only chuckled.

Chapter 2

The next morning, Jet needed to go into the office to get a few things done before she took the rest of the day off. She said that Ashley was welcome to come in with her or wait for her at the house. Ashley was curious about where Jet worked, so opted to go in with her.

Ashley noted that Jet was dressed casually, with jeans, lace-up flat black boots and a black baseball style jersey shirt. The shirt had a picture of a skull wearing a baseball hat that said "POLICE" on it. The words "LAPD" were above the skull and the words "Help Donate Blood – Run" were below the skull, both in large silver-gray letters. It was an interesting shirt.

"Nice," Ashley said, gesturing to the shirt.

Jet grinned. "Gotta have a sense of humor, right?"

"Do they run a lot?" Ashley asked.

"All the damned time," Jet said, her tone exasperated. "I tell them every time, 'don't run, you'll just go to jail tired.' But they don't listen."

Ashley laughed. Once again she was finding that Jet had a really great sense of humor. She always had in high school, always making some funny comment or pointing out things that were ironic.

In the kitchen, Jet poured coffee into a large thermal cup, then gestured to Ashley.

"I'm sorry, I didn't even think to ask, do you want coffee?"

"Sure," Ashley said, nodding.

Jet reached for another cup, but then hesitated. "I should warn you, this stuff is kind of strong. Is that okay?"

"How strong is strong?" Ashley asked.

Jet handed her a cup, and poured a little bit into it.

"There's cream and sugar there," Jet said, gesturing to the counter where two containers sat.

Ashley added some sugar and cream and then tasted the coffee.

"Oh my God, I think my heart rate just shot up," Ashely said, making a face.

Jet laughed. "Yeah, sorry, it's Arabian coffee, it's designed to be strong."

"Holy cow, you're not kidding!" Ashley said, setting down the cup.

"There's a shop at the office, we could grab you some there," Jet said.

"That works," Ashley said, smiling and nodding.

She then watched as Jet put the lid on her coffee, without added any sugar or cream.

"You drink that stuff black?" Ashley asked.

"Yep!"

"So, quite literally Jet fuel," Ashley said.

"Ha!" Jet said, pointing at her. "That's good!"

They walked out to the garage then, Jet opened the passenger door for Ashley. Once again, Ashley realized she should have known that Jet's gallant ways had to do with her being gay. Women weren't usually so attentive to such things with other women.

As Jet started the car the stereo came on and she immediately started tapping her fingers to the beat.

"You're always listening to music, aren't you?" Ashley commented. She'd noted the night before Jet had music going even in her room until she'd apparently gone to bed.

Jet grinned, nodding. "I gotta," she said as she backed out of the garage and then reached up to hit the button to close the garage door.

Ashley canted her head. "You mean that, don't you?"

Jet nodded. "Yeah, it keeps the ADHD at bay."

"You have ADHD?" Ashley asked, surprised.

"In spades," Jet said seriously. "Adderall doesn't really do a lot, but I didn't like the Ritalin, so… I deal with it other ways too."

"You had it in high school too?" Ashley asked, knowing that it was a disorder that usually started in childhood.

"Oh yeah," Jet said, nodding. "They said I was 'highly intelligent'," she said, using air quotes to indicate what she thought of that statement. "So that's why it didn't affect my school work. I got stuff done before my brain got bored and moved on." She shrugged to indicate that she didn't really believe that.

"Well, highly intelligent sounds right," Ashley said.

"Does it?" Jet asked, grinning.

"You were the number one in the class, Jet, you know it does," Ashley said her tone chiding.

Jet looked back over at her, narrowing her eyes slightly, then shrugged. "Anyway the music gives my mind a place to focus so I can pay attention to other stuff. Otherwise it's like a pack of wild dogs off the leash, running everywhere at the same time."

Ashley nodded, thinking that must be exhausting. It was yet another thing she'd never known about the dynamic Jet Mathews.

"Isn't that hard?" Ashley asked Jet.

"What?" Jet asked, her mind elsewhere already.

"Having your mind run everywhere at the same time," Ashley replied, using Jet's words.

Jet looked back at her, her look considering, then she shrugged. "Yeah, but it's how my mind has always worked, so I'm used to it."

Ashely shook her head, thinking she didn't think she could handle something like that in her daily life. She watched as Jet reached over to pick up her coffee and then take a drink.

"Doesn't that make it worse?" she asked. "All that caffeine."

"Actually, caffeine calms ADHD down, that's what Adderall and Ritalin are: stimulants. For whatever reason it has the exact opposite effect on the ADHD brain."

"Really?" Ashley asked, surprised. "You know a lot about this disorder."

"Gotta love the demon to manage him."

Ashley was surprised by that statement, but then Jet was surprising her a lot on this trip already.

"So you actually like the ADHD?" Ashley asked, knowing there was more to that statement.

"Oh, I love it," Jet said, her eyes sparkling. "It's who I am."

"Who you are?" Ashley asked.

"The off-the-wall, passionate, nut that I am," Jet said, grinning. "That's the ADHD."

Ashley looked back at Jet, watching her as she drove and seeing how she moved all the time, feet or hands, fingers or head, she was very energetic. There was a definite pull to Jet. She had a way of drawing people in to her, she'd always been that way in high school, Ashley had seen it time and time again.

Physical education was murder for fat people, was all Ashley could think when the teacher wanted them to run laps. Surely the woman was trying to kill her. Jet, who'd already run the required four laps in a ridiculously short time, was kicking around a soccer ball. As Ashley came around from her first lap, she saw a quick grin flash on Jet's face.

"Heads up," Jet said, kicking the ball toward her.

Ashley had astounded herself by managing to kick the ball back in Jet's general direction.

"Come on," Jet said, dropping into an offensive stance, passing the ball back and forth between her feet.

"I gotta... laps..." Ashley gasped.

"Screw that," Jet said, grinning. "Come on..." she said, again, her black eyebrows waggling mischievously.

"Okay," Ashley said, happy to stop running and she walked over to where Jet stood.

"Go over there," Jet said, gesturing to the other short side of the field.

Ashley did, grinning as others stopped running and started to watch. Jet started to move, kicking the ball and moving and swerving, she then surprised one of the spectators by passing the ball to her. The girl stopped the ball with her hand and looked back at Jet quizzically. Jet nodded to the girl, grinning.

"Come on," Jet said, gesturing to the girl with her fingertips.

The next thing Ashley knew, she and Jet were defending against the ball. Others kept joining in, some on Ashley and Jet's side, others on the opposing side. In the end, the PE teacher attempted to break up the game.

"Why?" Jet has asked the teacher, always more than happy to challenge authority.

"Because I told you to run, Mathews," the teacher said, annoyed. Jet Mathews was forever challenging her authority.

"Well, in case you weren't aware," Jet said, gesturing to the field. "We were running. Soccer involves running, just not in stupid circles." She said the last with a smug look in her eyes.

Everyone in the class cheered at that point. The teacher looked at her students, even the ones that were usually good students were standing there with Jet Mathews.

"Mathews in my office!" the teacher snapped, then turned and walked away.

Ashley looked over at Jet and saw that her look hadn't changed. Jet's eyes connected with hers, and she winked at her.

"Guess class is over, huh?" Jet asked her tone flippant, as she started to follow the PE teacher.

Someone started a chant then. "Jet! Jet! Jet!" And the whole group joined.

Jet threw up a V for victory sign over her head, causing everyone to get louder. Ashley stood watching Jet go, shaking her head.

Later, she saw Jet in the hallway. "What happened?" she asked, having been worried that Jet would get into trouble.

Jet grinned. "She's going to call my parents about me inciting a rebellious act in her class," she said, in her most officious tone.

"Are you going to get into trouble?" Ashley asked, thinking her own parents would kill her if they got a call from the school.

Jet laughed. "Yeah, if she could even get ahold of my parents," she said. "They wouldn't care any way; teachers annoy them almost as much as they annoy us."

Ashley shook her head. Jet Mathews could get out of anything!

At one point during the drive, the song "Brave" came on, and Jet sang the words, looking over at Ashley pointedly as she sang. Ashley noted that the words talked about how she could basically be anything she wanted. She could put up with the way people treated her or she could start standing up to them and saying what she wanted to them.

Ashley focused on the words that followed, phrases that talked about how words could truly hurt if you let them get under your skin, but that there was a way out of that kind of thinking. They hit home a bit.

Jet sang the chorus to her, telling her she wanted to see her be brave. The bridge of the song said what she'd been doing wasn't working, and shouldn't she just try telling people what she really thought? Jet sang every word, looking over at her as she did.

"I guess you're trying to tell me something, huh?" Ashley said, when the song ended.

"Yep," Jet said, nodding.

Ashley looked back at her, she wanted to ask Jet why she cared, but she knew she really didn't need to ask. It seemed to be who Jet Mathews was to her very core.

They arrived at the office, and after signing her into the building, Jet walked Ashley straight up to the coffee shop. Along the way, Jet was greeted by any number of people; it seemed she was quite popular at work as well. At one point Jet caught Ashley's grin when another person greeted her by name.

"Shut up," Jet said quietly to her, grinning.

Jet waited as Ashley got her coffee, tapping her fingers on the counter to the music on in the coffee shop. At the register, Ashley started to reach into her purse for her wallet. Jet's hand on her arm stopped her. She pulled a set of bills out of her pocket, pulling out a twenty dollar bill and handing it to the cashier.

The cashier smiled warmly at Jet, handing her the change. Jet dropped a dollar into the girl's tip cup.

"Thanks sweetie," the girl said, winking at Jet.

"Any time," Jet said.

As they walked back downstairs, Ashley looked over at Jet.

"Do you flirt with every girl you see?" she asked.

Jet's lips curled into a grin, "Maybe," she said, her tone teasing.

Later in the office, Jet had her iPhone plugged into her computer and her music played; she occasionally turned up songs she liked. Ashley watched as Jet pulled a leather-bound book out of her gear bag and set it open on the table. Ashley could see handwritten notes and pieces of paper sticking out randomly. Jet looked at it often as she typed on the computer. Her fingers flew over the keys at a dizzying speed, all the while she moved either her head or her feet to the music playing on her speakers.

"And Jet's in the office…" said a male voice from a cubicle next to Jet's.

Jet started laughing, as a man stuck his head up over the cubicle wall. "Thought you were off today, Mathews," he said.

"I am," Jet said, grinning.

"And yet, here you are," he said, smiling.

"I had a couple of things to handle, but I'm leaving soon, *Dad*."

"Can't get the kid to take a damned break," the man said, as he walking around the cubicle wall. "Hi, I'm John Evans," he said to Ashley as he extended his hand to her.

"John, that's Ashley," Jet said, her eyes still on the computer as she typed.

"It's nice to meet you," Ashley said, smiling up at John.

"You too," John said, glancing at Jet, and shaking his head. "The kid is in serious need of a vacation."

"Or a valium," came another male voice.

"Valium doesn't work on me…" Jet said, her voice singsong. Without looking up from her computer she said, "Curry, this is Ashley, Ashley, Nick Curry."

"Charmed," Nick said, grinning at Ashley.

Suddenly Jet stood up. "I need a cigarette," she said, nodding her head toward the back patio of the office.

Ashley stood up, smiling at both men, and then followed Jet out to the patio.

"How many girls a month does Jet date?" Nick asked, as he and John watched the two go.

"Helluva a lot more than me," John said, shaking his head.

They both adored Jet, she was smart and damned good at her job, they welcomed her happily to the group. However, they'd yet to figure out how she managed her love life with seemingly no drama. She was with a different girl regularly, on the phone, via text, they'd drop by the office, but rarely the same girl more than twice.

"They seem nice," Ashley said, as she watched Jet light a cigarette.

"Yeah, they're pretty cool," Jet said.

They'd been outside for a few minutes when another man walked out onto the patio. Ashley saw him first; Jet was looking down at her phone, texting someone.

"Jet Fire…" Sebastian said, smiling, winking at Ashley.

Jet's head snapped up and she smiled widely. "Baz!" she exclaimed, jumping up and tossing her cigarette aside and then moved to hug him.

Sebastian was a big man, at six three and 225 pounds, all of which was muscle. He easily picked Jet up off her feet as he hugged her.

"How are ya, kid?" he asked her, grinning.

"Baz, you're like eight years older than me," Jet said.

"Yeah, but all the energy you have, makes me feel a lot older," he said.

He looked at Ashley then, his gray-green eyes curious about her friend.

"Sorry, I'm a dumbass," Jet said. "Baz, this is Ashley, Ash, this is Special Agent Supervisor Sebastian Bach."

Sebastian extended his hand to Ashley his smile warm. "Ashley, it's nice to meet you."

"You too," Ashley said, smiling. "And I agree with you on the energy thing, she and I are the same age and she makes me tired."

"Hey…" Jet said playfully, as she tried to look offended.

"It's exhausting, isn't it?" Sebastian said..

"Entirely," Ashley said, laughing softly.

"So you looking for Kash?" Jet asked.

Sebastian gave her a chastising look. "Maybe I was looking for you…"

"Were you?" Jet asked.

"No, but I could have been," Sebastian said, grinning. "Of course I'm looking for Kash, have you seen her yet?"

"Nope, not yet," she said, glancing at her watch. "Hell, it's already ten?"

"In everyone else's world, little one," Sebastian said, grinning.

"Bite me, Baz," Jet shot back.

"I'm not your type," Sebastian replied, winking at her.

"It wasn't an offer." "So it was a threat?" Sebastian asked, raising an eyebrow at her.

"Only if you plan to file," Jet said.

Sebastian narrowed his eyes at her, wrinkling up his nose, and Jet did the same. It was obviously something they did often.

"Well, when you see her can you tell her to call me?" Sebastian asked.

"I'm not here today," Jet said.

Sebastian gave her a sideways glance. "So you're like a fig newton of my imagination."

"Yep," Jet said, nodding with a chuckle. "Technically I'm on vacation today."

"You do know that being on vacation means you don't come to the office, right?" Sebastian said, shaking his head at her and rolling his eyes.

"What can I say? I'm a dedicated public servant."

"You say dedicated… I say obsessive…" Sebastian said, his voice trailing off as he looked over at Ashley. "Promise me you will drag her out of here within the next hour."

Ashley smiled, enjoying the way Jet and Sebastian bantered. "I'll try, but she's pretty strong."

Sebastian leaned close to Ashley, putting his lips right next to her ear. "The trick is to take her music. She'll follow you anywhere if you have that."

Ashley was surprised by the shiver that went through her at the proximity of this man. He was definitely handsome, and he smelled really good too. Reminding herself firmly that she was married, she smiled up at Sebastian.

"Good tip," she said, nodding.

Jet watched the exchange, her cop instincts vibrating, but she said nothing about it. She did, however, reach over and swat Sebastian on the back of the head.

"Not cool, dude," Jet said then. "You're as connected there as I am."

"True," Sebastian said, his eyes sparkling, "which is why I know where your Achilles heel is."

Jet shook her head, and walked inside, leaving Ashley and Sebastian standing in the patio.

"Well, it was nice to meet you," Ashley said, smiling up at Sebastian.

"You too," he said, nodding, as he moved to open the door for her.

As she walked through, he found himself watching her. *Jet Mathews always scored the hottest women…*

Ashley managed to get Jet out of the office just under than an hour later. Not before Kashena Windwalker-Marshal walked in however. Kashena walked into Jet's cubicle, her look quizzical.

"I vaguely recall signing a leave slip for you today…" she said, already grinning, her dark blue eyes shining with humor.

Jet started to chuckle, even as she saved the document she'd been working on.

She looked up then. "I'm getting ready to leave, right now."

"Baz told me he gave your friend a deadline," Kashena said looking over at Ashley.

Jet stood from her chair stretching, and nodding toward Ashley.

"Kash, this is Ashley, Ash this is my boss, Special Agent Supervisor Kashena Windwalker-Marshal."

"Hi," Kashena said, smiling at Ashley.

"Good morning," Ashley said, smiling too.

"You're from Jet's hometown right?" Kashena asked.

Ashley nodded. "We went to high school together."

"And how was that?" Kashena asked, winking over at Jet.

"Amazing," Ashley said, surprising both Kashena and Jet.

"Wow," Kashena said, grinning, looking at Jet to see her reaction. She saw that Jet was shaking her head and rolling her eyes. "Guess there's a story there I need to hear sometime…"

Jet laughed, and then cleared her throat. "We're gonna go now," she said, her look pointed.

Kashena chuckled. "Have a nice half day off," she said, looking at her watch. "And I'll put four hours back on your timesheet," she said, narrowing her eyes.

Jet shrugged. "Doesn't matter," she said. "Hey are you and Sierra coming tonight?"

Kashena considered. "I think we might make it," she said. "Colby's at some school thing all weekend."

"Cool," Jet said, nodding. "Ash is hoping to meet Jericho."

"Well you know her and Zoey always make it," Kash said, grinning.

"Yeah, I figured as much."

"We'll see you tonight then," Kash said, smiling.

"You got it," Jet said, moving to pick up her gear bag, and gesturing for Ashley to precede her out of the office.

Kashena watched the two walk out. She, like everyone else that had met Ashley that morning, was trying to figure out the nature of their relationship. Jet changed women like she did her socks, but Jet had told her that Ashley was married, to a man no less. The girl definitely seemed to have, at the very least, a girl crush on Jet. It was going to be an interesting evening.

Jet lit a cigarette on the way out to her car, when they got to the car she opened Ashley's door and stood outside of the vehicle finishing the cigarette, then she got in on the driver's side.

"I take it you don't smoke in your car," Ashley said.

"Who's dumb enough to smoke in a hundred and eighty thousand dollar car?" Jet asked, looking aghast at the very thought.

Ashley laughed. "I guess not you."

"Hell no," Jet said, shaking her head and starting the car.

"So can I ask a personal question?"

"Sure," Jet said without hesitation.

"How can you afford this car?" Ashley asked.

Jet grinned, surprised Ashley hadn't asked that sooner.

"One of the last things I did in the Army was a job for an outside contractor. When I got out I had a nice fat check waiting for me. I blew it on the car and my motorcycle."

"Oh," Ashley said, widening her eyes, "outside contractors pay that good?"

"You bet they do," Jet said, rolling her eyes. "I thought my dad was going to have a stroke when he heard about the car…" she said, her voice trailing off as she grinned. "Waste all that money on a car…" she said, her voice imitating her father's. "You should have invested it…" She said the last rolling her eyes. "I didn't want to invest it, I wanted to buy a cool car and work for a living. Jesus, it's not like I used my trust fund money or anything…"

Ashley smiled.

Jet looked over at her. "And there you have my parental issues for the day."

"Everyone has parental issues," Ashley said.

"Yeah? Tell me yours."

"Oh, mine are the usual, mom thought I was fat, dad thought I was his little princess, blah, blah, blah."

"That sounds more fun," Jet said, grinning.

"Believe me, it wasn't."

"So what do you want to do now?" Jet asked, as they stopped at a red light. "We definitely need lunch, anywhere special you want to eat?"

"Wherever," Ashley said, shrugging.

"Do you want to stay on the non-gay side of town?" Jet asked, grinning.

"Stop it!" Ashley said. "I don't care about that, sheesh! We can eat wherever you want."

"Fine, West Hollywood it is," Jet said, winking over at her.

They were quiet for another few minutes as they drove. Then Ashley looked over at Jet.

"Why does your Facebook page say 'Jet Blue'?" she asked.

Jet shrugged. "I'm a cop. I really don't want my whole name out there. I mostly have that page so my parents know how to get ahold of me."

"Your whole name?" Ashley asked.

Jet looked over at her. "My middle name is Blue."

"It is?" Ashley said, surprised.

"Yeah, I chalk it up to my parents being high on something when they named me."

"Oh, my God, stop!" Ashley laughed.

They had lunch at Katana Robata, a Japanese restaurant and sat out on the patio. The waitress who came to take their order recognized Jet.

"Oh my God, how are you!" the girl said, smiling and leaning over to hug Jet, her cleavage on full display.

"I'm alright," Jet said, smiling. "Sara this is Ashley, she's a friend of mine."

"Hi," Sara said smiling at Ashley too.

"Hello," Ashley said, and then looked over at Jet who widened her eyes slightly.

"I'm sorry, so what can I get you?" Sara asked.

They ordered their food, and she left with a swish of her short skirt. Jet's eyes followed the girl appreciatively. When she looked up she saw that Ashley was giving her a narrowed look.

"What?" she asked, a grin starting on her lips.

"You are a dog," Ashley said.

"No," Jet said shaking her head. "A dog would have slid her hand up that skirt, like she was inviting me to. I'm a gentleman."

Ashley looked back at her, thinking that the word gentleman did seem to fit Jet pretty well. She got to see more as lunch went on. Two girls were walking by when one of them saw Jet and apparently also knew her. The blond squealed excitedly and ran over to Jet, who stood immediately. The girl barely took a breath before she launched herself into Jet's arms hugging her.

Ashley noted that Jet's hands stayed right at the girl's waist, even though the girl was definitely pressing herself very close. When she pulled back to look up at Jet, she pressed her lips against Jet's in a fairly deep kiss. After a long minute, Jet pulled her head back to break the kiss and smiled at the girl.

"Amy, this is my friend Ashley," Jet said, stepping back to give Amy the hint.

Amy didn't miss a beat, and she turned smiling brightly at Ashley. "Oh, hi," she said. "I'm sorry, I haven't seen Jet in months!"

"She does seem to have that effect on people," Ashley said, her tone reasonable.

"Doesn't she?" Amy said, laughing.

Jet remained standing, her look polite. Amy finally got the hint and retreated.

"Good lord, how many women do you know?" Ashley asked.

Jet only grinned.

By the time lunch was done, no less than five women had found it necessary to say hello to Jet. Still other women were watching her intently.

"You are one hot commodity," Ashley said, looking around them as Sara brought over the check and handed it to Jet. "And you are not paying that check," she said as she saw Jet reach into her pocket.

"Wanna bet?" Jet said, as she pulled out some money, and handed it to Sara, giving her a wink.

Ashley just stared at Jet, exasperated. "You don't get to pay for everything Jet Mathews."

"Watch me, Ashley Foster," Jet replied.

"Simmons," Ashley replied.

"Oh yes, the husband," Jet said, nodding as she moved to stand.

Ashley caught the slightest hint of sarcasm in Jet's voice and wondered about it. But she didn't want to sound crazy if she was imagining things, so said nothing.

After lunch they walked around looking in shops, and eventually got back in the car to head back to the house.

"So, Kashena…" Ashley began hesitantly.

"Yeah?" Jet asked, glancing over at her as she drove.

"Is she… um…"

"Say it…" Jet said, her eyes sparkling.

"Gay, is she gay?" Ashley said.

"Yes, she's gay too."

"Do you think that a lot of women who are police officers are gay?" Ashley asked.

Jet considered the question. "I think that more women that are cops are likely to be gay, yeah," she said. "It's a pretty tough job for a woman, and butch women tend to do well in the men's arena. Like firefighters, any man-type job, really."

"I don't know if I really get the whole butch thing," Ashley said looking over at Jet. "How does that work?"

"Well, you have two main types of women," Jet said. "You've got the more feminine women, who wear makeup and all that kind of stuff; they're considered femme. Then there are the women who are more like men; no makeup, kind of a masculine personality,"

"Like you?" Ashley asked.

"Yeah," Jet said nodding. "Fixing cars, carrying heavy stuff, construction, stuff like that."

Ashley nodded. "How are they different from men then?"

Jet curled her lips in a derisive grin. "Yeah, we butches hate that comparison, I gotta tell ya."

Ashley looked immediately contrite. "I'm sorry," she said, "I didn't mean anything by it."

Jet shook her head. "It's okay, I know you didn't, but I wouldn't suggest you say that to any other butch. We are nothing like men, at least no true butch is. We respect women, we treat them the way they should be treated. In a way that if men treated them even half as good, there might not be as many lesbians as there are these days."

Ashley looked back at her. "How do you think a woman should be treated?"

"Like she's the most fragile, beautiful thing you've ever seen, and that you'd walk over hot coals to be her boi."

Ashley found that she couldn't speak for a moment. It was the most amazing thing she'd ever heard and it didn't surprise her one bit that it came from Jet.

"Wow," Ashley said, blinking a couple of times.

"And that's what I mean," Jet said, seeing the look on Ashley's face. "Your woman should always look at you like that, and if she doesn't, you're not doing something right, man or woman."

Ashley shook her head, unable to believe that someone thought this way in this day and age. But Jet Mathews wasn't just anyone, and Ashley had always known that.

They were both quiet for a bit. Then Jet looked over at Ashley.

"So," she said, grinning, "what's hubby like?"

Ashley pressed her lips together, glancing over at Jet.

"What?" Jet asked, her look quizzical.

"I'm not sure I want to tell you," Ashley said, her tone tentative.

"Why?"

Ashley shook her head, still pressing her lips together.

"Don't tell me, let me guess, I'm more butch than he is…" Jet said.

Ashley laughed, then grimaced.

"Seriously?" Jet asked, her look poker-faced.

Ashley grimaced again and nodded.

"Jesus, Ash…" Jet said, sounding exasperated.

"He's very sweet…" Ashley said.

"Sweet?" Jet repeated, her tone indicating that she thought 'sweet' wasn't a positive description for a guy.

"Yes," Ashley said.

"What does he do for a living?" Jet asked.

Again Ashley hesitated, knowing how this was going to go.

"Ash…" Jet said, looking over at her as she exited the freeway.

Ashley sighed. "He's an accountant."

"Oh my God!" Jet said, her tone both shocked and disgusted at the same time. "Are you kidding me?"

"No," Ashley said, looking embarrassed.

Jet blew her breath out, shaking her head. "No wonder you hadn't said word one about him until I asked."

Ashley bit her lip. She didn't realize she hadn't yet mentioned her husband, Greg. Did that say something? The fact was she really hadn't thought about him at all up until this conversation.

Jet looked over at her, raising a black eyebrow. "What does he drive?" she asked, like that would be the final factor on whether or not her husband was a complete zero.

Ashley looked up at the ceiling of the car, not willing to answer the question.

"He drives a Prius, doesn't he?" Jet said, like it was the worst possible car that her husband could drive.

"No, it's a Nissan Leaf," Ashley said triumphantly.

Jet burst into laughter. "It's the same fuckin' thing, Ash!"

"It is not!" Ashley said, starting to laugh herself.

Jet just shook her head, feeling sorry for the girl.

Chapter 3

That night, Ashley walked down the stairs to Jet's foyer trying not to feel self-conscious. She'd had a hard time deciding what to wear, not wanting to appear like she was dressing up for meeting Jet's friends, but at the same, not wanting to look sloppy. She'd gone somewhere in between wearing a pair of nice fitting jeans, a blue shirt that brought out the blue in her eyes and three inch black heels. She'd left her hair loose in curls and added a little darker color to her eye makeup, lips and cheeks. She wore silver hoop earrings and a looped silver chain around her neck. She had been pretty pleased with the look, but now she was starting to feel like she'd over done it.

Jet was standing in the backyard smoking. Ashley stood at the back sliding door staring at Jet. She wore all black from head to toe: Opaque black jeans that were snug but boot cut, black rocker-style studded boots with a two inch heel, and a black button up shirt, open at the throat with a silver byzantine-style chain with a black iron cross hanging on it. In her ears she wore two sets of small silver Irish knot style hoops, and in the lowest hole she wore black studs. As she'd said she sometimes did, she wore the slightest smudge of black eye liner; just enough to make her eyes stand out even more than they did normally. Ashley couldn't take her eyes off the woman as she opened the slider to step outside.

Turning around Jet took in the sight of Ashley.

"Wow…" Jet said, her light green eyes sweeping over her appreciatively. "You're so gonna get hit on tonight," she said, grinning.

"Stop," Ashley said, smiling. "You look pretty amazing."

"Thank you," Jet said, inclining her head, moving to step closer. She leaned her head down. "I may hit on you myself," she said, her voice a low murmur.

Ashley felt her breath catch in her throat. She bit her lip, wishing she didn't feel her stomach flutter at Jet's proximity, but wishing didn't help.

After a couple of long seconds, Jet stepped back, looking down at her.

"Ready to go?" she asked, her tone completely normal.

"Y-yes," Ashley stammered.

The drive to the bar was mercifully without much conversation. Unfortunately, it didn't keep Ashley from inhaling the slightly different musk scent that Jet wore, which combined with the smell of leather in the car. When they got to the bar, Ashley ordered a double shot of tequila from the bartender. The woman provided it quickly with a wink. Ashley looked back at the woman, surprised.

"Told you," Jet said from behind her, her lips right next to her ear.

Ashley shook her head, and picked up the shot, drinking it as quickly as she could, and wincing as the alcohol burned her throat.

"Jesus, babe," Jet said, handing her a lime.

Ashley sucked the lime, trying to get the taste of tequila out of her mouth. Jet watched her with a slight grin on her lips.

Looking over at the bartender, Jet held up two fingers. "Casa Noble," she said. "Run my tab, will ya, Jen?" Jet said, pulling out her credit card and handing it to the bartender.

"You got it, Jet," Jen said, smiling.

Jen handed over two shot glasses and Jet handed one to Ashley. "Now," Jet said, and she licked the spot between her thumb and forefinger and shook salt onto it, looking at Ashley.

When Ashley didn't respond, Jet shook her head and reached down to picked up Ashley's hand. Leaning over, she licked the same spot on Ashley's hand she had on hers and shook salt on it, her eyes looking into Ashley's as she did.

Ashley stood staring at Jet, unable to believe where she was, and what she was doing.

"Now," Jet repeated, her look at Ashley pointed. "Lick" she said.

She licked the salt on her hand, waiting for Ashley to do the same, Ashley finally did.

"Drink," Jet said, and threw back her shot.

Ashley did the same, noting the tequila didn't burn near as much this time.

Jet handed her a lime slice. "Suck," she said, her light green eyes widening slightly.

Jet took the lime in her mouth, sucking on it, her eyes on Ashley's, as Ashley followed suit, starting the feel the first shot taking effect.

"Better," Jet said, grinning.

"I feel a disturbance in the Force…" came a voice from behind them. It was Devin, with Skyler behind her. "Oh, no," Devin said, glancing back at Skyler, "Jet's here, that explains it."

"You're not right, Devin…" Jet said, grinning, as she leaned down to kiss Devin's cheek, and then extending her hand to Skyler.

Devin grinned up at Jet. "You know I love you," she said, her green eyes sparkling.

"You say that now, but you're marrying that one in like six months, right?" Jet said, nodding toward Skyler.

"Yep," Skyler said. "Six months and counting."

"Dev, Sky, this is Ashley," Jet said, stepping back so they could see each other.

Ashley looked at the couple that Jet was introducing her to. Devin had black hair with purple streaks, multiple piercings and a bright smile. Skyler seemed more reserved, her light blue-green eyes warm even as she extended her hand to Ashley.

"Nice to meet you," Ashley said, smiling, feeling a bit tipsy already.

Jet noted the glazed look in Ashley's eyes. "Come on," she said, taking Ashley's hand and leading her over to one of the tables.

Skyler and Devin followed. Skyler moved to pull another table over to the first, creating a space for the group. Jet got the attention of one of the waitresses and ordered appetizers for the table.

Two tables later, there was finally enough room for the rest of the group as they started to arrive.

Jet got Ashley a bottle of water, and made sure she ate some of the appetizers that came out. Ashley felt better immediately, thanking Jet for helping her.

"Too much, too fast, baby girl. But that was my fault," Jet said, grimacing. She leaned in close, putting her arm around Ashley. "I'll take better care of you, I promise," she said, her tone apologetic.

Ashley leaned against Jet for a moment, closing her eyes and just enjoying the feeling of being there at that moment. Skyler and Devin exchanged a look. Jet had told them who Ashley was, but she'd also told them that Ashley was married. They all knew that Jet respected lesbian relationships, but as far as she was concerned, men were "on their own" when it came to whether or not she'd mess with a married woman. They wondered if they were seeing just that.

By the time the rest of the group got there, Ashley was feeling much more stable. She was sipping a glass of wine. A number of women walked by greeting the group. At one point, Jericho arrived with Zoey, her fiancée. Jericho was an imposing figure, tall at five foot nine and even taller in the two inch heeled boots she wore. With long dark hair worn in a ponytail, and bright blue eyes, she had a very exotic look. Zoey, her fiancée, was a classic Californian-looking beauty with blond hair and hazel eyes and a tiny perfect figure. It was obvious from the way Jericho treated Zoey that she was very much her protector.

When she met Quinn and Xandy, she saw exactly what Jet had been talking about; butch women took care of their ladies. Even Kashena, who seemed somewhat feminine in the office with her long blond hair, had a wife who was even more feminine and petite. Sierra Youngblood-Marshal, as she was introduced, was a dark haired American Indian beauty in the classic sense. And Kashena danced attendance on her, often touching her hand, or simply putting her arms around her, holding her from behind as they talked in the group.

Raine and Natalia arrived. Natalia, a beautiful Latina, immediately dragged Raine out onto the dance floor. Raine was also very cute in what Jet called a "soft butch" way, with her long curly red hair.

"Hi! Bye!" Natalia called, laughing.

Raine followed her girlfriend to the floor, shrugging to the group with a grin.

"You think she'd get tired of dancing, wouldn't you?" Jericho asked.

"I don't think Nat ever gets tired of dancing with Raine," Quinn said, grinning.

The group laughed. Ashley was able to see that Raine was definitely more butch than Natalia, although her long curly red hair made it more difficult to be sure.

She did have a harder time with Cat and Jovina. Catalina Roché was the Special Agent Supervisor in charge of another part of LA IMPACT, and was very beautiful with long blond hair, sky-blue eyes and a great figure. Jovina was yet another Latina beauty, and very feminine. Jet told her that Jovina was a songwriter. Catalina seemed to take care of Jovina, getting her drinks, and letting her sit in the bar stool, standing next to her, her arm around her shoulders.

Ashley found herself watching all the couples there that night, seeing exactly what Jet had said and admiring it. At one point Jet excused herself to go and smoke a cigarette. The group watched Jet leave, and not too long after Jet sat down at a table on the back patio the comments started.

"Oh… there's Tabby, is she still after Jet?" Devin asked Skyler.

"I think that ship's already sailed…" Skyler said, grinning.

"Seriously?" Xandy asked, rolling her eyes.

"The girl's no slouch," Quinn said, grinning.

"You were just as bad, as I recall…" Xandy said.

"Uh-huh," Quinn said, grinning.

"All caught now," Skyler said.

"Shut it," Quinn muttered, causing the group to laugh.

"So, exactly how many women *does* Jet know here?" Ashley spoke up, surprising the group.

She'd just seen yet another woman approach Jet, who leaned down to kiss her and slid her hand through Jet's hair seductively. It was the sixth woman since Jet had gone outside less than five minutes before.

The group exchanged looks, some of them grinning.

"Well…" Cat said, her voice trailing off as she looked to the rest of the group.

"Okay, how many of those women has she been with?" Ashley asked, curious now despite how ridiculous she might sound to Jet's friends.

The looks became distinctly more uncomfortable at that question, except for Quinn, whose grin widened.

"I think it would be a shorter list if we told you who out there she hasn't been with," Quinn said.

"Pretty much," Devin agreed, nodding.

"Yeah, that seems accurate," Cat added.

"What seems accurate?" Natalia asked as she and Raine walked up.

"Jet's track record," Quinn said,

"Jodonton," Natalia said, whistling softly.

"Stud," Raine translated.

"Gonna go smoke too," Skyler said, moving to stand.

She walked outside, sitting down in the chair across from Jet.

"You know they're in there talking shit, right?" Skyler said, grinning.

Jet laughed. "Yeah, figured as much. How much bullshit are they telling Ash?"

"So far, not a thing that ain't true," Skyler said, smiling.

"Be good, Skyler, you're getting married soon…" said a girl walking by.

"Yeah, no fair monopolizing the one that isn't engaged," said the other girl with her.

"Just remember girls," Skyler said, her grin wicked, "I had her first."

"Ohhhh…" Jet exclaimed, laughing.

Jet had been in Iraq for a week before she was finally assigned to a base. Her first encounter was with a Blackhawk pilot and her crew, who were her transport to her new unit. She was greeted first by a guy about her age, who was all smiles and blue eyes.

"I'm Benny," he said, smiling at her. "You're new, huh?" he asked as she handed him her duffle and climbed up into the helicopter.

"Yeah," Jet had said, "I'm Jet."

"Good to meet ya," Benny said, glancing over his shoulder. "Sky and them should be here in a minute."

"No worries," Jet said, sitting on the bench of the Blackhawk, her legs extended in front of her, her ankles crossed casually.

Next to arrive were two men; one named Jams, a good looking guy with blond hair and blue eyes, and another with brown hair and glasses, who they called Radar.

"'Cause his last name's O'Reilly," Benny told her.

Jet liked Benny right off, he seemed like a fairly happy guy, and without a lot of bluster, which was rare for helicopter crew members. A couple minutes later the pilot arrived. She was cussing a blue streak.

"Fuckin' damn ass motherfucker, I swear to all that is not holy in this land that the man is just trying to piss me off..." Skyler said, climbing onto the helicopter, then seeing the soldier sitting on the bench seat. "Oh," she said, grinning. "Sorry, my CO is on a break and his ball-breaker of a second in command is an asshole."

"It happens," Jet said.

"Way more than it should," Skyler said, then she extended her hand to Jet. "Skyler Boché."

"Jet Mathews," Jet replied with a grin.

"Where you headed?"

"First infantry HQ," Jet said.

"We'll get you there in relatively one piece," Jams said.

"You'll be fine," Skyler said, winking at Jet. "He's just a copilot. I do the flying."

"I feel better already," Jet replied, her light green eyes looking directly back into Skyler's blue-green ones.

Skyler's chin came up slightly as she recognized the come on, but she said nothing.

A half hour later they touched down at the camp, and Jet thanked them for the ride. She watched as the Blackhawk lifted off, and thought that it hovered a few seconds longer than necessary, but she couldn't be sure, then it flew off.

It was a week before Jet saw Skyler again, and by that time she'd all but forgotten the hot pilot. She was in her office, looking over some reports she'd just received. The door to the office had opened, but she'd assumed that it was one of her fellow soldiers returning from a break.

"How's it going in here?" Skyler finally asked.

Jet turned, surprised to see her.

"Oh, you know," Jet said, her tone wry. "Same shit, different day."

Skyler grinned, nodding.

"You had dinner yet?" Skyler asked.

"Is it that late?" Jet asked, looking at her watch. "Wow, time flies, huh?"

"Oh yeah, in this fun place," Skyler said, rolling her eyes.

They walked over to the mess hall then, eating and talking companionably. Afterwards, they walked around the camp talking for a bit. Skyler told her she was from Baton Rouge, Louisiana and they talked about crawfish boils and things like that.

"Jesus, it's hot here," Jet said at one point. "Does it ever cool off?"

"Not often," Skyler said, they'd stopped walking, having reached the back of the camp.

"I'm from Seattle, it doesn't get this hot there," Jet said.

"You'll get used to it," Skyler said, staring directly into Jet's eyes.

Jet caught the look, and felt her breathing become heavier. She swallowed nervously, even as her lips parted in anticipation. She'd known from the moment she'd met Skyler Boché that she wanted her to be the first, she just hadn't known if she could pull it off. She hadn't counted on Skyler having her own agenda.

Skyler took a step toward Jet, testing to see if the younger woman would retreat. Jet held her ground, her head tilting up slightly, her lips parting as her eyes connected with Skyler's again. That was all Skyler needed to see, and taking another step closer, bringing her right up to Jet, Skyler slid her hand around Jet's waist, pulling her closer, as her mouth closed over Jet's.

The kiss was hot, and Jet immediately felt her body tremble. She reached up, sliding her hands through Skyler's hair, and pulling Skyler even closer, deepening the kiss. Skyler responded, by pushing her back against the wall to the barracks. Thankfully there was no back door and no one could see them where they were.

Skyler's hands pulled at Jet's shirt and Jet recklessly pulled it off over her head, wanting Skyler's hands on her. Skyler obliged and Jet groaned softly, pressing closer to Skyler, pulling at her, wanting to feel everything. Jet's fingers bit into Skyler's shoulders as Skyler's lips moved to her neck, then moved lower. Jet had to bite her lips to keep from crying out when Skyler's mouth closed over a hard nipple. She felt Skyler's hands at the waist to her pants, and she wanted nothing more *than to be naked at that moment, but she knew they were already risking their careers by doing what they were.*

When Skyler's hand slid inside her pants, touching her, Jet came immediately, grasping at Skyler and exalting in the feeling, wanting more. Afterwards, she leaned against the building, breathing heavily. Skyler leaned into her, her lips on Jet's shoulder and in the curve of her neck.

"My God..." Jet breathed, still trying to catch her breath.

Skyler lifted her head, looking down at Jet. "What?" she asked.

Jet bit her lip, grinning. "That was my first time," she said softly..

Skyler felt a sexual jolt run through her, the likes of which she'd never experienced before. It had her leaning in to kiss this girl's lips again. This time, Jet moved away from the wall, turning Skyler to put her back against the wall instead. Jet took the time to do all the things she'd dreamed of doing to another woman for more than a year now. Skyler found herself coming with abandon, her hands in Jet's hair and feeling insanely protective of this girl suddenly.

Their friendship with benefits lasted a full two years, even though Skyler had a girlfriend back home in Los Angeles, it hadn't mattered. They were both far away from home, and took refuge in each other's arms whenever they felt the need. Neither of them was looking for a love match, they just needed to feel needed and wanted, and it worked for them.

When Skyler's Blackhawk had gone down, Jet had been frantic to find her. When she'd heard that Skyler had lost both Benny and Radar in the crash, her heart broke for her friend, knowing that Skyler would blame herself because they were her crew. When Skyler and Jams were found, Jet had seen Skyler for only a few minutes before she'd been medevacked out to the hospital.

She'd known that Skyler would never be the same; she'd seen it in her eyes. She'd kissed her on the cheek, whispering, "I'm sorry my friend," as tears had streamed down her cheeks. Skyler had simply nodded, looking like she was hundreds of miles away. It had been one of the saddest days of Jet's life.

Jet looked over at Skyler, remembering their time in Iraq, but also seeing that Skyler was now happy and Jet knew beyond a shadow of a doubt that Devin was the reason for that. It made Jet happy to know that Skyler had finally found love. It also made her sad in a way too.

Back inside, Cat walked over to the bar, winking at Jen. "Give me a couple of shots of Casa Noble, will ya?"

"You're drinking tequila?" Jen asked, knowing she usually drank Jack Daniel's.

"It's for Jet," Cat said.

"Oh," Jen said, nodding. She poured the shots and handed them to Cat. "Twenty, Cat,"

"Jesus, Jet has expensive taste," Cat said, grinning as she pulled a ten and a twenty out, tossing them on the bar. "Thanks," she said, winking at the bartender again.

"Any time, sweetie," Jen said, loving their group, they were all good tippers.

Cat walked over to where Ashley sat, watching Skyler and Jet talk.

"Here," Cat said, handing one shot to Ashley.

Ashley looked back at Cat, her look confused.

"Drink it," Cat said, her tone commanding.

Ashley did as she was told and drank the shot.

"Now," Cat said, handing her the other shot, "take this out to Jet."

"And tell Skyler she needs to get her ass in here," Devin said, smiling sweetly.

Ashley nodded, standing up and walked toward the back door, noticing that she was getting a lot of looks from women in the bar. It made her feel a little more confident as she opened the back door and walked outside.

Walking over to the table where Jet and Skyler sat, Ashley looked at Skyler. "Devin wants you inside," she told her.

"Oh, you are in trouble…" Jet said, grinning.

"Damn it," Skyler said, grinning all the same and getting up, offering Ashley her chair.

Ashley moved to sit down, handing Jet the shot. "Cat sent this out for you."

Jet grinned, knowing Cat was known to be a matchmaker. Jet drank the shot, and chased it with a drink of her beer. Sitting back, she lit another cigarette, looking at Ashley.

"So how are you doing," Jet asked, her look searching.

"Okay," Ashley said. "Your friends are funny."

"Are they?" Jet asked, her look amused.

"Yeah, according to them, you've slept with almost every woman out here," Ashley said, her smile wide.

Jet looked surprised, and like she was about to protest, but then she looked around, even turning around to look behind her at the far corner of the patio. Finally, she sat back, blowing her breath out.

"Yeah, they're right," Jet said, nodding.

"Oh my god!" Ashley said, laughing. "You are such a slut!"

"No, honey," Jet said. "Sluts will fuck anyone, I'm very particular," she said, her look direct.

Ashley felt her breath quicken, but then narrowed her eyes.

"All of these girls, that's particular?" she asked.

Jet licked her lips slowly, looking around. "Do you see even one that isn't hot?"

Ashley looked around the patio, seeing the different women, and she had to admit there wasn't one slouch.

"And they have to be hot?" Ashley asked.

"It definitely helps," Jet said, winking at her.

"I see," Ashley said, nodding her head.

"No," Jet said slowly, "I don't think you do."

"What does that mean?" Ashley asked, her tone challenging.

"You still think I invited you to stay at my house because I'm a lesbian and you're female," Jet said.

"No," Ashley said, shaking her head, "because you still thought I looked like I used to. I wouldn't have qualified."

Jet narrowed her eyes at Ashley for a second. "You're right, I had no idea what you look like now when I invited you to stay at my house."

"What if you had known what I look like now?" Ashley asked, feeling brave with the tequila running through her veins.

She saw the quick flair of Jet's eyes widening, then Jet curled her lips in a grin.

"What?" Ashley asked.

"Tequila's doing a pretty good job on your confidence right now, isn't it?" Jet said.

"Answer the question."

"You don't want to hear the answer."

"Yes I do," Ashley said. "Answer the question."

Jet looked back at her, her eyes staring right into her. "If I'd known what you look like now, yes I would still have invited you to stay with me." Her eyes widened slightly, which should have warned Ashley, but she held fast. "But I would have invited you to stay in my bed."

Ashley stared back at Jet, completely at a loss for words.

Jet signaled the waitress. "Give me another Casa Noble for the lady."

"So," Jet said, settling back with her beer and cigarette, "let's talk about you for a minute, okay?"

"What about me?" Ashley asked, thinking she probably shouldn't have started this.

Jet's eyes stared right into hers as she asked, "Do you come when he fucks you?"

Ashley's mouth dropped open, her eyes widening. Jet started to grin, knowing she'd taken her completely off guard.

"I can't believe you asked me that," Ashley said, stunned.

"Why not?" Jet asked, her tone mild. "You asked me about my sex life, I get to ask you about yours. That's how this game is played."

Ashley looked back at Jet and realized that she was right. She had asked Jet about her sex life, and it really hadn't been her business. So turnabout was fair play, even if the question had shocked the socks off of her.

"What was the question?" Ashley asked, as the waitress arrived with the shot.

Ashley picked up the shot and downed it, setting it back on the waitress' tray.

"Put it on my tab, hon," Jet said to the waitress, smiling at her, then looking back at Ashley. "Do you come when he fucks you?" she repeated, her tone as mild as before, her eyes still staring directly into Ashley's.

Ashley looked distinctly uncomfortable, but then shook her head. "But no one comes every time," she said.

Jet's grin was sardonic and Ashley narrowed her eyes at her. "What?" Ashley asked.

"They do with me," Jet said simply.

"Maybe they fake it," Ashley said, her tone showing the effects of the shot she'd just done.

Jet looked back at her for a long moment, then looked around the patio. "Do you want me to ask one of them?"

"Stop it," Ashley said, grinning.

"Okay," Jet said, settling back in her chair again, her look still direct, "So how often do you come with him?"

Ashley blew her breath out. "I don't know."

Jet's look was almost comical. "Honey, if you don't know, he's not doing it right."

"I mean, I know, but I don't like count," Ashley said.

"Let's say out of ten times you have sex with him," Jet said, circling her finger to indicate the ten times. "How many times do you come?"

Ashley hesitated, looking like she was calculating. Jet looked back at her, waiting.

"Like two," Ashley said.

"You're kidding me, right?" Jet said, her voice serious.

"No," Ashley said, suddenly very serious about this conversation.

"And how long does that usually take?" Jet asked.

"Oh my God… like… I don't know a half hour, maybe an hour."

Jet looked back at her, completely flabbergasted. "So, out of those two whole times you come, does he make you come or do you?"

Ashley had to swallow against the sudden dryness in her mouth. She could not believe she was having this conversation at all and with Jet Mathews no less!

"Ash?" Jet queried.

"I don't know," Ashley said, not willing to tell Jet this part too.

Jet narrowed her eyes, but decided to leave that one alone. Sitting back she lit another cigarette, then looking at Ashley she said, "Five minutes."

"What?" Ashley asked, feeling suddenly really tingly from the tequila, and thinking she'd missed something.

"I can make you come in five minutes," Jet said confidently.

"Ha!" Ashley said, her tone challenging. "I don't think so."

"You don't?" Jet asked, her look direct, but easy.

"No, I'm sorry, but no. There's no way," Ashley said, shaking her head.

"What if I told you that I could make you come in five minutes without removing a single article of your clothing," Jet said then.

"I'd say you're nuts," Ashley said, her look arrogant.

Jet licked her lips again, then took a drink of her beer.

"Let's make it interesting," Jet said. "Let's bet on it."

"What are we going to bet?" Ashley said, her confidence building.

Jet looked considering for a moment, taking a long drag off her cigarette and blowing the smoke out slowly. "You like my Stang right?"

"The Fastback?" Ashley said, looking stunned. "Hell yeah."

"Okay, I'll bet you that Stang," Jet said confidently.

"Are you nuts?" Ashley said, thinking confidence was one thing, but Jet was just being crazy now.

"Not at all," Jet replied, her tone even. Jet leaned forward then, her eyes looking up into Ashley's. "Let me ask you something."

"Okay…" Ashley said, suddenly feeling less brave than she thought.

"That day, in my car," Jet said, moving a little closer, her lips closer to Ashley's now, "did you want me to kiss too?"

Ashley had to swallow against the sudden feeling that she couldn't breathe. Her eyes stared back into Jet's and she knew she couldn't lie at that moment. Finally, she nodded slowly. Jet nodded too. Picking up her beer she drained it and then stood up, holding out her hand to Ashley.

"Let's go," Jet said.

"Where?" Ashley asked, even as she took Jet's hand and let her tug her out of the chair.

"Home," Jet said, her look heated.

Once again Ashley's mouth went completely dry, so she nodded her head. Jet led her to the back door of the bar. She had a vague impression of saying goodbye to people and then they were outside and in Jet's car. The drive home was quick and before Ashley had time to think, they were inside the garage. Jet opened Ashley's door and held her hand out to help Ashley out of the car.

Taking her hand, Jet led her inside, turning off the alarm as she passed it. She led Ashley upstairs and into her bedroom, turning to press her against the bedroom door as it closed.

Jet's lips found hers and Ashley was sure the entire world had just turned upside down. The feel of Jet's lips as they moved over her lips was a surprise; they were like silk, soft, wet and with a pressure that had every nerve in her body tingling. Jet deepened the kiss then, sucking at her lips her hands sliding through Ashley's hair, gently grabbing a handful and using it to pull her face closer. Ashley moaned against her lips, and Jet pressed her body closer, making Ashley writhe as her body became a mass of nerve endings.

Suddenly Jet stepped back, taking Ashley's hand and leading her over to the bed, where she backed her up until she sat on the bed, facing Jet. Jet's lips took possession of hers again, as she moved forward, pushing Ashley back onto the bed with the simple pressure of her lips. Ashley was surprised when Jet lifted her slightly, pulling her up further on the bed, but she forgot that surprise a moment later as Jet's body pressed against her. Jet moved, pressing her hips downward, making Ashley breathe faster, her hands grasping at Jet's shoulders.

"Jet, Jet…" she whispered heatedly, as her body pressed up to meet Jet's.

Jet's hands were on either side of her head, her upper body raised, so that her hips could move expertly. Within a minute, Ashley was crying out, gasping and moaning as she felt her body explode in ecstasy. Jet's lips were on hers again, her body still moving against her and within minutes she was orgasming again.

"Oh my god… my god…" she moaned, feeling like her body could simply melt and flow away at that moment.

Jet's mouth moved down her throat, kissing and nuzzling. Ashley lay, feeling absolutely sated and wondering where this feeling had been her whole life.

"My god, you are good," Ashley said, smiling up at the ceiling.

Jet moved slightly to her side, looking down at Ashley, her eyes sparkling.

"I tried to tell ya," she said, grinning.

"You were right, you win," Ashley said, smiling.

"I usually do," Jet said, smiling too, then she moved to get up. "I'll give you a minute," she said, "I'm gonna get another drink."

With that, Jet got up and left the room. Ashley lay on the bed, her mind a swirl of questions and sensations. She could not believe that Jet had been able to excite her that much. She'd known that Jet was kind of a thing for her, but she didn't really believe that it was sexual. She really thought she admired Jet to the point of wanting to be her. Now she wondered what this meant, was she gay? Did she like women? Was that the problem with sex with her husband?

"Does the fact that I enjoyed the hell out of that, make me gay?" she asked, when she went downstairs to find Jet sitting on the couch.

"No," Jet said, shaking her head. "It makes you someone whose husband only makes her come twenty percent of the time and who needed to get off in the worst way."

Ashley looked back at her for a long moment. "Tell me how you really feel," she said, grinning.

"How long have you two been married?" Jet asked, her tone serious.

"A little over two years," Ashley answered.

"And does he make you come? Or do you take care of it yourself?"

Ashley bit her lip.

"That answers that," Jet said, her tone disgusted. "After two years, Ash, the man should know how to make you come. So either he doesn't care, or he's just really inept."

Ashley took a deep breath, blowing it out slowly. "How do I know?"

"You go home and make him fuck you like I just did," Jet said, her tone strong.

Ashley's eyes widened at Jet's words, but then she realized what Jet was saying.

Jet blew her breath out, shaking her head. "Ash, I'm sorry. But I think sex in a relationship is too damned important to be left up to whenever he gets around to it."

She stood up, walking over to where Ashley stood, and slid her hand around Ashley's waist, pulling her in close to her. Ashley's pulse quickened immediately, her breathing increasing in excitement.

"That's how he should make you feel," Jet said, her eyes staring down into hers.

Ashley blinked a couple of times, nodding her head, then moving to rest her head on Jet's shoulder. Jet's hand came up, touching her cheek gently.

"Come on," Jet said then, turning toward the stairs and reaching over to turn off the lights.

"Where are we going?" Ashley asked.

"To do this right."

She took Ashley back up to the bedroom, this time taking her time to seduce the girl, making love to her for hours until they both fell into a deeply sated sleep.

Chapter 4

The next morning Ashley woke to find that Jet had already gotten up. She found her in the backyard working.

"Good morning," Ashley said, smiling.

Jet glanced over her shoulder, smiling. "Morning," she said.

Straightening from the squatting position she was in, she walked over to Ashley, keeping her hands out to the side, since they were muddy, and she leaned down kissing Ashley on the lips.

"Did you see there was coffee?" Jet asked. "I even found some Starbucks, so it's not my stuff."

"I didn't, but I'll go get some," Ashley said. "Did you need anything?"

"Nope, I'm good."

"Yes, yes you are…" Ashley said, her smile wide.

Jet chuckled, shaking her head.

A few minutes later, Ashley walked back outside, moving to sit in one of the chairs with her coffee. She watched Jet for a while. As always, music played from the stereo, and Jet sang with most of the songs.

An hour later, Jet took a break. She sat down next to Ashley, pulled a cigarette out of the pack on the table, and reached into her jeans for her lighter. Her light green eyes looked at Ashley through the smoke.

"So, how are you feeling this morning?" Jet asked.

Ashley thought about her answer. "I'm really not sure how to feel at this point," she answered honestly.

Jet nodded, taking another drag off her cigarette. She'd wondered if Ashley was going to feel guilty, or ashamed. Jet imagined that what had happened between them the night before was likely a jarring event for someone like Ashley, who was so staid and stable.

"How does this go, moving forward?" Ashley asked cautiously.

Jet looked back at her. "That depends on you."

"On me?" Ashley asked.

"How do you want this to go moving forward?" Jet asked.

Ashley looked back at her, her look surprised.

"Within limits, of course," Jet added, her look pointed.

"What are your limits?" Ashley asked.

Jet sat back in her chair, taking another drag off her cigarette, her look direct as always.

"I don't do love, I don't do jealousy, and I don't do permanent house guests," Jet said simply.

Ashley nodded. "So, you're not in love with me, no boiling your bunny and I can't come live with you if my marriage blows up when I get home," she said, her tone succinct, making Jet chuckle.

"You got it," Jet said, inclining her head.

"What's that called?" Ashley said. "Friends with benefits, right?"

"Right," Jet said, nodding.

"Does that kind of thing work for you?" Ashley asked.

"It has before," Jet said.

"Really?" Ashley asked, curious now.

"Yep, you met one of them last night," Jet said, her eyes sparkling with humor.

"Who?" Ashley asked, her look surprised.

"Skyler."

"Really?" Ashley asked, definitely surprised now. "Are you two still?"

"Oh, hell no," Jet said. "I don't fuck with relationships. I stay away from women who are involved."

Ashley looked back at Jet, her face reflecting confusion.

"Oh, except for women who are involved with men. Men are on their own," Jet said, an edge to her voice.

"Especially ones that don't make their wife come?" Ashley asked.

"Damned right," Jet said, her tone serious.

Ashley couldn't explain it, but it somehow made her happy that Jet had such a strong opinion on what was appropriate, even if it didn't make sense to anyone else.

"So Skyler, huh?" Ashley asked. "When was this?"

"When we were in the Middle East together, years ago," Jet said.

"You were in the Middle East?" Ashley asked.

"Yeah," Jet said, nodding.

Ashley noted that Jet wasn't expansive on the subject so she left it alone.

Devin opened the door to her and Skyler's Malibu home, smiling at Jet. It had been two months since she'd met Jet at the party at Kashena's, but she already liked her.

"I'm glad you made it," Devin said, smiling and leaning in to hug Jet.

"Thank you for the invite," Jet said, handing Devin a bottle of wine as she walked inside.

Devin looked at the bottle of wine, whistling softly. "Nice…" she said, knowing that the bottle was likely about a hundred dollars.

Jet winked, looking around the house.

"Beautiful place," she said, nodding appreciatively.

"We like it," Devin said, gesturing for Jet to precede her. "Sky's in the backyard with Benny."

"Benny?" Jet asked, her look odd.

"Our dog," Devin said, but saw Jet's look, "You knew him, didn't you?" she said then.

Jet nodded, looking somber. "Yeah, he was a really nice kid," she said.

"You knew Sky then… before…" Devin said, referring to the crash.

Jet nodded, her eyes sad.

Devin shook her head. "I don't know how you all did what you did over there," she said, her tone affected. "What Sky went through," she said, shaking her head sadly.

"Yeah, it's a lot," Jet said, nodding. "I'm glad she has you though," she said, then. "You seem like you've brought her back."

Devin smiled softly. "Well, believe me, she tried to push me away with both hands for a while," she looked wistful for a moment. "But she finally got the idea that I wasn't giving up on her and let me help."

Jet nodded. "I'm glad. She's one of the good ones. You're very lucky."

Devin looked back at the other woman, detecting a bit of sadness and wondered at it.

"Were you in love with her?" Devin asked, no anger in her voice.

Jet drew in a deep breath, looking like she was considering the idea. "I think in a way I was," she said. "But I think it had more to do with where we were, and how fragile life was there."

Devin nodded, understanding that idea completely. From the stories Skyler had told her, she knew that things were always tenuous and dangerous. Having someone to hold onto was probably the best possible thing there.

"How long were you over there, after…" Devin asked.

"About a year," Jet said.

Devin nodded.

"Hey…" Skyler said, coming in from the backyard.

A gray and white streak headed towards Jet.

"Benny, sit!" Skyler called.

The big husky's butt hit the floor immediately, and Jet grinned, looking down at the dog.

"Hi Benny," Jet said, kneeling to pet the dog.

Benny happily slobbered all over Jet's hand, shirt, jeans.

"Oh my God, Benny, stop!" Devin said.

"He doesn't speak English babe," Skyler said, grinning as she walked over, and put her hand out to Jet to help her up. "Benny, easy!" Skyler said. Benny immediately calmed.

"If I could get women trained that way…" Jet said, grinning.

"Hey!" Devin said, laughing.

Jams joined them a little while later.

"Thought you were bringing the latest…" Skyler said to Jams when he arrived.

"I decided I needed a break," Jams said, grinning. "Jet, it's good to see you," he said, smiling and leaning over to hug her.

"You too," Jet said, smiling up at him.

She'd always liked Jams. He was a nice guy and he definitely looked out for Skyler and she liked that about him.

They all sat down at the table in the backyard, having drinks and talking.

"So where are you from, Jet?" Devin asked.

"Seattle area," Jet said.

"Do you have family there?" Devin asked, catching Skyler's grin even as she did.

"My parents live there," Jet said, grinning.

"Okay, what?" Devin asked, looking between Skyler and Jet.

"She hates her parents," Skyler said.

"With the passion of a fiery sun, is the term I heard once, wasn't it?" Jams added.

Jet laughed, nodding her head. "They probably bugged me that particular day. But yeah, I really don't get along with them. I stay out of their way, they stay out of mine."

Devin nodded, thinking that it was no wonder Jet and Skyler had hit it off. Skyler had a hate, hate relationship with her parents too. Which reminded her...

"Sky, didn't Sebo say he was going to try to stop by?" Devin asked Skyler.

"Yeah, he did, let me text him," Skyler said.

"The Sebo?" Jet asked, grinning.

Skyler laughed, nodding.

"The thorn in my side, pain in the ass Sebo?" Jet asked then.

"Excuse me," said a man's voice from behind them.

"Speak of the devil..." Skyler muttered as she stood up. "Hi baby brother," she said, grinning as she hugged him.

Then she turned to Jet, who stood up, her eyes on Sebastian Boché, Skyler's younger brother, who she'd heard a lot about. He looked a lot like Skyler; he was a handsome man.

"Sebo, this is Jet Mathews," Skyler said.

Sebastian nodded his head. "Good to meet you, how do you know my sister?"

"Right to it, I see," Jet said, her grin wry.

"Pretend you have manners, Sebo," Skyler said.

"It's okay," Jet said, her eyes staring directly back into Sebastian's, which were the exact same color as Skyler's. "She and I were in the Middle East together."

Sebastian narrowed his eyes slightly, then nodded, satisfied with that answer. He really liked Devin, and didn't want anyone coming between her and his sister, and this woman was very obviously gay and a stranger to him.

"Jesus, Sebo, relax!" Skyler said, shaking her head and rolling her eyes.

Sebastian smiled then, moving to grab a beer from the cooler and sitting down next to his sister. He watched Jet, though, as the rest of the group talked.

"So how long after," Jet said cautiously, referring to the crash, "did you two meet?" she asked looking between Devin and Skyler.

"About a year and a half," Skyler said, glancing at Jams, who nodded.

Jet nodded. "You two look good together," she said, grinning.

"Thank you," Devin said, smiling.

"How much longer did you stay in?" Jams asked, his look mild.

"About a year," Jet said. "Got out about a year ago."

Jams nodded. "Heard you were WIA too." Skyler's head snapped around looking at Jet stunned. "You were wounded?"

Jet looked back at Jams for a long moment, then looked at Skyler nodding.

"Jesus, when?" Skyler asked, her tone shocked.

"Just before I got out." Jet said, shrugging her eyes looking away.

Skyler narrowed her eyes, she knew Jet well enough to know that she was downplaying the incident and Skyler knew better than anyone how dangerous that could be.

"What happened?" Skyler asked.

Jet didn't answer for a long moment, then shrugged. "IED," she said simply.

"Jesus..." Skyler breathed.

An improvised explosive device was responsible for many deaths in the military, especially in the Middle East. Hearing about one happening to someone you cared about was terrifying.

Jet said nothing, really not wanting to discuss the matter.

"How bad were you hit?" Skyler asked, her eyes scanning Jet as if she could see it for herself.

Jet's light green eyes met hers. "I'm still here, aren't I?" she said, her tone light.

Skyler narrowed her eyes, she'd had no idea that Jet had been wounded, she'd never heard anything. She looked over at Jams then, and he held up his hands. Then she looked back at Jet again.

"We're not done talking about this," she told the younger woman.

Jet lit another cigarette, narrowing her eyes, but not saying anything. They moved on to other topics then, but Jet could feel Skyler gazing at her a number of times.

Later after everyone left, Devin looked over at Skyler as they cleared the table in the back yard.

"How bad do you think she was hurt?" Devin asked, concerned.

Skyler looked over at her fiancée, smiling. Of course Devin wouldn't be jealous, that wasn't her style and Skyler loved that about her.

"I think she's making light of it on purpose," Skyler said.

Devin nodded. "She needs you," she said simply.

Skyler looked back at her, reaching over to touch her cheek. "Are you okay with me being there for her?"

"Of course, Sky," Devin said.

"You're pretty awesome, you know," Skyler said, pressing her lips against the side of Devin's head.

"I can't know what it was like for you guys over there," Devin said, looking up at Skyler, "but I do know that you are close to the people you were over there with and if you can help her, I want you to."

"And it doesn't bother you that she and I were a thing?" Skyler asked, her eyes searching Devin's.

Devin looked back into Skyler's eyes. "I love you," she said, "and I trust you."

Skyler smiled, nodding. "Good."

Pinning Jet down to a time to talk was nearly impossible. She was busy all the time. Skyler kept asking, bound and determined to get together with the girl, even if it took time.

Jet was splitting her time between spending time with Ashley and work, though recently, work had kicked up significantly.

One night, a few nights after that night at the bar, Jet got in late. She took a shower and dropped into bed and was asleep minutes later.

Ashley knocked lightly, and then saw Jet lying on the bed naked but partially covered by the bed sheet. Jet stirred, opening her eyes.

"Hey," Jet said, grinning.

"Hey," Ashley said, smiling.

"Come here," Jet said, holding out her arm.

Ashley moved to lie down next to Jet, putting her head in the hollow of her shoulder. Jet's arm immediately encircled her shoulders, pulling her close and leaning up to kiss her lips softly.

"How was your raid?" Ashley asked her.

"It was okay, ups and downs," Jet replied, as she reached up to rub her eyes tiredly.

Ashley caught side of a freshly-stitched gash on her forearm.

"Would one of the downs be that gash?" Ashley asked.

Jet lifted her arm looking at it. "Yeah, razor wire sucks."

"I don't think you're supposed to go over fences with that stuff on it," Ashley said, grinning.

"Yeah, well, your suspect goes over, you go over," Jet said, her tone matter-of-fact.

"Ouch," Ashley said, wrinkling up her nose.

"Yep," Jet said, grinning again. "So how was writing?" she asked. Ashley had been working on her story about Jericho for the past few days.

"It was good," Ashley said.

"Good," Jet repeated tiredly, closing her eyes and turning her head to the side.

Ashley looked down at Jet, trying to ignore the stab of disappointment. She sighed.

Jet opened her eyes, turning her head to look at Ashley.

"What?" she asked.

Ashley looked back at her. "I didn't say anything."

"You sighed," Jet said, her look searching. "Why?"

Ashley shrugged, shaking her head. "Nothing."

Jet narrowed her eyes slightly. "Tell me," she said simply.

"It's nothing," Ashley said, her tone placating.

"Don't… do… that," Jet said, her words measured, her eyes pinning Ashley with a look. "Tell me," she said, her tone stronger.

Ashley took a deep breath, blowing it out as she shook her head. "I just missed you the last couple of nights and…" She let her voice trail off as she looked away.

Jet's hand brought her face back to hers. "If you want something," she said, her tone even, "you take it, you don't ask for it."

Ashley stared back at her, knowing that Jet was trying to get her to be more assertive.

"What do you want?" Jet asked her then.

"You," Ashley said simply.

"Show me," Jet said, her eyes still staring directly into Ashley's.

Ashley lowered her head, kissing Jet's lips, Jet responded, but didn't move to touch her. Drawing her courage, Ashley slid her hand over the sheet covering Jet's chest, touching a nipple through the sheet. Jet jumped slightly in reaction, her breath quickening. Emboldened, Ashley deepened the kiss, moving to press her body closer to Jet's. Jet's arm on her shoulder moved down, her hand pressing at the small of Ashley's back, caressing and grasping at the nightgown she wore. Ashley reached up, pulling the nightgown off and pulled the sheet aside she could get to Jet's skin.

They were making love heatedly a few minutes later. Afterwards they lay together. Ashley was gasping for breath, and she realized that Jet hadn't had an orgasm.

She looked up at Jet, who lay with her eyes closed, looking perfectly relaxed.

"You didn't…" Ashley said, her voice trailing off.

Jet's lips quirked in a grin, but her eyes stayed closed. "Say it," she said.

Ashley grinned, Jet was forever trying to get her to say words she wasn't comfortable saying. To Jet's way of thinking, you had to be able to use the words you needed to use to ask for what you wanted.

"You didn't come," Ashley said.

Jet opened her eyes, looking down at Ashley. "Sometimes I don't, it doesn't matter."

"How can it not matter?" Ashley asked.

"Another major difference between butches and men," she said. "We don't always care if we have an orgasm, as long as our lady does."

"Really?" Ashley asked.

Jet chuckled, closing her eyes again, and nodding.

Ashley shook her head, she wasn't sure if she was ever going to understand everything about the lesbian world. What she did understand was that Jet excited her beyond all experiences that she'd ever had, and that was what mattered right then and there.

Moving to sit up, she pulled the hair tie out of her hair, since it was all askew anyway, and that's when she saw the tattoo on Jet's chest. She hadn't seen it before and it surprised her. It was a fairly good sized tattoo, at least five inches in diameter. It was a dark green medallion, with a tiny detailed border around the outer edges and with odd characters and symbols in the middle.

"What's this?" Ashley asked, touching the tattoo lightly with her fingertips.

Jet sighed audibly. "It's a Shia symbol."

"Which is what?" Ashley asked.

"Shia is a religion in the Middle East," Jet said, her tone not inviting any more questions, but Ashley didn't catch that tone.

"Wait, you're religious?" Ashley asked, looking confused.

"No," Jet said. "That's not what it's about."

Ashley was running her hand over the tattoo, and felt the rough texture in parts. "Wait, this is scarring…" she said, her voice trailing off as she looked down at Jet. "What happened?"

Jet looked back at her, her face completely closed off at that point.

"You don't want to talk about this, do you?"

"Not really, no," Jet said, her tone cool.

Ashley nodded, finally noticing the ice in Jet's eyes. She moved to lie down, putting her head back on Jet's shoulder. She had a hard time sleeping that night. It had been the first time Jet had been chilly to her and it worried her. She hadn't meant to upset her, but the tattoo had been a shock. Thinking about it, she realized that Jet rarely let her see her naked. It hadn't seemed deliberate, but now Ashley was wondering if it had been. She was really curious about the scars, but she wasn't sure she was brave enough to ask Jet again.

Light and sound exploded all around her. She heard her men yelling, someone screamed, was it her? She felt intense heat, the Humvee was on fire. She moved to get out but something to her right distracted her. She turned and that's when the blast threw her off her feet. She was unconscious before she hit the ground.

The next time she woke, she could feel a thin mattress under her, there were smells and sounds, but all she could focus on was the extreme pain in her chest and the fact that she couldn't breathe. Was this how she died? The thought slammed around in her head. Opening her eyes, needing to know where she was she jumped at the black completely veiled form that hovered over her.

"It is okay," said a woman's voice.

"Who are you?" Jet demanded, her tone commanding.

"I am called Fadiyah," the woman said.

Jet shook her head, her pain overriding her ability to process anything else. She could feel blood trickling down her side. Glancing down she saw that her chest was bloody; she couldn't even tell where it was coming from. The woman was trying to dab at the blood with a rag.

"Tawaqqaf 'urjuk," Jet said in Arabic, asking the woman to please stop. Every touch of the rag was sending shockwaves of pain through her body.

"You speak Arabic?" the woman asked, surprised.

"Some," Jet gasped out, starting to feel light-headed.

Closing her eyes, she started seeing stars, moments later she lost consciousness.

Fadiyah Antar's hands shook as she did her best to clean the wounds on the soldier's chest. She could see that the woman had fainted and was grateful for that. She didn't want to cause the woman pain, but she wanted to help in any way she could. Her father had brought the woman in. There had been blood everywhere. He'd told her that he'd found her on the road and that her fellow soldiers were dead.

He had told her, "I do not know if we can save her, but we have to try."

Fadiyah knew that her father was doing what her mother would have done and that he liked the soldiers because they had been kind to her mother and to her brother as well.

As she looked at the woman's face, Fadiyah recognized her. She had been the woman that had played soccer with her brother Abdul in the streets a few days earlier. She remembered the woman laughing and calling to the kids who were playing. She had very kind eyes, such a beautiful green color, like a very light jade. Now, looking at the woman who was lying bleeding on her bed, Fadiyah knew she had to use the few skills she'd acquired to try and save her.

Jet came to again, the same pain screaming in her lungs as she tried to breathe. Trying to breathe and not being able to caused her to panic, but that made it harder to breathe.

"You have to breathe slow..." said Fadiyah.

Jet shook her head, trying to get up.

"No please!" Fadiyah cried, putting her hands on Jet's shoulders. "You must not, you will bleed again!"

"Can't, can't," Jet repeated over and over, shaking her head.

"Please lie back," the woman said, sounding frantic.

In truth Fadiyah could not believe this woman was so strong, and she was terrified that she would overpower her and try to leave.

Jet used her hands to try and push herself up off the bed. "I need to go, I need to get back…" Jet was saying. "Can't die here, not here…"

"Please!" Fadiyah exclaimed again. "Please do not… please…"

Something in Jet's mind heard the pleading in the woman's voice and she yielded. She was still panting heavily, her breath coming in gasps. She fainted again.

She woke again, this time it was just getting light outside. Turning her head sideways she saw the woman was kneeling, doing prayers. That's when she saw it. The woman's hands were flat on her thighs and her arms were extended … It was the difference in the way the Shiites prayed versus the Sunni way and Jet recognized it immediately. This family was obviously Shiite. Also known as Shia.

"Oh Jesus…" Jet breathed, starting to lever herself up again, crying out with the pain it caused.

"No!" Fadiyah cried, seeing blood again immediately. She jumped to her feet and did her best to push the soldier back down.

"I can't stay here," Jet said. "I can't stay here… You have to let me go…" she said her tone desperate. "I can't stay here…"

"Please! You are hurting yourself more, stop!" Fadiyah cried.

Jet dropped back onto the bed, gasping at the pain the jarring caused, her eyes were wide with fear. "Don't you understand? I can't stay here! They'll kill you all, I can't stay here… please… just let me go…" Her voice faded as she grew weak again. "You're Shia…" she whispered just before she lost consciousness again.

Fadiyah looked down at the woman, shaking her head sadly. She knew what the soldier meant and what she was worried about. They were in occupied territory, Raqqa. The city just down the road from where they lived was occupied by ISIL, an extremist group that was known to execute Shia, also known as the Shiites.

ISIL were Sunni and the Sunni wanted nothing more than to exterminate the few Shia left in the country. Being caught hiding an American military soldier would give the ISIL a perfect excuse to slaughter the whole family.

Fadiyah took heart in the fact that the soldier seemed to be afraid to cause that fate for her family. It meant that her father had been right about trying to save this woman. She was honorable and deserved their help.

Jet started to wake, seeing an older man standing over her.

"What... who..." Jet said, her voice soft as she looked past him to the woman again.

"He is the village doctor," Fadiyah told her.

"Jesus... no..." Jet said, shaking her head. "No, you can't..." she gasped.

"He is Shia, he will not tell anyone," Fadiyah assured her.

Jet shook her head, shifting in the bed and gasping for air at the same time.

"Please let him help you..." Fadiyah said, her voice beseeching.

Jet was feeling light-headed again, so she didn't respond. She felt the man's hand on her shirt and the sound of cloth ripping. His fingers touched the ripped and bleeding flesh where the shrapnel had cut into her skin, Jet jumped in response wincing in pain.

The man uttered something in Arabic as he turned to draw out an object that resembled a scalpel.

Jet gave a short guttural laugh, glancing at the woman. "He said this is going to hurt, right?"

"Yes," Fadiyah replied.

Jet took a deep breath, steeling herself for what she knew was going to be painful. She had no idea how right she was. As the scalpel slid across her skin it felt like it was on fire. She gripped the sheets under her, groaning loudly. She could feel the blood sliding down her sides as he reached for another implement. As he probed for shrapnel Jet did everything she could to keep from screaming. Biting her lower lip, she drew blood, gasping and groaning she squeezed her eyes shut, her entire body shaking with the effort not to scream. She knew that making too much noise could bring people and that would be disastrous.

Fadiyah watched the soldier writhing in pain and she couldn't stand it, she reached out to try and take the woman's hand.

"No!" Jet exclaimed. "I'd break your hand..."

There was one last jolt of pain that seared through her as the doctor probed deeper. Jet came off the bed a few inches, giving out a short scream and then mercifully fainted again.

"Okay, I gotta hand it to you," Skyler said, grinning over at Jet, "it's a damned hot car."

They were in Jet's car on their way to the store for Devin. It was the first time Skyler had been able to get Jet alone to try and talk to her.

Jet smiled, nodding. "Yeah, I know."

"So, how much did it cost?" Skyler asked, there'd been a lot of debate among their friends.

"One eighty," Jet said, looking over her shoulder and changing lanes.

"Thousand?!" Skyler exclaimed, her eyes wide.

Jet laughed. "No shit," she said, shaking her head.

Skyler shook her head. "Son of a bitch. How the hell did you afford a hundred and eighty thousand dollar car?"

Jet grinned again. "Outside contractor with the Army."

"Son of a..." Skyler muttered. "I heard it was good money..."

"Oh yeah," Jet said, nodding.

They were both quiet for a bit, Jet tapped on the wheel, her music on, but not loud. She knew what was coming, she was dreading it.

"So tell me," Skyler said finally.

"I'd rather not," Jet said.

"Tough," Skyler said simply, her light blue-green eyes brooking now argument.

Jet blew her breath out. "What do you want to know?"

"Tell me what happened," Skyler said.

"We were headed back to Balad, from Tikrit," Jet said, knowing that Skyler would know the landmarks. "We were just outside of Raqqa when we hit the first one."

"First?" Skyler choked out.

Jet grimaced at Skyler's tone, but nodded. "The Vee caught fire, we got out, and that's when the second one blew."

"Oh my God…" Skyler said, swallowing against the feeling of nausea that wanted to push up her throat. "How bad were you hit?"

Jet looked over at Skyler, feeling bad for putting her through this. Blowing out her breath, she pressed her lips together for a moment.

"If it hadn't been for a family in a village outside of Raqqa, I'd have been done."

Skyler blinked a couple of times, shocked at how badly this hurt to hear. But she knew Jet needed to get it out.

"A village…" Skyler said, her tone appalled, knowing that meant Jet was in a house with no running water.

Jet knew what Skyler was thinking and she couldn't tell her she was wrong.

"How long were you there?" Skyler asked, desperately wanting to hear that the Army had stormed in and taken her to a hospital.

"About three weeks," Jet said, laying waste to Skyler's hope.

"Jet…" Skyler said, shaking her head sadly. "I'm so sorry I wasn't there…"

"You were long home by then, Sky," Jet said, shaking her head.

Skyler looked back at her, knowing she'd heard the slightest edge to Jet's voice. She blew here breath out, shaking her head.

"I left you there…" Skyler said, her tone sad.

"Sky, you went through hell," Jet said. "You couldn't worry about me."

"But I should have…" Skyler said, her voice gravelly suddenly.

"You almost died, Skyler!" Jet exclaimed. "You almost died. Two of your crew did die. I wasn't that important, Jesus!" There were tears in her eyes now, fortunately hidden by her sunglasses, but Skyler had heard it in her voice.

Jet refused to admit that she'd been completely lost without Skyler there, especially knowing that Skyler would blame herself. That's how Skyler was, always taking everything onto her shoulders. Skyler saw Jet as her responsibility, just like she'd seen her crew as her responsibility.

Skyler looked back at Jet, knowing that her leaving had affected the girl. It had affected her too, she'd missed Jet like crazy, but she'd felt that it wasn't something she had the right to miss. Her men had died, one had died trying to protect her. She didn't have the right to miss the woman who'd shared her bed for two years. It wasn't as easy to justify to herself now though, not seeing that girl now, and knowing what had happened in her absence.

"I should have been there," Skyler said, simply.

"You couldn't have done anything."

"I would have come looking for you."

Jet didn't respond. She remembered having that thought at some point during her time with the Antars, that she wished she'd hear a Blackhawk overhead. It had been a ridiculous dream and it irritated her now that she'd even thought about it.

Jamming her foot down on the accelerator, the Maserati shot forward. Jet drove expertly, zig zagging in and out of traffic. Skyler refused to put her hand out to indicate her alarm. She knew Jet needed to get it out of her system, she'd felt the need to risk her life so many times after the crash. Part of Skyler wondered if it would be what she deserved, getting killed in an accident with Jet.

When Jet slowed down, Skyler looked over, and saw a single tear slide down Jet's cheek. It made Skyler feel like crap, but she knew there was nothing she could do to change the past. All she could do is control what happened now.

"So, I take it this is how you're dealing with it?" Skyler said, gesturing to the car.

Jet shrugged, then picked up her cell phone, tapping a couple of keys and then handing it to Skyler.

"What's this?" Skyler asked, looking at the phone and seeing a map.

Jet looked over at her, and reaching over, she touched a spot on the phone to zoom the map in. Skyler saw that it was a Google map of the area around Raqqa, Iraq.

"What are you trying to do?" Skyler asked, mystified.

"To find them," Jet said.

"Who?" Skyler asked.

"The family that saved my life," Jet said, her look serious.

Skyler blinked a couple of times. "Raqqa is ISIS controlled right now…"

"And they're Shia."

"Holy shit," Skyler said, knowing the gravity of that problem right away.

"It was bad enough when ISIL was in control, they at least needed an excuse to kill Shia. ISIS doesn't have that problem."

"What do you think you can do?" Skyler asked, her tone both shocked and exasperated.

"I want to go back and get them out," Jet said, her tone serious.

"You…" Skyler began, her voice trailing off as she realized how crazy that idea was. "How the hell do you think you're going to do that?"

Jet pursed her lips in disgust. "That's been the problem so far," she said. "I can't figure out how to get back, not even the Reserves will let me."

"It's ISIS fucking controlled Jet!" Skyler exclaimed. "The Army isn't going to send you back there so you can get slaughtered on Al Jazeera TV!"

Jet winced at not only the volume of Skyler's voice, but her words as well.

"I can't leave them there, Sky…" Jet said, her voice tremulous.

"Jet, they might be dead already…" Skyler said, her voice gentle.

"I know, I know," Jet said, nodding. "But I need to know. I've reached out to every contact I still have over there, and nothing… Raqqa's gone completely dark."

"That's what ISIS does, Jet…" Skyler said, her look searching.

Jet shook her head, swallowing against the lump in her throat.

"You don't understand…" Jet said, her tone more dismal than Skyler had ever heard it.

"Help me understand," Skyler said.

"They had a daughter," Jet said. "She took care of me. They'll rape her until she's dead."

Skyler closed her eyes against the image that Jet's words image conjured. It was true, young women would be gang raped by ISIS members until they literally died. It was a fate worse than death for any woman.

Taking a deep breath, Skyler looked over at Jet.

"Who have you talked to?" she asked.

"Everyone I can think of," Jet said. "The Army, the State department, the American embassy, the fucking Iraqi embassy… No one will listen."

"Maybe we need a bigger stick," Skyler said.

Jet looked over at Skyler as she pulled up to the store.

"What kind of bigger stick?" Jet asked.

"Like an Attorney General that hates the idea of women being targeted," Skyler said, starting to grin.

"You think Midnight Chevalier would do anything?" Jet asked, not daring to hope at this point. "She doesn't even know me."

Skyler shook her head. "No, but your boss knows her. Hell, the way I hear it, Kashena saved Midnight's life once… So, she might just listen."

"Do you really think so?"

"I really think we need to find out."

Jet looked back at her friend, astounded as she realized her fight for the last year had just become Skyler's fight too.

Chapter 5

Jet returned from her ride with Skyler her mind going in a hundred different directions. Pulling into her garage, she took off her black cover shirt, exposing the black tank top underneath. She then pulled the holster and holstered gun out of the small of her back and set it aside. Taking her phone out of her pocket, she set it in the iHome in the garage and cranked the music. She then popped the hood on the Mustang and spent the next two hours working on her car, letting her mind go over everything, allowing herself to remember…

Jet came to slowly, the first thing she noted was that she was breathing easier. The pain was still there, but she could breathe easier. She opened her eyes slowly, staring up at the ceiling for a long moment; she tried to reconcile her situation. She was at least forty clicks from her base and she was fairly sure that her two other team members were dead. She was in a primitive part of the country, where there were no hospitals anywhere close, and even if there were, an American soldier would be reported immediately and God only knew where she'd end up then. Essentially, she was screwed.

There was movement to her side, she turned her head and was shocked to see a young woman looking back at her. Jet figured she was in her early twenties, she was definitely Iraqi with olive skin and dark eyebrows, her hair was covered by a hijab, but her eyes were what had Jet captivated, they were almost silver.

The young woman smiled, and then she spoke. "You are awake."

"You?" Jet asked, surprised that this was the young woman who'd been the veiled presence before.

Fadiyah smiled softly, inclining her head.

"But your veil..." Jet said, knowing that she was breaking every rule the Army had given her about communicating with the female population of Iraq.

"I felt that what we just went through," Fadiyah said, gesturing to the bandages on Jet's chest, "would equate to a formal meeting."

Jet gave a short laugh in response, which unfortunately resulted in a coughing fit which left her weak and hurting desperately again.

"I am sorry," Fadiyah said, looking contrite.

"It's okay," Jet said, her voice weak, as she breathed heavily.

Fadiyah picked up a cup and moved to help Jet take a drink of water.

"Shukraan," Jet said, nodding.

"You speak Arabic well," Fadiyah said, smiling.

"I'm still learning it," Jet said. "You speak pretty good English."

Fadiyah nodded. "I learned at the university, before they closed it."

Jet's lips twitched, it annoyed her that ISIL was purposely making it impossible for young women to improve themselves. It was part of her biggest issue with being in the Middle East, the way women were treated.

"What were you studying?" Jet asked.

"Nursing," Fadiyah said, smiling.

"Well, good thing for me, huh?" Jet said, grinning.

They were both silent for a few minutes, then Fadiyah looked at her for a long moment.

"You are called Mathews?" she asked, pronouncing the surname like "mat-hues."

"Mathews," Jet pronounced. "And that's my last name."

"What is your given name?" Fadiyah asked.

"Jet," she replied.

"Jet?" Fadiyah repeated, emphasizing the 't'.

"Yeah, like the plane," Jet said, grinning.

Fadiyah smiled, nodding her head.

"Fadiyah!" called a man's voice, making Jet jump which had her hissing in pain again.

"It is my father," Fadiyah said, moving to stand and walked out of the room.

Jet overheard part of the conversation spoken in such quickly spoken Arabic she could only catch a few words.

She heard words like "safe" and "honor." She also heard Fadiyah's father ask about her veil and heard Fadiyah tell him that since Jet was a woman, she had no need of the veil. Jet rolled her eyes thinking, 'good thing they don't know I'm gay.'

Fadiyah returned to the room, smiling at Jet.

"My father wanted to know how you are doing," she told Jet.

"Yeah, and when the hell I'm getting out of his house," Jet said, grimacing when she realized she'd cursed. "I'm sorry," she said quickly.

Fadiyah smiled at Jet's grimace. "It is okay. He is not asking when you will get the 'hell' out of his house."

Jet grinned at the way Fadiyah had repeated her words, but then she drew in a deep breath, blowing it out, her look becoming serious.

"This really isn't safe for your family, Fadi," she said, shortening the girls name unconsciously. "If they find me here, they'll kill all of you."

Fadiyah looked back at Jet, her face composed. "You and your fellow soldiers come to my country to try to help us fight extremists who would destroy us all. You risk your lives for all of us, this is the least we can do to repay that sacrifice."

Jet stared back at the girl, unable to formulate a sufficient reply. She had no idea how old Fadiyah was, but what she did know was that this girl had grown up in a country torn apart by war and hate, and it had definitely had its effect on her.

"You must rest, Jet," Fadiyah told her then, seeing that Jet was fighting to keep her eyes open.

Jet nodded, allowing herself to fall asleep again.

Ashley found Jet in the garage, having heard the music and a few swear words. Walking out into the garage, Shock Top in hand, Ashley waited until Jet moved to get another tool and saw her.

Ashley offered Jet the beer.

"Thanks," Jet said, smiling. She took it gratefully and took a long drink.

Ashley watched her; things between them had been strained since the day before when she'd asked about the tattoo.

Jet caught Ashley's look, knowing that she'd been a little hard on her and feeling bad for it. Leaning in, she kissed Ashley's lips, and then pulled back to look down into her eyes for a long moment.

"I'm sorry," Jet said, her look contrite.

"I didn't mean to upset you," Ashley said softly.

"I know, and you couldn't have known," Jet said.

"Will you tell me about it sometime?" Ashley asked, her tone cautious.

"I'll try," Jet said. "But I'll probably need to be drunk."

"I can arrange that," Ashley said, grinning.

"Can you?" Jet asked, grinning too.

"Mmm Hmm," Ashley murmured, moving to slide her arms around Jet's waist, kissing her again, her lips demanding.

Jet groaned, even as Ashley deepened the kiss.

"Babe, I'm filthy…" Jet murmured against Ashley's lips, her voice affected all the same.

"I don't care," Ashley said, her hands pulling Jet's tank top out of her jeans and taking it off.

Jet reached over, setting the bottle of beer down and grabbing a rag to do her best to wipe off her hands, her lips never leaving Ashley's. Ashley's hands were grasping at Jet's waist, trying to pull her back.

"Patience…" Jet murmured.

"Uh-uh," Ashley said, smiling as she moved her lips down Jet's neck.

Jet's hands slid around Ashley's body then, pulling her close, her hands making quick work of Ashley's top, her lips taking possession of Ashley's again. Ashley moaned against her lips as Jet reached over closing the hood of the Mustang. She lifted Ashley up to sit her on the hood, moving to stand between Ashley's leg, her lips more intense on Ashley's.

Jet made love to her on the hood of the car, and Ashley enjoyed every second of it.

There was no denying that Jet was beyond exciting as a lover, but Ashley also felt like Jet was a source of strength for her, she hoped that Jet would let her be that for her as well.

Later that night they went out with the girls again and Jet indulged in a lot of shots of her favorite tequila.

"Someone get her keys," Jericho said as they watched Jet walk over to the bar to order another drink.

"Got 'em," Ashley said, smiling.

"Good girl…" Skyler said, from beside her.

"Not that I can drive that car," Ashley said, grinning.

"I can," Quinn said, grinning.

"Me too," Skyler said.

"I volunteer!" Cat added.

"Love to!" Kashena agreed.

Ashley laughed, shaking her head. "We'll have to figure something out, she won't leave it in the lot."

"That would be blasphemy," Skyler said, shaking her head.

"She'd trust you with it," Devin told Skyler.

"Yeah," Kashena said, nodding her head.

"Then I guess I win," Skyler said, smiling widely.

"Hate you," Quinn said, her eyes sparkling humorously.

"Who hates who?" Jet asked, walking up and handing Ashley her wine, another bottle of beer in her hand.

"I'm driving you two home tonight," Skyler informed Jet.

"Uh…" Jet said, looking confused.

Skyler simply clinked the bottle of beer she had with Jet's, her look inarguable.

"Ma'am, yes, ma'am…" Jet said, grinning.

Skyler nodded.

Skyler enjoyed the feel of the Maserati, but took it easy because Devin was following her in her 370Z and she knew if she pushed the speed too much she'd hear about it later.

"Come on…" Jet goaded from the passenger's seat. "Gun it."

"You're gonna get my ass beat," Skyler said, as she accelerated, the car responding beautifully. "Oh my God…" Skyler muttered reverently.

Jet laughed, knowing exactly what Skyler meant. They both loved cars, speed and power; it was one of their many bonds.

Ashley watched from the backseat, she easily sensed how close Jet and Skyler were. She knew that Skyler was about six years older than Jet, and it was obvious that Skyler was protective of the younger woman. She wanted to know more about them.

After Skyler and Devin left them at the house, Jet took a beer out of the refrigerator and walked out into the backyard to smoke, turning on the stereo as she did. Ashley walked out after her, moving to sit in the chair next to her.

Jet glanced over at her, blinking slowly, a slight grin on her face.

"Go ahead," she said, "ask whatever you want."

Ashley smiled softly. "How close were you and Skyler?"

"Over there?" Jet asked.

"Yeah," Ashley said, nodding.

Jet took a deep drag on her cigarette, blowing the smoke out a few moments later, her look considering.

"It's different over there," Jet said, her tone solemn. "There's none of this day-to-day shit that gets in the way. You do your work, your missions, your jobs and when you have downtime you spend it the best way you can. Some people have people at home that they talk to, write, text, whatever. Sky and I had each other."

Ashley nodded. "So it wasn't just sex."

"It's never just sex," Jet said, her look sentimental. "We were friends, we hung out, we drank, we talked, we laughed. Sometimes we hung out with her crew. They all knew she was gay, so it was comfortable and easy."

"How long were you two together?" Ashley asked.

Jet blew her breath out, reaching for another cigarette and lighting it. "About two years," she said, her look pensive.

"What changed?" Ashley asked.

Jet smiled sadly. "Skyler's Blackhawk went down, two of her crew were killed, and she and Jams were taken prisoner."

"Oh my God," Ashley said, not having expected that answer.

"I went out of my mind trying to help plan a rescue, but Skyler got them out. She was shot and injured from the crash…" Jet's voice trailed off as her throat clogged with tears at the memory of hearing what had happened.

Her hands shook as she lifted the cigarette to her mouth again. Ashley saw it and grimaced.

"But she got them back to her base." Jet said, her voice gruff with emotion. "I saw her once before they transferred her Stateside to recover… She was already gone."

Tears sprang to Ashley's eyes at the last words. It was obvious how much the incident had affected Jet, and it broke Ashley's heart to see it so clearly on her face.

Jet saw the tears in Ashley's eyes and leaned forward to touch her cheek in gratitude for her empathy.

"Were you able to keep in touch?" Ashley asked, hopeful.

Jet exhaled in a short humorless laugh. "It was the last time I talked to her until about seven months ago when I joined LA IMPACT and saw her at a party at my boss' house."

Ashley looked back at Jet shocked. "That must have been surprising."

"It was," Jet said, "but I was past it by then."

"Past it?" Ashley asked.

"It didn't hurt anymore," Jet said honestly.

Ashley shook her head, knowing that she wouldn't have been as easy going about things as Jet seemed to be.

"But does it now?" Ashley asked, her look probing.

Jet smiled softly, her eyes downcast. "It has its moments."

Her answer was completely honest, and Jet knew that the alcohol in her veins was leaving her wide open and she was betting herself that she'd regret it later.

Ashley nodded having sensed a lot more hurt in Jet's voice than she was letting on.

"Do you want to tell me about the tattoo?" Ashley asked gently.

Jet chewed at her lip, her look brooding. "Not sure," she said quietly.

Ashley looked back at Jet, her looked pained. "I don't want to push you," Ashley said, her tone still tender.

She could tell that Jet was being more open with her than she wanted to be. She was afraid that if she took advantage of that, Jet would resent it later when she was sober.

Jet's eyes searched hers for a long moment. Ashley felt like she was looking for deception on her part. She made a point of looking back at Jet, letting her see whatever she needed to in order to feel more comfortable.

Finally, Jet nodded, and moving to stand, she held her hand out to Ashley. Ashley took it without hesitation. Jet led her into the house and up to her bedroom. There Jet turned on her music low, then turned to Ashley.

They stood a few feet apart. Jet lifted her hand and crooked her index finger at Ashley, her look mischievous, her light green eyes intent. Ashley bit her lip as she took a couple of steps to close the distance between them.

Jet proceeded to slowly remove every article of clothing Ashley had on, then she turned her to face the full length mirror that hung on the bedroom door. Standing behind her, Jet's eyes were on hers in the mirror as her hands touched her sensually.

"This…" Jet said, her voice a sultry whisper right next to Ashley's ear, "is an incredible body," she said, as she slid her hand up Ashley's side and kissed the crook of her neck. "And with this, you can get anything you want, from anyone you want." Her light green eyes stared deep into Ashley's in the mirror.

Jet's hands continued to touch Ashley's body, making her writhe.

"When you want something…" Jet said, her voice husky with desire. Her hands moved to Ashley's hips, pulling her back against her sharply, her arm sliding around Ashley's waist to hold her there. "You use this body to take it," she said, her mouth moving over Ashley's skin.

Ashley moaned loudly, her hands grasping at Jet's arm that encircled her, her head back on Jet's shoulder. Jet reached over, turning the music up on the stereo and proceeded to make love to Ashely until she screamed over and over again.

Picking up the remote for the stereo, and putting it between her teeth, Jet picked Ashley up in her arms and carried her to the bed. Using the remote to turn the stereo down a bit then setting it aside, Jet smiled down at Ashley who was watching her with heat in her eyes.

Climbing onto the bed, still fully clothed in jeans, boots and a black collared shirt, Jet began kissing Ashley again. It was a long, long night and neither of them slept until the wee hours of the morning.

Three days later, Jet was at work, and was sitting out on the patio smoking. She was listening to music on her phone, and had her back to the double doors, so she didn't hear them open.

"Heads up, Jet Fire," Sebastian said from behind her.

Jet turned her head, and was shocked to see Midnight Chevalier standing there looking at her. She immediately dropped her cigarette, stubbing it out with a booted foot as she turned toward the Attorney General.

Even at over fifty years old, Midnight Chevalier was a beautiful woman with long strawberry-blond hair and gold-green eyes, perfectly smooth skin and an enviable petite body. She was also known to be extremely dynamic and considered by many to be the best Attorney General California had ever had. She was what was considered a 'cops cop.' She had grown up in law enforcement, moving through the ranks of San Diego PD to become it's youngest chief and then being asked to run for Attorney General to become the State's "top cop." It was impossible to be a woman in law enforcement and not know who Midnight Chevalier was.

Jet inclined her head respectfully to Midnight. "Good morning, ma'am," she said, praying she didn't sound like a complete idiot.

Midnight narrowed her eyes slightly at Jet, she'd heard a lot from Kashena about this one. Kashena considered Jet Mathews her best asset in her unit, and with her experience and abilities, Jet was proving to be just that. Jet had developed more confidential informant sources single-handedly in six months than the entire unit had in the two years previous. The girl had a gift. And, from what Midnight had been told, a problem.

"Call me Midnight, Officer Mathews," Midnight said, moving to sit down, gesturing for Jet to do the same.

"Then call me Jet," Jet said, grinning, glancing at Sebastian who nodded to her.

"I understand you're itching to go to the Middle East," Midnight said.

"*Back* to the Middle East," Sebastian put in, moving to sit in another chair.

Midnight nodded, her eyes still on Jet. "Tell me why," she said then.

Jet took a deep breath, expelling it slowly. "Because a Shia family over there saved my life and I now believe them to be in mortal danger."

"You were wounded?" Midnight asked.

"Yes, I was hit with an IED blast that should have killed me," Jet said, seeing Sebastian grimace.

Midnight's eyes flickered with empathy, nodding again. "And this family saved you?"

"Yes, at a huge risk to their own safety."

"What do you mean?" Midnight asked.

"They're Shia," Jet said and immediately heard Sebastian suck his breath in.

Midnight glanced at Sebastian seeing his reaction, then looking back at Jet.

"What does that mean?" Midnight asked, her look pointed.

"Sorry, ma'am," Jet said, grimacing. "In this particular region there are two religions that are violently adversarial; there is the Shia, or what are commonly known as Shiites and there are Sunni. The Sunni are the majority and are usually the rulers of the area and they use any excuse they can to execute Shia. By taking in an American soldier and saving my life, this family put themselves at great risk."

"How long ago was this?" Midnight asked.

"Just over a year ago," Jet said.

"So why now?" Midnight asked.

"Well, it isn't just now," Jet said. "I've been trying to get back there since ISIS took over the region. I just haven't been successful yet."

"What changed with ISIS?" Midnight asked.

"The ISIL would at least need an excuse to kill Shia, ISIS doesn't bother," Jet said.

Midnight grimaced. "How can you be sure they haven't already been killed?" she asked, her tone gentle this time.

"I can't," Jet said. "I've reached out to all of my contacts in the region and Raqqa is completely dark."

"So, you have no idea if they're even alive, but you're willing to risk your life to check?" Midnight asked, her tone concerned.

"Yes, ma'am," Jet said.

"Why?" Midnight asked, knowing there was more than Jet was saying.

Jet didn't answer for a long moment, glancing at Sebastian who narrowed his eyes slightly, then nodded. Jet looked back at Midnight then.

"Because there's a young woman," she said. "She's the one that took care of me and if the Sunni get ahold of her they'll kill her, slowly and horrifically."

Midnight swallowed convulsively, but nodded, understanding the impetus now. She put her hand on the table in front of her, her look intent.

"I don't know what I can do," Midnight said, "but I will do everything that I can to help you."

Jet blew her breath out, blinking slowly. She looked at Midnight. "Thank you," she said, her tone full of gratitude.

Midnight nodded, moving to stand.

"I'll be in touch," Midnight said, extending her hand to Jet.

Jet stood, taking Midnight's hand, shaking it as she nodded her head.

Midnight turned and left. Jet looked at Sebastian who now stood when Midnight did. He curled his lips in a sardonic grin, his eyes on her.

"If anyone can help you, it's Midnight," Sebastian said, his tone strong.

Jet nodded, "Any help is something," she said.

"That it is," Sebastian said, winking at her. "Catch you later," he said as he walked back into the building.

Jet stared after him, feeling the starting of hope in her heart.

Just hang on guys... she thought, closing her eyes and sending that thought over 7,500 miles.

Jet woke with a groan, besides the ever present pain in her chest, her back was now in a huge knot, and most likely from the jolt she'd taken over a week earlier in the blast.

"What is it?" Fadiyah asked, moving to stand to look down at her patient.

"I need to turn over," Jet said, gritting her teeth.

They'd gotten less formal over the last week, chatting occasionally about minor things. Jet was much more comfortable with her so didn't have a hard time asserting herself at this point.

Fadiyah shook her head. "You are still healing, it is not good."

Jet blew her breath out, her face contorted in pain. "I can't stay like this," she said, gasping as she tried to shift.

"Then please let me help you," Fadiyah said, her tone both motherly and nurse-like.

"Getting that tone down pretty good now…" Jet said, grinning, even as Fadiyah gave her a narrowed look.

Fadiyah stepped closer to the bed and put one hand on Jet's shoulder and the other on her hip, gripping to try and help her roll.

Jet started to move, but Fadiyah lost her grip quickly. She tried to recover by grabbing at the material of the BDUs that Jet wore. Instead, however, Jet ended up falling back onto her back again, taking Fadiyah with her due to her tenuous grip on the BDU material. They ended up face to face with Fadiyah leaning over her.

Jet stared up at Fadiyah for a long moment, her eyes slightly widened, but they narrowed as she remembered where she was and who she was staring at this closely.

Even so she couldn't resist saying, "God your eyes are beautiful…"

She'd been thinking it for days, ever since Fadiyah had taken off her veil, but she hadn't said it until now. Now she wondered if she was stupid for having done so, but Fadiyah smiled softly.

"So are yours," she said quietly.

They looked at each other for another few seconds, and Jet knew she needed to break the tableau lest she do something incredibly stupid like kiss the girl.

"How about you let me do this?" she asked then, grinning.

Fadiyah immediately pressed her lips together in a playful dirty look. "Fine!" she said, moving to stand. "Al'amirkiuwn dayimaan 'an tafeal al'ashya' dhatiha…" she muttered, saying in Arabic that Americans always had to do things for themselves.

"Damned right," Jet said, grinning.

Fadiyah opened her mouth in shock. "I thought you were still learning Arabic," she said, her tone accusatory.

"Learning to speak it, honey, not learning to understand it," Jet said, her grin wide.

Fadiyah made a disgusted noise in the back of her throat, and rolled her eyes, which had Jet laughing. Then she gave Jet a quizzical look.

"Honey?" she asked, smiling companionably.

"Uh," Jet stammered, grimacing. "It's a term of endearment," she said, "I use it a lot."

Fadiyah closed her lips, pursing them, then nodded, and said, "Okay."

Jet blew her breath out, thinking she'd gotten out of that one thankfully. She often forgot that she was dealing with an Iraqi woman and needed to be careful about, not only the way she spoke, but how she looked at the girl, smiled at the girl. And she certainly by any stretch of the imagination shouldn't flirt with the girl! It was difficult sometimes, because Fadiyah did have a playful side, and Jet couldn't help but want to tease her and make her smile. The problem was, the lesbian in her was quite attracted to the girl, and that lesbian had a big mouth.

The soldier was ever mindful of the fact that if and when she left this house, she would never see this girl again and she could not in any way cause her to shame her family. Girls in Iraq could be killed for bringing shame to their family and it was the last thing Jet wanted to do. She'd already established that Fadiyah's mother had died three years before, and that Fadiyah was the one taking care of her younger brother, Abdul, and her father, Farshad. Thus far, neither of the males in the household had even looked in on her. It was traditional that a woman's area was never entered into by the males of the household. It was for that reason that Jet and Fadiyah were able to talk freely without too much concern of offending the men in the house.

Jet steeled herself and levered herself up on her left elbow, hissing in pain as both her back and chest complained. She grabbed a handful of mattress with her right hand and pulled herself over so she lay on her left side. She relaxed then, breathing heavily from the effort of moving. A sudden feeling of nausea hit her then, and she closed her eyes against the onslaught.

"What is it?" Fadiyah asked, seeing Jet pale suddenly.

Jet shook her head, her eyes still closed as she fought the nausea. "Just moved too fast I think," she said, out of breath.

"Then rest," Fadiyah said, moving to sit again, her eyes on Jet.

Jet nodded, trying to blow her breath out slowly to ease the sick feeling. She fell asleep a little bit later.

Images were flashing in her mind: her parents, their house in Edmonds, the explosion, the image of Skyler the last time she'd seen her, and then came that familiar ache. The images continued to flash through her mind, even as something else pushed into the foreground of her consciousness, it was hot, it was so hot… Why was it so hot? You're in a desert, idiot, her mind said. Skyler had always reminded her of that, "You're not in Seattle anymore, babe…" But this was a different heat, it was moist… humid… Why was it so hot?

Fadiyah saw Jet's head starting to move around. Her hair fell over her cheek and Fadiyah immediately reached out to brush it back. That's when she felt the fever.

"Oh no…" Fadiyah whispered to herself.

She could see that Jet was sweating, putting her hand more firmly on Jet's forehead she gasped at how hot her skin was.

"No, no…" Fadiyah said, moving to get up and going into the other room to get water and a rag.

After wetting the rag, she began pressing it to Jet's face in a desperate attempt to cool the fever. She watched helplessly as Jet started to writhe, moaning softly. Fadiyah reached out, brushing her hand over Jet's hair, noting that even her hair was hot. She put the wet rag to Jet's neck, remembering what she'd been told about pulse points. She stroked Jet's hair, trying to soothe her, even though the girl wasn't conscious.

Jet's feet moved and that's when Fadiyah realized that Jet was still wearing her combat boots.

Fadiyah pushed the leg of the BDUs up and unlaced each of the boots, taking Jet's boots and socks off. Getting up she got another rag, wet it and put it to the soles of Jet's feet. That was when she noticed the tattoo on Jet's ankle. She stared at it fascinated for a moment, but knew there were more important things to worry about.

She moved back to Jet's head, and continued to change the rag, wiping her face and putting the rag on her neck, stroking her hair all the while. It worried her that the fever had come on suddenly, and she was afraid that an infection was setting in. Fadiyah knew if Jet got an infection at this point, she would most likely die. They had no antibiotics or ways to fight an infection. She did not want this woman to die; she was her friend now. Tears stung the back of Fadiyah's eyes, not wanting to lose anyone else in her life.

Jet's eyes opened, and she felt Fadiyah's hand on her cheek, and saw tears in Fadiyah's eyes. She immediately covered Fadiyah's hand on her face with her own, her fingers lacing through the other girls. Fadiyah smiled sadly at the gesture.

"You have a fever," Fadiyah told her. "You need to conserve your strength…"

"You're worried," Jet whispered.

Fadiyah looked back at her, wanting to deny it, but unable to lie. She nodded.

Jet closed her eyes for a moment, swallowing convulsively, then nodded as she opened them again to look at Fadiyah.

"If I don't make it," Jet said, her voice gravelly.

"Do not say that," Fadiyah gasped.

"Fadi," Jet said, her tone strident. "You need to listen… You need to burn my uniform and just get rid of the body, bury my dog tags somewhere far away…" She was out of breath, but she continued, her words halting as she began to feel dizzy. "Don't try to tell the military, do you understand?"

Fadiyah shook her head, she wouldn't listen to this, she couldn't.

"Fadiyah!" Jet gritted out. "You have to understand."

Fadiyah's tears spilled over, and she looked away. Jet closed her eyes, she couldn't handle tears right now. She felt Fadiyah's hand on her cheek again, and took it in her own, kissing Fadiyah's palm. Her lips lingered against Fadiyah's skin for a few extra moments. Then she put her head back down on the pillow, giving in to the desire to pass out.

Jet started awake to the feeling of a cool finger on her ankle. The fact that she felt it on her bare ankle made her realize that she was no longer wearing her boots. The fever seemed to have abated, but her head still ached madly. Moving her head to look down toward her feet, she saw that Fadiyah was looking at her ankle closely. Jet closed her eyes, knowing exactly what had Fadiyah fascinated.

"What happened to my boots?" Jet asked.

Fadiyah turned her head to look at Jet, smiling brightly. "You are awake," she said, her voice happy.

"So it seems," Jet said, grinning.

"The fever has gone," Fadiyah said.

Jet nodded, her look expectant.

Fadiyah looked down at Jet's ankle again, and then looked back at her. "I took your boots off to help cool you down," she explained. "What is this?" she asked then, touching Jet's ankle.

Jet licked her lips to wet them, stalling. "It's a tattoo," she said.

Fadiyah gave her a foul look. "I know that," she said. "But what does it mean?"

Again Jet hesitated. Glancing at the small table next to the bed, she saw a cup of water sitting there. Reaching out she picked up the cup, and Fadiyah immediately moved to help her take a drink.

"Thank you," Jet said, dropping her head back against the pillow.

Fadiyah nodded, then looked at her, waiting for an answer to her question.

Jet's arms were up near her face. She rubbed her chin against her arm, trying to think of a way out of this line of questioning.

"It's, um," Jet said, stammering, "it's a symbol for people like me." She hoped that would end the questions. It didn't.

"People like you?" Fadiyah queried. "Americans?"

Jet grinned. "Well, yeah, some of us are Americans."

"What do you mean?" Fadiyah asked, ever curious.

Jet rubbed her entire face against her arm, for once in her life not happily admitting her lifestyle. She was afraid that it would ruin the bond she had with this girl. She'd never been in that position before.

"Jet?" Fadiyah queried again.

Jet blew her breath out in a burst. "It means I'm gay," she said.

"Gay?" Fadiyah repeated, her look perplexed.

"Homosexual," Jet clarified, knowing it was more likely a word Fadiyah would recognize. She was right.

Fadiyah blinked a couple of times, then nodded slowly. Jet waited for her look to change to one of disgust or anger, but it didn't. Jet bounced her foot in subdued agitation as she waited to see what Fadiyah would say or do next.

Fadiyah noticed Jet's foot moving repeatedly, she looked at Jet in askance.

"I have ADHD," Jet said.

"ADHD?" Fadiyah repeated.

"Didn't get to that part in the classes?" Jet asked, grinning despite her tension.

Fadiyah just looked back at her blankly.

"It's a cognitive disorder," Jet said. "It means that my mind goes too fast and tries to be everywhere at once. A lot of times it comes out in some kind of repeated movement," she said, gesturing to her foot.

Fadiyah looked surprised. "Is it painful?"

Jet burst into laughter then, shaking her head. "No, hon, it's mental, it's…" Her voice trailed off as she shook her head, at a loss for trying to explain something that was part of her.

"It's me."

Fadiyah nodded again. "How do you slow your mind down?" she asked, moving to sit down in the chair next to the bed again.

"Right now," Jet said. "I don't, really. Usually I take medication that helps. Or listen to music to give me something constant to focus on remotely while I focus on what I need to somewhere else."

"That sounds very hard," Fadiyah said.

"It definitely has its moments," Jet said, nodding.

Fadiyah smiled at her then, and Jet returned the smile, relieved beyond words that Fadiyah seemed okay with the fact that she was gay.

The night before Ashley was supposed to leave to go back to Washington, Jet took her to dinner and they sat talking for hours. Once back at the house, they made love and lay together afterwards. Ashley glanced at the clock, it was two in the morning.

"You have to work tomorrow," she said, grimacing.

Jet grinned. "Don't worry about it."

Ashley was lying in Jet's arms, and she couldn't begin to imagine how strange it was going to be to go home to Greg. She hadn't been kidding when she'd told Jet that she was more butch than her husband. She had called him a total of once during her time in Los Angeles; it had been about a three minute call. In the end she'd hung up thinking that she wasn't sure if she could even face him.

"How am I going to do this?" Ashley asked, her thoughts on going back.

Jet's fingers stroked her bare shoulder, as she looked up at the ceiling.

"Go back and tell him you want out, if that's what you want," Jet said.

Ashley moved to look up at Jet. "I want what this feels like," she said, indicating to their bodies lying together.

A grin tugged at the corner of Jet's mouth. "Are you gonna get this with him?"

"I doubt it," Ashley said, "and part of me doesn't even want to find out."

"Why?" Jet asked.

"Because," Ashley said, "because I feel connected here." Again. she indicated to their bodies and put her hand on Jet's chest, touching the tattoo again.

Jet looked back at her, her look somber.

"But you know there's no future here," Jet said, her tone cautionary, "with me."

Ashley moved to lever herself up on her forearms. "Yes, I know," she said, her tone clear. "You don't do love. But I want this… this kind of thing. To feel a deep connection with someone and have passion and heat… and love too."

Jet nodded, understanding what Ashley meant. In her heart of hearts, she wanted that too, but she didn't think it was something she'd ever have, so why bother thinking about it?

"It's up to you, babe," Jet said. "I can take you to the airport in the morning. You can go home, tell him you want a divorce and be back in time for dinner if you want. I just don't want you to leave him thinking that something's changed here…"

"I know," Ashley said again, feeling like Jet was trying to push her away and irritated by it.

Jet detected the irritation and narrowed her eyes slightly, Ashley caught the look and returned it.

"I get it, okay?" Ashley said. "I'm not leaving my husband thinking I'm going to come back here and build a love nest with you, okay? Jesus…"

Jet couldn't help but grin at the ire she heard in Ashley's voice. It was amazing how much she'd changed in just the two weeks she'd been there. She had more confidence and was aware of her own value. Jet honestly hoped that something had clicked inside Ashley, something that told her she didn't have to settle for mediocre to be loved.

"Don't you grin at me Jet Blue Mathews…" Ashley said, narrowing her eyes.

"Then don't be so fuckin' cute when you're mad," Jet replied.

"I swear to God, I'll hit you…" Ashley said, scrunching up her face.

"Yeah, that'll hurt…" Jet said, rolling her eyes.

Ashley started laughing then, and the spent the rest of the night talking about whatever came to mind. They both finally fell asleep at four in the morning, and the alarm went off at six.

"Oh God…" Jet said, groaning. "I changed my mind. Divorce him in a text and let's go back to sleep…"

Ashley chuckled, turning over and looking at Jet. Her eyes surveyed this handsome, wonderful woman in amazement. Two weeks before, she wouldn't have believed how different she felt. She was still completely dazzled by Jet Mathews, but for a completely different reason. She now knew more about Jet and in knowing more, she found that Jet was even more incredible than she'd believed before. She'd also discovered that Jet was human with hurts and wants like anyone else; it had endeared her more to Ashley.

Laying her hand on Jet's cheek, she looked down at her.

"You are so amazing," she said, her blue eyes shining.

Jet looked back at her, her face tranquil. "I'm just me," she said.

"And who you are, is amazing," Ashley said.

"Okay," Jet said, not looking like she believed a word of it, but also too tired to argue.

Ashley looked considering for a moment, then gave Jet a direct look.

"Will you tell me about this?" she asked, touching the medallion tattoo.

Jet looked back at her for a long minute. "It was an IED in Iraq."

Ashley stared back at her in shock.

"It would have killed me, but a Shia family took me in and saved my life." She touched the tattoo that she'd already told Ashley was a Shia religious symbol. "They did it despite the fact that if I'd been found in their home, they would have been slaughtered like cattle."

"Oh my god, Jet…" Ashley said, shocked more than she'd thought possible.

Jet nodded. "Yeah," she said simply.

"I guess I can understand why you don't talk about it much," Ashley said, her tone gentle. "Thank you for telling me though."

Jet smiled softly. "Figured you should know."

Two hours later, Jet walked her to the security checkpoint. Turning, Jet took her in her arms, pulling her close and leaning down to kiss her softly on the lips. Then pulling back she looked down at her.

"You do what feels right when you get there," Jet said. "I will be here for you, no matter what, okay?"

"Okay," Ashley said, suddenly feeling tearful.

Jet saw the tears in her eyes, and gathered her in her arms again, holding her close.

"It'll be okay, Ash…" Jet said.

Ashley nodded her head, forcing herself to step back and look up at Jet.

"Thank you," she said, her eyes looking up into Jet's. "For everything."

Jet nodded, smiling.

Ashley turned and determinedly walked up the ramp to head to the security checkpoint. There were a few times when all she wanted to do was run back down the ramp and back into Jet's arms, but she knew she needed to do this herself.

She landed at Seattle Airport three hours later. She texted Greg to tell him her plane had landed. Walking to baggage claim, Ashley felt almost numb. She'd texted Jet to tell her she'd landed as well.

Jet had texted back quickly. "Good flight?"

Ashley had sent back a sad face.

"You can do this, babe," had been Jet's response.

She'd yet to hear from Greg. Standing at baggage claim she finally got a text from him, "At the curb."

So romantic, was Ashley's thought.

She hauled her bag out to the curb. Seeing the light blue Nissan Leaf, she almost wanted to laugh. Compared to Jet's Maserati, the Leaf looked pitiful. As she walked up to the car, Greg popped the trunk, then proceeded to sit in the car and wait for her to put her bags in the back.

Ashley thought about Jet, and how she would never let her touch a heavy suitcase. Shaking her head she rolled her bag to the back of the car and after barking her shins a couple of times, got the bag in the trunk. Finally, she got in on the passenger's side of the car. Looking over at Greg, she saw the straggly brown hair and the boring brown eyes. It was everything she could do to stay seated in the car, he didn't even lean over to kiss her hello.

"Thanks for your help with the bags," Ashley said sarcastically.

Greg looked back at her for a second, then shrugged. "I didn't want to get a ticket."

"Uh-huh," Ashley said, thinking that Jet wouldn't have cared.

"Greg…" she said as he carefully signaled and pulled away from the curb at the dizzying speed of five miles an hour. "We need to talk."

Two hours later she was on the phone to Jet as she threw stuff into a suitcase.

"I hope you were serious this morning," she said, her voice out of breath, "because you have completely ruined me for wussy men."

Ashley ran back into Jet's arms eight hours after she'd landed in Seattle. Jet grabbed her up, kissing her and laughing.

"You're nuts!" Jet said.

"I wasn't kidding," Ashley said. "I couldn't see one redeeming thing about him after spending two weeks with you. You know he didn't even help me with my bags, he popped the trunk and that was the extent of his assistance."

Jet looked at her as she loaded Ashley's suitcases into the back of the Maserati. "Seriously?"

Ashley held out her leg with bruises on the shin. Jet knelt down, taking her leg and kissing the bruise while Ashley laughed and did her best to balance.

"Come on," Jet said, taking her hand to lead her over to the passenger side of the car.

They were back at Jet's house an hour later. Jet had made up the guest bedroom closest to hers, per their discussion. In the end, though, they ended up in Jet's bed making love. Ashley was happy to be back.

Jet had Ashley with her the next morning when she went into the office, because Ashley was still working on her stories about the department. She wanted to see if she could score a few minutes with Jericho to ask a few more questions. As it turned out, Jet got called to Jericho's office on an unrelated matter right before lunch.

"Ah shit, what did I do?" Jet asked, grimacing after she hung up the phone.

"What?" Ashley asked from behind her. She was working at the small table in Jet's area.

"That was Jericho's secretary, she wants to see me, now…" Jet said, looking a bit worried.

"What did you do?" Ashley asked, her eyes widening.

"Thanks!" Jet said, giving her a dirty look.

Ashley laughed. "Stop it. She's probably going to give you a medal or a promotion or something."

"Yeah, I'm sure that's it," Jet said as she stood and stretched.

Ashley stared at Jet appreciatively; she wore well-fitting faded jeans and a black fitted tank top and lace up boots. At her throat she wore a simple silver byzantine-style chain and small silver and black hoops in her ears. Regardless of the simplicity of the outfit, she looked really good, especially to Ashley.

"Quit it," Jet said in an aside, seeing Ashley watching her.

Ashley chuckled, nodding her head and Jet left the area.

An hour later, Jet still hadn't come back, but Sebastian came by.

He knocked on the side of the cubicle, causing Ashley to turn and look at him. He grinned at her, his gray-green eyes twinkling.

"I've been instructed to take you to lunch," Sebastian said, smiling.

"Instructed?" Ashley queried.

"Yeah," Sebastian said, leaning casually against the cubicle wall, "by this mean little girl with fiery-green eyes."

Ashley chuckled. "You can't mean Jet…" she said sarcastically.

"That sweet angel?" Sebastian said, grinning. "Of course not." He canted his head at her then. "Would you like to have lunch?"

"Sure," Ashley said, smiling.

She stood up, realizing that she was a bit stiff from sitting all morning. She arched her back stretching. Glancing over at Sebastian, she saw that he was smiling and watching her appreciatively. When he saw that she'd caught him ogling her, he closed his eyes in a comical wince.

"My partner would smack me for doing that," he said, his tone contrite.

"Well, it's probably a good thing she's not here," Ashley said, reaching for her purse.

"How much do I have to pay you for your silence?" Sebastian asked, as he gestured for her to precede him.

"Oh, I don't know…" Ashley said, smiling. "I'll have to get back to you on that one."

Sebastian grinned, opening the door to the office for her and holding it until she passed through. They walked out to the parking lot and he led her over to a black Hummer. She canted her head at him.

"A left over from my Ranger days," he said, shrugging.

He opened the passenger door for her, holding out his hand so she could hold it to step up into the vehicle. Ashley smiled, thinking that Rangers had some serious manners.

He got in on the driver's side, then looked over at her. "What would you like?" Ashley looked like she was at a loss. Finally, she shook her head. "You pick."

"Okay," he said, narrowing his eyes at her.

"What?" Ashley asked, self-consciously.

"Trying to figure out if you're of the salad set," he said, a grin playing at his lips.

"I've been known to eat salad too, but I'm more of a beef kind of girl," Ashley said.

"Oh, I think I'm in love," Sebastian said, his smile wide.

Ashley laughed as he started the vehicle, and put in gear. He reached for his cigarettes, then grimaced, holding up the pack. "Do you mind?"

"No, go ahead," Ashley said.

"Scoring points left and right…" Sebastian muttered as he took out a cigarette. He lit it and then dropped his lighter in the cup holder.

Ashley reached over and picked it up looking at it. It was a Zippo like Jet's, but it had a black bereted skull with a knife in its teeth, with a black banner over it that said "Ranger" and lettering on the back that said "Mess with the best, die like the rest."

Sebastian glanced over, seeing that Ashley was looking at his lighter. He was curious about this one; he knew she was seeing Jet, but she just didn't seem like a lesbian to him and he usually had good instincts about that. He'd also heard that she was married to a man, but he knew that never said anything necessarily. Kashena's wife, Sierra, had been married to a man too, a Marine.

"You really were an Army Ranger?" Ashley asked, looking over at Sebastian.

Sebastian grinned. "Yeah," he said, nodding. "Army for ten years, Ranger for six, Captain for four."

"Wow…" Ashley said, her eyes reflecting admiration.

"You should be getting used to all the ex-military around here," Sebastian said, grinning.

"Well, I know that Jet was Army," Ashley said, narrowing her eyes, "and that Skyler was Army too… Who else?"

"Kash was a Marine," Sebastian said.

"Oh!" Ashley said. "I don't think I knew that."

"I won't tell her you said that," Sebastian said, grinning.

"Damn, there goes my leverage," Ashley said, snapping her fingers.

"Oh, I think you probably still have some…" Sebastian said, grinning.

Ashley laughed. "What leverage could I still have?"

"Oh, beautiful women always have leverage," Sebastian said, his tone sure.

Ashley looked back at him, thinking he was kidding, but she could see that he was serious. She looked out the passenger window, biting her lip. She had to admit it felt good to hear that from someone other than Jet, who she felt was biased.

At the restaurant, Sebastian got out and walked around to open her door for her, again holding his hand out for her so she could get out without ending up flat on her butt. He even held open the restaurant door for her. He was definitely a gentleman, because Ashley didn't feel that any of his actions were out of the ordinary for him.

Once they were seated at the table, and had ordered their lunch, Ashley excused herself to go to the restroom, and Sebastian stood when she did. It was almost jarring to have a man act like that around her. She was used to men like Greg, who didn't have a gallant bone in his body. In the bathroom, Ashley found herself checking her makeup and her hair, glad she'd taken the time this morning to look nice. She knew it was silly, but she wanted to look good, if nothing else so people didn't wonder what Jet was wasting her time on her for.

As she walked back up to the table, Sebastian once again stood, and even held her chair out for her.

"Thank you," Ashley said, smiling up at him.

"No problem," he said, smiling back at her.

After a few minutes, he looked over at her. "So how long have you known Jet?"

"Since high school," Ashley said, smiling fondly.

"Did you have a crush on her then too?" Sebastian asked, smiling.

Ashley laughed softly. "You know, I really think I did. I just didn't recognize it."

"Well, I've only known her for about seven months now, and I gotta say, I love the girl."

"She kinda has that way with people," Ashley said. "In high school she was almost legendary."

Sebastian laughed at that, nodding. "I believe that."

"Don't get me wrong, she was a troublemaker too, a little rebel."

"No wonder I like her," Sebastian said, grinning.

"Oh… were you a rebel too?" Ashley asked.

"Well, I got into trouble a lot, if that counts," he said, his look having a hint of seriousness to it.

Ashley looked at him. "What kind of trouble?"

Sebastian shrugged slightly. "The kind where you get arrested."

"Really?" Ashley said, not able to see that in this man. She shook her head. "I really can't picture that."

Sebastian's smile was wry. "Oh, trust me. I got arrested for holding a knife to my father's throat and threatening him."

Ashley looked shocked, but then started to shake her head. "He must have done something to warrant that."

Sebastian canted his head. "What makes you say that?"

Ashley looked back at him, seeing the almost amused look in his eyes. She thought about it for a few long moments and finally, she shrugged.

"I guess because from what I've seen of you, you're this complete gentleman. I also know that Jet likes you, and she's always a really good judge of character. Besides, you were an Army Ranger, that says a lot."

Sebastian found himself grinning by the end of her answer. "All that, huh?"

Ashley laughed self-consciously. "I'm sorry, I ramble when I'm nervous."

"And why are you nervous?" Sebastian asked, his gray-green eyes looking back into hers.

Ashley bit her lip, knowing she'd just backed herself into a corner and not sure how to answer his question. She dropped her eyes from his, nervously rearranging the silverware in front of her. His hand on hers stopped her. She looked up at him and saw that his look was kind.

"You don't need to be nervous around me," he told her. "I'm fairly harmless."

"I don't know that I believe that for a second," Ashley said, amusement in her eyes. "But thank you."

Sebastian nodded, sitting back in his chair and taking a drink of his beer.

"Do you know what kind of trouble your girlfriend is up to at this moment?" he asked her then.

"Jet's not my girlfriend," Ashley said, far too quickly. "I mean, she wouldn't call herself that, she's a non-relationship type of person."

"Her loss…" Sebastian muttered.

Ashley laughed softly at his comment. "So what kind of trouble is our girl into?"

"Oh, she's in the director's office right now, working on getting her and the Attorney General to send her back to Iraq," he said, the look on his face indicating what he thought of the idea.

Ashley looked at him, shocked. "Why would she do that?" she asked, but then quickly realized exactly why. "Because of that family…"

Sebastian nodded, his look not pleased. "She's gonna get herself killed."

"What do you mean?" Ashley asked.

"The area she'd need to go into is ISIS controlled right now. They even smell her and they'll send twenty insurgents to kill her."

Ashley drew in a sharp breath. "Certainly they won't let her go back over there, she's not even in the Army anymore, is she?"

"She's in the reserves."

Ashley pressed her lips together, her look worried.

"I'm sorry, I probably shouldn't have said anything, if she hasn't," Sebastian said.

"She just told me about when she was injured, the night before last, so…" Ashley said.

"So she probably hadn't gotten around to it yet," he said, grimacing.

"Or she wasn't going to tell me."

"Maybe not until she knows if it's a go or not," Sebastian said. "It's not going to be easy to get her over there, especially not *there*. Even the Army steers clear of ISIS controlled territories unless it's an all-out offensive."

Ashley blew her breath out, nodding.

It took everything Ashley had not to ask Jet about her plans to go back to Iraq, until much later that night. They lay in bed, having just made love.

"So when were you going to tell me you're trying to go back to Iraq?" Ashley asked quietly, her eyes looking down.

Jet pursed her lips, she wondered if Sebastian was going to say something when he took her to lunch. He hadn't been pleased that Midnight had come to discuss the matter further with Jericho and Jet. That had been why Jet had suggested that he go take Ashley to lunch, hoping to distract him with a pretty girl. It had half worked.

"I just don't know if it's going to happen at this point or not."

"But you were going to tell me?" Ashley asked, her tone cynical.

"Well," Jet said, grinning, "I would have said I was leaving."

"Uh-huh," Ashley said, nodding her head. "That's what I thought."

"I just didn't see the point in worrying you, Ash."

Ashley moved to sit up, pulling the sheet up with her. "I don't understand why you feel like you need to do this."

Jet looked back at her for a long moment, trying to think of a way to explain it to Ashley.

"Let me ask you this," Jet said. "If tomorrow I saved your life, risking my life to do it, and then you found out a year from now I was in danger, would you do whatever you could to help me?"

"Well, yes, but..." Ashley said, shaking her head.

"There's no but, Ash," Jet said. "Those people risked their lives to save mine, and I can't leave them in that place and not try to do something."

"What if you're killed doing that?" Ashley asked.

"Then maybe I was meant to die then, and I cheated death," Jet said, her tone reasonable.

Ashley shook her head, unable to understand what drove these people to risk their lives. She knew it was an admirable quality, but it scared her all the same. The idea of losing Jet to some unseen, evil force in a distant country made her feel sick.

Chapter 6

As Jet healed, she got more and more restless.

"I need to get up," she said one morning to Fadiyah as she walked into the room.

"Okay," Fadiyah replied. "Will you let me help you?"

Jet grinned, remembering how Fadiyah trying to help her had ended last time.

"Are you sure you want to repeat that folly?" Jet asked, raising a black eyebrow.

"I do not want you to hurt yourself again," Fadiyah said, her tone even.

"How about you stand there, and if I need you I'll say so," Jet said, subduing a grin.

Fadiyah did not look pleased by this suggestion, but she'd already learned how headstrong this particular woman was, so she didn't bother to argue.

Jet carefully shifted her weight to swing her legs over the side of the bed, wincing in pain a few times, but pushing on.

Fadiyah stood by, looking worried. Jet caught her shifting her weight back and forth nervously.

"Will you stop that?" Jet asked, her tone cajoling.

Fadiyah bit her lip instead, doing her best not to pace in agitation.

When her feet were finally on the floor, Jet pulled off the remnants of her khaki colored t-shirt, fully revealing the black exercise bra that was partially covered by bandages. She sat for a long few moments taking slow deep breaths, both to relieve the pain she was feeling from her back and her chest and also to gather her strength.

Finally, using her arms to push herself up, she teetered slightly, and Fadiyah moved to support her. Jet's hand reached out gripping Fadiyah's shoulder as gently as she possibly could. She was breathing heavily with the effort of holding herself steady. She was also thanking the daily sit-ups, push-ups and hours of cardio and weight lifting that provided the strong core muscles that supported her now.

When she finally calmed her breath again, Jet took a step, wincing as the movement shifted still healing wounds on her chest and angered muscles in her back. Gritting her teeth she took another step, forcing herself to keep from groaning at the pains shooting down her body from her chest and back. She couldn't control the panting that resulted from her body's effort to deal with the pain.

Fadiyah looked over at Jet, feeling the way her arm was shaking, and hearing her panting. She knew that Jet was overdoing it, and probably hurting herself a great deal. It worried her.

She was just about to tell Jet that she needed to stop, when Jet stumbled, starting to fall. Fadiyah cried out, moving to try and catch Jet with her other arm before she crumbled to the floor, but she wasn't fast enough. Jet lay unmoving for a few moments, gasping in pain, and really wishing she'd been smarter about the whole walking thing.

"Jet!" Fadiyah queried anxiously, kneeling on the floor, her hands grasping at Jet's shoulders to try and help her up.

"Wait, wait..." Jet said, holding up one shaking hand. "Please..." she said, gasping.

After a couple of minutes, she moved carefully, turning over on her back and looking up at Fadiyah, who still kneeled over her.

"I'd say this mission was a fail," Jet said, her breathing still somewhat heavy.

Fadiyah looked down at her, her look circumspect.

Jet started to laugh then, a warm raucous laugh that was so contagious that Fadiyah found herself laughing too. When they'd exhausted themselves with their laughter, Jet dropped her head on the wooden floor, closing her eyes.

"I'm just going to stay down here," Jet said, her tone tired.

"You cannot," Fadiyah said, shaking her head. "It is not clean."

"Don't care," Jet said, sounding like a petulant child.

"La yakun alttifl..." Fadiyah said, telling Jet not to be a child in Arabic, forgetting for a moment that Jet understood Arabic.

"Can if I wanna," Jet said, grinning and opening her eyes to look up at Fadiyah, her eyes sparkling with humor.

Fadiyah closed her eyes, shaking her head, then opened them again, and looked down at Jet. "You must get up," she said, her tone brooking no argument.

"Fine," Jet said, exasperated.

Fadiyah moved to help her but Jet held up her hand.

"I can do this."

"Like you could stand and walk by yourself?" Fadiyah asked, her own eyebrow raised.

"That's just wrong," Jet said, narrowing her eyes at Fadiyah.

"What is wrong?" Fadiyah asked, still trying to get accustomed to Jet's phrases.

"You kickin' a sista when she's quite literally down," Jet said, quirking a grin.

"I did not kick you," Fadiyah said, her look aghast.

"Never mind," Jet said, too tired to try and explain

Once again, using her hard acquired upper body strength, Jet pushed herself into a sitting position. She waited until her breathing calmed again, then she reached up, grabbing the end of the bed's wood base. Tightening her grip and then concentrating on nothing but sending every ounce of strength she had to her stomach muscles, she pulled herself up to standing.

Fadiyah watched in amazement, seeing the muscles in Jet's arms and stomach contracting and straining with the effort. It was obvious that Jet Mathews was very strong, despite being so badly injured.

It took a few more minutes, and her allowing Fadiyah to help her take the steps back to the bed, but Jet made it.

"That was fun," Jet said breathlessly. "Let's do that again in about three hours."

"No," Fadiyah said simply.

Jet chuckled at the look on Fadiyah's face.

"Four?" Jet queried.

"No," Fadiyah answered.

"Five?"

"No!" Fadiyah exclaimed, a grin starting on her lips.

"Okay fine, tomorrow," Jet said, sighing.

"Maybe," Fadiyah said.

It took another week, but Jet was eventually able to get up and walk with relatively no effort. She had to stay in the room they were in, though. She couldn't be observed either by the men in the household, or more concerning, anyone outside that could tell ISIL about her.

It was two more days, before Jet told Fadiyah that she needed to leave.

"Leave?" Fadiyah repeated, looking worried.

"Fadi, I need to get back to my unit," Jet said. "Every day I stay here, I'm putting your family in greater danger."

"How will you get back?" Fadiyah asked.

"It's only about a forty click hike," Jet said, shrugging.

Fadiyah looked back at Jet like she thought Jet was insane, which indeed Fadiyah was wondering if that was the case.

"I can do it, Fadi," Jet said. "You don't have to worry."

Fadiyah shook her head, not wanting to think about Jet trying to walk all that way or what would happen if she failed.

"Did I get here with anything?" Jet asked. "My pack, my gun?"

"Yes", Fadiyah said, nodding as she got up and left the room. She came back in with both Jet's pack and her rifle.

Jet moved to sit up, taking the M16 rifle in her hands. Fadiyah watched in fascination as Jet removed the ammunition magazine from the rifle, checked it and then set it aside. She then began turning nobs, and pulling the trigger as well as the charging handle on the top of the weapon.

What is that you are doing?" Fadiyah asked, pointing to the rifle.

"I'm doing what's called a function check," Jet said. "It's to make sure this baby fires when it's supposed to. It can be the difference between a long healthy life and a quick death by enemy fire."

Fadiyah nodded, surprised that she'd somehow managed to forget for a few moments that Jet was a soldier. Not that it was an easy thing to forget, she still wore the camouflage uniform pants and her dog tags.

Jet slid her ammunition magazine back into the bottom of the rifle and pulled back on the action handle to chamber a round, the weapon pointing downward the entire time. After clicking on the safety, she set the rifle aside and reached for her pack. She pulled out a khaki colored tank top and pulled it on over her head. She then rummaged through the pack, pulling out MREs, water packs, extra ammunition clips, a Kabar knife and sheath which she also set near her rifle. She also pulled out a first aid kit, and extra socks. Unfortunately, her radio had been in the Humvee when it had burned, having just used it to communicate with the base before they'd hit the first IED.

She looked at Fadiyah and saw that she was watching her with wide eyes.

"It's not as bad as it looks," Jet said, as she started to put things back in her pack.

"It does not look bad," Fadiyah said. "I have never seen this up close. Only on soldiers going by our village." She smiled softly. "Do you remember the day you played with the boys in the village?"

Jet canted her head. "You were there?" she asked, surprised. She realized she shouldn't be, since there had been a few fully veiled women watching the minor soccer match she'd conducted. It had involved Jet and three other soldiers against at least ten of the village children.

"I remember your smile that day," Fadiyah said. "And how you laughed and teased the children, making them giggle and scream in laughter. My little brother Abdul was one of those boys."

"He was?" Jet asked, having not remembered that, although she'd only glimpsed the boy since she had been in the house.

"Yes, and he was so happy that day," Fadiyah said, smiling fondly. "It was the first time I had seen him smile and laugh so much since our mother died."

Jet smiled sadly. "I'm glad I could help," she said. Then she gestured to her rifle. "I wish this wasn't the only way we could help your country."

"I wish that too," Fadiyah said.

They exchanged a sentimental look then.

Jet moved to stand, setting her pack down next to her rifle.

"When will you go?" Fadiyah asked, her tone subdued.

"Tonight," Jet said, picking up her watch and putting it on. "Late, so hopefully everyone is asleep."

Fadiyah nodded, her look sad.

Jet smiled, taking solace in the thought that Fadiyah might miss her a little bit.

At midnight, Jet put on her boots and clean socks. She pulled on her camouflage jacket that still had her blood on it. Fadiyah stood watching her, her face full of concern.

Jet looked at Fadiyah, seeing that she was upset, and wanting to do something to help, but not sure what was wise or safe. Finally, throwing caution somewhat to the wind, she stepped over, holding her arms out.

"Will you permit me?" *Jet asked Fadiyah, her tone respectful.*

Fadiyah nodded sadly and stepped into Jet's arms. Jet hugged Fadiyah to her, one hand on her upper back the other holding Fadiyah's head gently. She felt Fadiyah tremble, and heard her sniffle.

"No tears…" *Jet said softly.*

Fadiyah nodded, keeping her head against Jet's shoulder.

"I will miss you, Jet," *Fadiyah said.*

"And I will miss you," *Jet said, putting her finger under Fadiyah's chin to turn her face up to hers.* "Thank you for saving my life," *she said, her tone grave.* "I will never forget this kindness."

Fadiyah pressed her lips together, tears in her eyes again.

"Stop that," *Jet said, smiling, even as she felt a lump rising in her throat.*

She hugged Fadiyah again, then stepped back.

"I better go," *she said, pulling on her pack, and then picking up her rifle.*

Fadiyah surprised her by reaching her hand up to touch her cheek. "Please be careful, Jet Mathews."

"You be careful too," *Jet said, her look serious.* "Make sure you use the double veil every time you leave the house, never forget."

Fadiyah looked back at her for a long moment. She knew that Jet was telling her that for her own safety and it warmed her heart just a little more toward this brave soldier.

"I will not forget," Fadiyah said, nodding.

"Good," Jet said, smiling.

Jet walked to the door of the room. She looked back one last time, seeing Fadiyah standing in the middle of the room, her hands clasped together in front of her, her look still worried.

Jet winked at her, then stepped out the door. She left the house moments later, moving carefully to avoid making any noise. She spared one last glance at the house she'd been in. Taking a deep breath, she blew it out slowly. Then set her mind to the long hike she had back to Balad base.

Jet and Skyler were in Jet's car the afternoon Jet heard that she was a go for going back to Iraq. She just needed to await final details.

"You should have them in the next two days or so," Midnight said.

"I can't thank you enough, Midnight," Jet said, her tone sincere, her eyes shining as she drove.

"Thank me by coming back in one piece," Midnight said, grinning at her end of the phone. "Kash will kill me if I cost her her best asset."

Jet chuckled. "Roger that, ma'am," she said.

"Be safe, Jet."

They disconnected then. Jet looked over at Skyler and could see Skyler's tension instantly.

"You know I gotta go, Sky," Jet said.

Skyler didn't answer for a long minute. She just looked over at her, her eyes searching Jet's face as she drove.

"You know that there's a high possibility they're already dead," Skyler said, her tone gentle, but knowing it needed to be said.

At a red light, Jet closed her eyes for a moment, blowing her breath out and nodding. "Yeah, I know that," she said, her tone hurried.

Skyler nodded. "You may not find anything at all."

Jet narrowed her eyes, still looking forward at the road, but nodded again.

"What's the plan?" Skyler asked. "If you do find them?"

"Get them to Balad, and then to Tehran."

"How?" Skyler asked, narrowing her eyes.

Jet shrugged. "Probably by chopper," she said and immediately saw the look in Skyler's eyes and started to shake her head.

"No!" she said sharply.

"A Blackhawk is faster than a Huey, Jet, you know it."

"No, Sky," Jet said, still shaking her head.

"I can get you to Tehran in three hours. A fully loaded Huey will take around five. How long you want to torture those people who've probably never been in a chopper? And how much chance of getting shot down do you want to take?"

"Fine, then I'll get a local Blackhawk pilot," Jet said, nodding.

"No," Skyler said, shaking her head. "No one else is flying this mission with you. You need me."

"I'm not dragging you into this, Sky, you've already done enough!" Jet yelled, as if her volume alone would change Skyler's mind.

Skyler face remained completely impassive, her light blue-green eyes simply looking back at Jet calmly, which only infuriated Jet more. She whipped the car into the parking lot of the store they'd driven to, threw it into park and jumped out. She immediately began to pace furiously, mad at herself for telling Skyler about taking a helicopter to Tehran. She should have known that Skyler would see that as a sign that she was supposed to help her. Skyler Boché was one of the best Blackhawk pilots Jet had ever seen, everyone said it. The accident that had downed her chopper had been unavoidable and should have killed the entire crew. The fact that three of them originally survived was a miracle and a testament to Skyler's flying skills.

"So fucking stupid!" Jet screamed at herself as she paced, her boot heels striking the pavement.

Skyler got out of the Maserati, standing with her arms folded on top of the car. She watched Jet pace back and forth furiously. Skyler had an amused look on her face and began nodding at people passing by who were staring wide-eyed at the crazy woman pacing and cussing to herself.

Finally, Jet turned to face her. "You can't go, that's it," Jet said authoritatively, making a cutting gesture with her hand.

Skyler simply curled her lips in a grin.

"Don't fucking do that!" Jet yelled, startling a little old lady walking by carrying a little dog in her arms.

"Jet…" Skyler began, trying to reason with her.

"Don't fucking *Jet* me either! You're not fucking going, Skyler. That's it!"

Skyler shook her head, watching and waiting for Jet to run out of steam. It took a while, but she finally did, and she lit a cigarette, taking long drags to try and calm her nerves.

"Figure it out yet?" Skyler asked, her tone mild.

"What?" Jet asked, her tone still sharp.

"That I'm going no matter what you say," Skyler said, her tone still even.

"Why?" Jet asked plaintively.

Skyler looked back at Jet, her look both considering and wretched.

"I left you once," she said, her tone serious, "I won't let you leave me now."

"Sky, you're getting married in two months," Jet said.

"I know," Skyler said. "Devin and I already talked about it; she's behind me on this too."

"Did you tell her it might be a one way ride?" Jet asked.

Skyler nodded, her look telling Jet that she should have known better.

"And she's okay with that?" Jet asked.

Skyler grinned slightly. "Well, I'm pretty sure she hopes I come back…"

A grin tugged at Jet's lips then, but she narrowed her eyes. "You're sure about this?"

"Yeah," Skyler said. "If you're going, I'm going."

"Oh, I'm going," Jet assured her.

"Then sign me up."

Sebastian stunned Jet the next morning when he said essentially the same thing.

"What?" Jet asked, her tone disbelieving.

"I said if you're headed over there, Jet Fire, then I am too."

Jet stared at him openmouthed, blinking a couple of times.

"Did you really think I'm gonna let a Military Information Officer go to an ISIS controlled area without a Ranger on hand?" Sebastian asked, his tone chiding.

"This MIO knows a thing or two about combat," Jet responded, her tone heated.

"I'm sure you do, little one," Sebastian said. "But Rangers lead the way."

Jet shook her head. "You're all fucking crazy…" she said, her tone flabbergasted.

Sebastian grinned. "Army sticks together, Jet Fire. You should know that."

Jet drew a deep breath in, blowing it out as she narrowed her eyes at him.

"You're sure about this?"

"Yep."

"You're doing what?" Kashena screamed at him when he walked into her office an hour later for lunch.

"I take it you heard," Sebastian said, grinning.

"Baz, I get the whole protective thing, believe me, I do…" Kashena said. "But you're going to an ISIS controlled territory on the hope that this family is still alive?"

Sebastian nodded. "Yeah, that's about the size of it."

"What the hell are you thinking?" Kashena asked him.

Sebastian canted his head looking at her. "I'm thinking that if this was you, I'd have your back in a minute. This is a kid, Kash, and she needs a team she can trust."

"She's thirty Baz, hardly a kid," Kashena countered.

"And you know that she's operating under a cloud of worry and concern," Sebastian said. "She's emotionally compromised on this one. She needs a safety net."

"And that's you?" Kashena asked, already knowing she was arguing a losing battle.

"Roger that," Sebastian said.

"And I hear Skyler's going too?"

"Sounds like it, yeah," Sebastian said, nodding.

Kashena shook her head slowly. "You'd kick my ass if I did something like this…"

"No, I'd go with you to watch your ass."

"True," Kashena said, knowing she couldn't argue with him on that.

Sebastian Bach took care of his own and the people he cared about. For whatever reason, he'd formed a quick and close bond with Jet Mathews. He also had a lot of respect for what Skyler Boché had been through in Iraq, so Kashena could see why he was volunteering for the mission.

"You bring those girls back," Kashena said, her tone serious. "And you better bring yourself back too."

"Ooah!" Sebastian replied, nodding.

That night Jet was surprised when she received confirmation details for the mission. She was going in as a reserve army officer; Skyler and Sebastian had also been classified as reservists. Jet wasn't sure how that had been achieved so quickly. They were to fly out in two days at noon. She couldn't believe it was finally happening. She just prayed that she wasn't too late.

It took Jet all night to hike the forty kilometers to the base. Reaching the gate she told the duty officer about the incident and that she'd been in Raqqa for the last three weeks.

"We had you listed as killed, Mathews," the duty officer said.

"Yeah, sorry," Jet said, tiredly, "still alive."

With that, she passed out. The duty officer barely had time to catch her. She woke in a hospital in Baghdad. The base doctors at Balad had taken one look at her still-healing wounds and immediately transferred her to Baghdad for surgery. She woke in pain, but was immediately given painkillers. After two weeks in the hospital, she was medically discharged from the Army, and she'd received a purple heart for her injuries.

The day before they were supposed to leave, Devin found Skyler outside washing her Nissan 370Z Nismo edition. She knew immediately that Skyler was mentally gearing up for the mission that lay ahead. Moving to sit on the driveway to watch her fiancée, Devin did her best to calm her nerves. Skyler had asked her about going with Jet, and while the thought terrified her, she also understood that Skyler felt a lot of guilt about not being there for Jet in Iraq.

Devin knew that Skyler fully accepted the reason she hadn't been there for Jet, having had horrific injuries of her own to recover from. However, to Skyler's way of thinking, she could have reached out to Jet after she'd recovered, but hadn't. It was that lack of action that had Skyler twisted in knots. Devin had only recently gotten all of Skyler's emotional knots about the Blackhawk crash untied; the last thing she wanted was her getting herself tied up in new ones. She knew it was a huge risk that Skyler was taking, but she also knew that if she tried to stand in Skyler's way, she was likely to lose Skyler anyway.

Their relationship had been quite rocky to begin with, because Skyler had been avoiding dealing with the loss of her crew members after the crash. In fact, Skyler had been avoiding all emotional entanglements, except for her best friend Jams, since the crash. Devin had accidentally stepped into a hornet's nest of pain and guilt. Skyler had continually pushed her away, a few times quite forcefully, but Devin had stayed put. Skyler had also been the one to rescue Devin when her vehicle had been caught in a mudslide on Highway 1 outside of Malibu. Skyler and her crew had come in a rescue chopper, pulling her out of the vehicle before it was pushed over the cliff by the encroaching mud. Skyler had literally saved her life. For that reason, and the fact that she loved Skyler Boché beyond all hope of reason, she'd stayed and helped Skyler through her emotional trauma.

Sitting watching her wash her car, Devin could see Skyler's mind working.

"Vehicular therapy?" Devin asked when Skyler looked over at her.

Skyler smiled, nodding. "Yeah."

Devin nodded, continuing to watch Skyler. A few minutes later, Jet drove up.

Getting out she grinned at Skyler. "You can do this one next."

"You can do it yourself," Skyler said, her grin wry.

"Uh-huh," Jet murmured as she walked over to Devin, who moved to stand.

Without a word, Jet took Devin into her arms, hugging her. Devin smiled, hugging Jet back, knowing it was Jet's way of thanking her.

Skyler watched the two with a regretful look in her eyes.

When Jet pulled back, Devin put her hand to Jet's cheek.

"You bring her back," she told Jet.

Jet nodded, looking reserved.

"And you come back too," Devin said then.

"Roger that," Jet said, smiling softly.

"You two want beer?" Devin asked then.

"Sure," Skyler said, nodding.

"Definitely," Jet said, smiling.

After Devin went into the house, Jet walked over, picked up the hose, and started rinsing behind where Skyler was washing. They were both silent for a while. Devin came back and handed them both bottles. She kissed Skyler on the lips, then went back into the house.

"You got a really good one there," Jet said, nodding toward the house and Devin within.

"I know," Skyler said, nodding.

Jet nodded, looking affected.

As she leaned down to dry the wheels of the vehicle, she glanced up at Skyler.

"I updated my will," she said, her tone serious.

"That's comforting," Skyler said, rolling her eyes.

"I left the Mas to you and Devin," Jet said.

"Well, now I might have to kill you myself," Skyler said, a sardonic grin twisting her lips.

Jet laughed at that. "Great!" she said, shaking her head.

That night there was a party at Jet's house. The entire group showed up, including Midnight, with her bodyguards Kana and Tiny, and their wives. There were introductions all around and Jet found herself feeling anxious about the trip. She'd walked inside, leaving everyone out in the backyard, wanting to be alone for a minute to get her head together.

Jericho Tehrani found her in a screening room ten minutes later. Jet was sitting in a recliner with her knees bent, almost to her chest. She was looking at her phone and looking forlorn.

"Hey," Jericho said, her bright blue eyes on the younger woman.

Jet looked up, smiling at the Director of the Division of Law Enforcement.

It still amazed Jet that she suddenly knew such important people, and moreover that they knew her and cared enough about her and her mission to help her. It was really insane.

"Hey," Jet replied.

"How are you doing?" Jericho asked, moving to sit in the recliner next to Jet.

Jet rubbed her face with her hand. "I think it's finally hitting me that this is happening…" she said, her voice trailing off as she shook her head. "And that I'm now going to have to deal with whatever I find over there."

Jericho nodded, her look understanding.

"I mean, Jesus," Jet said, holding up her phone. "I'm still on Google Maps trying to see into Raqqa, like I'm going to find them this way," she said, her tone indicating how stupid that thought was.

Jericho looked back at her. "You know the realities over there…" she said, her tone grave.

Jet nodded, closing her eyes for a moment. "Yeah, I do," she said.

Jericho nodded too. "So you need to be prepared," she said. "And you need to be ready to accept whatever you find and roll with whatever happens."

Jet nodded. She knew what Jericho was saying, and she knew that everyone was trying to prepare her for the very real possibility that the entire Antar family could be dead.

She blew her breath out in frustration, scrubbing her face with her hands. "I just wish I knew something…" she said, her fears coming to bare. "I wish we weren't going in there completely blind."

"But it's what you've got."

"I know, and that would be okay with me, but now I've got Skyler and Sebastian involved."

"Well, it sounds to me like they involved themselves," Jericho pointed out. "And that's because they care about you."

"That's what I'm worried about."

"That's not something to worry about, Jet," Jericho said. "Having people who care about you, and who you care about, is the whole point of this existence."

Jet looked back at Jericho, nodding. "But what if my insanity gets them killed?"

Jericho drew in a deep breath. "That's a responsibility you're going to have to put on them. They know the risks they're taking, Jet. They're both fully trained and have experience in combat. You know that," Jericho said, her tone chiding. "So you have to have faith in them that they know what they're doing and why they're doing it." She gave Jet a pointed look then. "What you are doing is for the right reasons, Jet. You have to have complete faith in that."

Jet looked considering for a long moment, Jericho's words rolling around in her head. Then she nodded, starting to feel better about things.

"Thank you," Jet said, "for everything. I know you used your connections to help me with a lot of this and I don't know if I'll ever be able to repay you."

"Don't worry about repaying me, you just go there and do what you need to and know that the people back here will be thinking about you and hoping for the best."

Jet inclined her head, feeling tears sting the backs of her eyes. She had no idea how she'd gotten so lucky as to find a group of people that included women like Jericho Tehrani, but she was very grateful she had.

Sebastian walked over to Ashley who was standing at the edge of the yard, looking out into the night.

"Hi," Sebastian said, his voice soft.

Ashley turned, looking up at him, he saw immediately that she'd been crying. He grimaced, putting his hand out to touch her cheek, his thumb brushing away a tear.

"I'll bring her back," Sebastian assured her.

She nodded miserably, feeling so desperately afraid she had no idea what to do.

Sebastian set his beer on a nearby table and stepped toward Ashley, taking her in his arms and holding her. She cried against his shoulder for a few minutes. He simply smoothed his hand down her back soothingly, letting her cry.

When she quieted, he looked down at her. "You have to trust me on this one, Ashley."

She looked up at him, her eyes searching his. "And what about you?" she asked. "Who's going to make sure you come back?"

"I will," he said. "Didn't I tell you? I'm bullet proof," he said with a cocky grin.

Ashley smiled, with tears still on her cheeks. "You are, huh?"

"Yep," he said, nodding. Then he touched her cheek again. "I will take care of our girl, okay? You can believe me on that."

Ashley drew in a deep breath, blowing it out as she nodded. "Okay, but I expect you to take care of all of you, including you."

Sebastian grinned. "Ooah," he uttered.

That night Jet took her time making love to Ashley. The thought rang in her mind that it could be the last time. It rang in Ashley's mind too, and stayed there as she clung to Jet as she orgasmed and lay in her arms afterward. It was the longest, hardest night of both of their lives.

The next morning, Jet woke early to go outside and to water the plants. Ashley found her there, and stood behind Jet with her arms wrapped around her, resting her head against her back, trying desperately not to beg her not to go. Jet's hand came up to cover one of her hands. At one point she dropped the hose and moved her other hand to cover both of Ashley's, stroking Ashley's fingers. They stood that way for a half hour.

Two hours later, Ashley walked into Jet's bedroom to see her sitting on the bed. She was wearing a black exercise bra and black boy shorts underwear. Her hair was already in a short ponytail, her desert BDUs hung on the door, and her boots were on the floor next to the bed. Jet's eyes were closed and she looked like she was doing what would be considered Yoga breathing. She opened her eyes, however, when she sensed Ashley there.

Ashley walked over to stand in front of Jet and, reaching out her hand, she touched Jet's cheek. Jet's put her hand over Ashley's and looked up at her.

"I'm coming back," she told Ashley.

"You better be," Ashley said, tears in her eyes already.

"I'll be bringing houseguests."

"I'll make sure the rooms are ready."

"I'll miss you."

Ashley's tears spilled over then, and she moved to straddle Jet's lap, hugging her close, her head down on Jet's shoulder. Jet held her for a long time, stroking her back and kissing the side of her head.

Jet glanced at the clock and knew she needed to get ready. Ashley sensed the movement, and looked at the clock too. She moved to get off Jet's lap and sat on the bed as Jet put on her uniform and boots. It was distracting how good Jet looked in BDUs, and Ashley found herself watching Jet as she moved around the room, putting things into bags, and preparing.

Before Jet walked out the front door, she turned to Ashley, taking her in her arms and kissing her one last time.

"I'll be back soon," she said, smiling.

"I'll be waiting."

The military flight took thirty hours on the first leg of their journey. They touched down at their first stop, Ashgabat, a refueling station in Turkmenistan. Skyler, Sebastian and Jet walked off the transport plane into the desert heat. It was four in the morning at the air base. They'd purposely chosen the time to arrive when there would be less movement on the base, so they drew less attention to themselves. There was no sense in taking chances with anyone at the base informing others about the arrival of three Americans. They were met by the base commander, Tom Juneau, who was fully aware of their mission, and also aware that these three had fairly influential people in the right places.

Regardless, he appreciated and understood their mission. He'd been injured during his time in Iraq and had been lucky enough to receive good care from locals during his time in the hospital. He had, in fact, married one of the Iraqi nurses who'd cared for him. He hated the fact that ISIS was silently and systematically slaughtering all Shia they discovered.

Commander Juneau showed them to a set of private barracks and told them to get some sleep, which they did gratefully. At three o'clock that afternoon, they got up and dressed in fatigues to go and eat. Afterwards, they got together in the barracks and went over the plan for that night.

"We should hike in the last half a click," Skyler said, pointing to where she thought they should come in from.

"Yeah, that's probably a good idea," Sebastian said, nodding. "Headlights in the middle of the night might look a little suspicious."

"Just a little," Jet said, grinning.

"Hopefully, the ISIS presence will be more concentrated in Al-Raqqa proper and not in the outlying villages," Sebastian said, then.

Jet drew in a deep breath, nodding.

They finished planning their operation then gathered their gear and headed out to the airfield, walking towards a Blackhawk helicopter that sat off to the side on a little used area of the station. Jet saw Skyler move her head around, stretching her neck. She knew that Skyler was tense about flying a Blackhawk again. It was one of the many reasons she hadn't wanted Skyler to make this trip.

Jet glanced at Sebastian, and saw that he too was looking over at Skyler, his eyes connected with Jet's and they exchanged an understanding look.

Inside the helicopter, Skyler climbed into the pilot's seat on the right side of the helicopter, blowing her breath out and refamiliarizing herself with the aircraft.

"Want some company?" Jet asked, poking her head into the cockpit.

"Can you fly?" Skyler asked, grinning.

"I can watch you do it," Jet responded. "I'll bet I'm pretty good at that."

Jet climbed into what would be the copilot's seat looking over at Skyler.

"You okay?" she asked her friend.

Skyler looked over at her. "I'm not gonna say it's not weird to be back in one of these," she said, gesturing to the aircraft around them. "But I'm glad I could be here."

Jet smiled softly. "Me too."

Skyler started up the Blackhawk and ran through her preflight. Jet watched, having always been fascinated by Skyler when she was in 'pilot mode.'

"Are you sure we should be here?" Jet asked, looking over at Skyler sitting in the pilot's seat.

"You said you wanted to see me fly," Skyler responded with a grin.

"I did, yeah, but it's not worth losing your commission over."

Skyler chuckled. "Don't worry, I got it covered," she said confidently.

As Skyler went through her preflight, Jet asked questions about what she was doing and why she needed to do it. Skyler patiently explained as much as she could.

When they lifted off, Jet felt a thrill go through her. It was surreal to watch someone you were so intimate with doing something they loved so much. She could see the elation on Skyler's face as she flew the Blackhawk. They flew out to a secluded area by the Kuwait Bay. Skyler landed, climbed out of the helicopter and took Jet's hand to help her down.

Walking over to the beach, Jet pulled off her clothes, stripping down to her exercise bra and black boy shorts and ran for the water. Skyler joined her not too long after that, and waded over to her. Their eyes met and Skyler slid her hand around Jet's waist, pulling her close and kissing her deeply. Jet slid her arms up around Skyler's neck, using a handful of Skyler's hair to pull her head closer, deepening the kiss.

Skyler groaned against her lips, never able to get enough of this girl. Her hands grasped at Jet, as Jet moved her mouth down to Skyler's neck and then moved lower. Shoving aside the bra that Skyler wore, Jet's mouth closed over a hard nipple. Skyler grabbed a handful of Jet's hair, holding her there as her body spiraled out of control. It always amazed her that Jet excited her so much. She wasn't sure if it was just the fact that they were in a strange place and they had each other to hold on to or if there was more. Either way, it didn't matter. She clung to Jet, making love to her and then moving them to the beach. They spent the day just enjoying each other, the sun and the water.

That evening as Skyler flew them back to base, Jet looked over at her. She never found Skyler less attractive, it seemed that the more time she spent with the woman, the more addicted she felt to her. Watching her fly the Blackhawk made her feel all twisted up inside and she just wanted more, but she knew that this was just a wartime romance. Skyler had a girl back home, although the woman was a bit of a hothead and broke up with her on a weekly basis.

On the way back to the base, there was suddenly the sound of gunfire from a remote area, and Skyler started cussing a blue streak.

"We're taking fire, hold on!" she yelled, taking the Blackhawk in a wide arc.

Jet had grabbed the flying straps and had hauled herself out of the copilot's seat, moving to the back of the Blackhawk.

"Jet, what the fuck are you doing?" Skyler yelled.

"I'm going to give you some cover fire, take this fucker out!" Jet yelled back.

Skyler began hearing M16 fire from the back of the helicopter and heard return fire from the ground.

"Son of a…" Skyler muttered, clamping down on her fear for Jet and reminding herself that Jet was a trained soldier, not just a Military Intelligence Officer. They'd all been trained in combat, now it was time to trust that training. "Put on a helmet!" she yelled back to Jet.

A few moments later she heard Jet in her earpiece. "They're on your three o'clock, come hard left…" Jet said.

"Coming left," Skyler said, automatically falling back on her skills and training.

She heard the report of M16 fire, and the reply, hearing bullets hit the side of the aircraft, wincing.

"Jet!" she yelled.

"Motherfucker!" she heard Jet yell, fortunately not into the mike, and then heard another burst from the M16. "Reloading, come right!" Jet yelled.

Skyler heard the clatter of the magazine clip hitting the deck of the helicopter. As she called, "Coming right," the aircraft bucked a bit. "Hold on!"

The hail of gunfire seemed to light up the sky. Skyler automatically pulled back on the stick climbing, putting the belly of the aircraft up to protect the rotors.

"Skyler, come left thirty degrees, I can see the greasy little bastard, get me in there and I can take him out."

"I'm not getting you too close to that, I can take him out with a Hellfire," Skyler yelled back.

"And let the military know we were playing with a Blackhawk. Do you want to hand them your commission?! Just get me down there, Sky, I'll take him out!"

"Goddamn it!" Skyler yelled. "Coming left thirty degrees, you be careful and keep your damned head down!"

The Blackhawk swung left, suddenly.

"Now just tip it about five degrees, on my mark" Jet said calmly into the mike. "Mark... coming down, coming down... right... there!" she said, letting go a burst of fire from the M16.

There was an explosion to Skyler's right, and she heard Jet let lose a yell. Skyler laughed, giving a sigh of relief. Jet reappeared in the cockpit a minute later, grinning.

"You're crazy, you do know that, right?" Skyler said her blue-green eyes sparkling in the setting sun.

Jet shrugged. "Sometimes," she replied with a sardonic grin.

As the Blackhawk lifted off the ground, Jet got the same old thrill. There was something exhilarating about the sights, sounds and smell of being in an Army aircraft. She knew the mission they were on was dangerous, but somehow it felt really good to be here again, in uniform and looking across the cockpit at Skyler.

"Remember our trip to the beach?" Jet asked grinning.

"I do," Skyler said, grinning back at her.

They exchanged a look, at that moment it was all about being a soldier and doing a job.

"Thank you for coming with me on this," Jet said, her tone sincere.

A soft smile crossed Skyler's lips. "Wouldn't have wanted it any other way."

Jet nodded, feeling the warmth of the friendship she'd shared with Skyler years before and holding on to it tightly. Glancing back she winked at Sebastian who was sitting in the back.

The sun was setting when the team touched down at the Balad Air Base five hours later. The base was an Iraqi Air Force base, but fortunately had enough American military traffic to make their arrival uninteresting to any prying eyes. Skyler put the Blackhawk down at the far edge of the field, purposely partially hidden by the older, less used hangars. Powering down the rotors, Skyler did her post-flight check as Jet got up and moved to the back of the aircraft.

"How's it going back here?" Jet asked, grinning at Sebastian.

"Got a good nap," Sebastian said, winking at her.

"Like sleepin' in a cradle, huh?" Jet asked him.

"Oh yeah," Sebastian said, the look on his face telling Jet he was feeling the same way she had earlier: good to be back.

"Comin' up on the right!" Skyler called from the cockpit.

Jet moved to her M16 looking out the sliding door window. She relaxed instantly as she recognized the man who drove the Jeep. He was their contact at the air base.

Abrahem Hairi got out of the Jeep. Holding his arm up to Jet, she opened the sliding door to the helicopter and got out.

"We have everything you requested in this hangar here," Abrahem said, nodding to Skyler and Sebastian as they climbed out of the helicopter.

"Thank you, we'll take it from here," Jet said to Abrahem, not wanting to involve him anymore than necessary.

Abrahem nodded, turned and got back into the Jeep and drove away.

They intended to make the short drive to Raqqa at midnight. They spent the next four hours going over the plan, and mentally gearing up for the mission. Jet found a quiet spot in the corner. She leaned against the wall with her headphones on, she cranked her music, and smoked. Sebastian and Skyler played cards, smoked and talked.

"How do you think she's doing?" Sebastian asked, looking over at Jet.

Skyler looked over at the girl too, her look measuring. Jet's head was moving to the music she was listening to, mouthing the words of the song with vehemence as she smoked.

"I think she's doin' alright," Skyler said. "That's kind of her pre-game warm up."

Sebastian grinned. "I get the music, I'm big into it myself," he said, nodding.

"Well, Jet has ADHD, so she needs to be able to focus that brain of hers. The music does that for her," Skyler said, her look fond as she looked back over Jet.

"So you two were a thing, huh?"

Skyler nodded, taking a deep drag off her cigarette.

"What happened?" Sebastian asked casually.

"My copter went down."

"What did you fly?" Sebastian asked, never having heard Skyler's story.

Skyler canted her head at the Blackhawk that could be seen through the doors of the hangar.

"What happened?" Sebastian asked. "If you don't mind me asking."

Skyler looked back at him, she would have minded a year before, but now she was used to telling the story. Her therapist said it was good for her to do so, that it desensitized it for her.

"RPG took out our tail rotor," Skyler said. "We spun out and went down hard," she said, her eyes narrowing slightly. "One of my crew was killed instantly, another one was wounded badly. We were all hurt."

Sebastian nodded, his look pained.

"Insurgents moved in, shot me, shot Jams my copilot twice, took all three of us prisoner."

"Fuck..." Sebastian breathed, knowing she was lucky to be alive.

Skyler nodded, looking grave. "Ended up almost being raped. Benny, one of my crew, tried to defend me and they killed him for it. I used the knife they used to kill him to take them all out." She said the last with her tone low.

"Ooah," Sebastian said, nodding.

"Ooah," Skyler answered.

"When we got back they sent us home," Skyler said, looking over at Jet again.

"And she stayed," Sebastian said, understanding now.

Skyler nodded.

"And that's why you're here now?" Sebastian said.

"Wouldn't you be here if Kashena was?"

"You know it."

"I owe her," Skyler said, her eyes serious.

Sebastian nodded.

"So why are you here?" Skyler asked him.

Sebastian grinned, shrugging. "'Cause my little Jet Fire needed the back up and Rangers always lead the way."

Skyler gave him a narrowed look. "You really feel protective over her, don't you?"

Sebastian nodded.

"Why?" Skyler asked.

Sebastian looked considering. "Lost a kid like her on my platoon a year into my time as a Captain. I guess I just want to make sure it doesn't happen again."

"I'm just hoping we don't lose her if she finds out they're all dead," Skyler said, looking over at Jet again.

"Lose her?" Sebastian queried, his look worried.

Skyler shrugged, "She's been holding on to this for a year now, Baz. Holding on to hope, thinking if she could just get back here… Now she's here… If they're dead I don't know how she'll take it."

"Well, she's going back in one piece, whether she likes it or not. I promised Ashley I'd bring her back."

"Ashley, huh?" Skyler asked, grinning.

"She's worried about her."

"Uh-huh…" Skyler said, grinning.

"Hey, she's Jet's girl," Sebastian said, holding up his hands.

"She's not Jet's girl. Jet doesn't have girls," Skyler said. "It's not her style anymore."

"Anymore?" Sebastian asked.

"Not since I've known her this time," Skyler said. "She flits from one woman to the next, never sticking around long enough for them to get their hooks into her."

"Sounds familiar," Sebastian said, grinning.

"Like you?" Skyler asked.

"Yeah…" Sebastian said, his look proud as he looked over at Jet.

"Yeah, well, it's not a fulfilling life," Skyler said, giving him a dirty look.

"Like getting married?" Sebastian asked.

"Yeah," Skyler said, grinning. "Actually, if anyone would have told me two years ago that I'd be getting married, I'd have turned them out."

"But you found the right one," Sebastian said.

"Yeah, I did," Skyler said, her eyes shining.

"Hopefully that's in the cards for all of us," Sebastian said. "Speaking of which, I call."

Skyler laid her cards down and she had a Royal Flush.

"Son of a mother…" Sebastian breathed, grinning.

"I'll take that," Skyler said, pulling the pot in with a rakish grin.

At midnight they drove out of the air base in a blacked out Humvee. They were all heavily armed, Sebastian was driving. It took them thirty-five minutes to reach the outskirts of the villages that ringed Raqqa. Sebastian pulled the vehicle over, looking back at Jet who sat behind Skyler. She was looking at the burned out houses at the edge of the village. It was beginning to occur to her that they really could have done all of this for nothing.

"Ready?" Sebastian asked, glancing at Skyler, then back at Jet again.

Jet closed her eyes, taking a slow deep breath and blowing it out slowly, then nodding as she opened her eyes. They got out of the Humvee and started jogging deeper into the village to where the Antar household resided. Sebastian stayed behind Skyler and Jet his eyes ever watchful. They were within a block of the house when Jet heard gunfire and a woman's scream split the night.

"Son of a bitch!" she growled, and took off toward the house.

"Damnit!" Skyler exclaimed as she sprinted to try and catch up with Jet.

She knew what Jet was thinking and also knew that Jet was as impulsive as a person could be. Sebastian caught up to her, with his longer stride, and snatched her up by the back of her vest, shoving her up against a house wall nearby.

"Hold on," he whispered furiously as she struggled against his hold.

He motioned for Skyler to take a look, pointing with two fingers. Skyler nodded, grateful to Sebastian for stopping Jet's headlong run. Dropping to a knee, Skyler peered carefully around the corner, she saw the Antar house and she also saw two insurgents outside of it. Pulling back she leaned against the wall, glancing up at Sebastian and nodding, an unhappy look on her face. She held up two fingers.

He dragged Jet down as he dropped to a kneeling position.

"You aren't going to do any of them any good if you get yourself killed, charging in," be told Jet.

Jet gritted her teeth, nodding.

"Okay, I'll take the one on the left," he said, peaking around the corner, then looking back at them. "Sky, you take the one on the right, on my mark. Quick shot, we don't need the rest of their friends heading this way. Jet, you hit the house, got it?"

Jet nodded, moving to stand. The three of them turned, their weapons at the ready. Sebastian held up three fingers, pulling each of them down, one at a time, then gave the move sign with his hand sideways. As one unit they moved. Skyler and Sebastian shot at the same time, taking down both of the men outside. They moved off, to secure the perimeter of the house, and Jet moved to the door.

She did a quick look inside, seeing Fahrshad lying on the floor dead. Leaning against the wall again, she steeled herself, then she heard Fadiyah scream again. She moved quickly, her M16 at her shoulder in the ready position. Moving to the backroom she was horrified to see a man trying to force himself on Fadiyah, she was fighting him mightily.

Jet stuck the muzzle of the M16 against the back of his head.

"Get off of her now…" Jet growled through gritted teeth.

The man froze.

"Move!" Jet roared, jamming the muzzle into his head, dying to shoot the man, but afraid she could hit Fadiyah in the process. She wouldn't take that chance.

The man slowly moved backwards, and Jet backed up to ensure she could cover him.

"Get your fucking hands up!" Jet yelled, then repeated it in Arabic, just I case he didn't get it.

He put his hands up, muttering in Arabic. Jet shoved the muzzle of the M16 into his face. "I don't think you want to talk shit about women right now, pal," she said, her eyes blazing with fury.

Jet refused to look over at Fadiyah until she knew the man was no longer a danger.

"Jet," Skyler said from the door to the sleeping quarters.

"Cover me," Jet told Skyler, Skyler nodded.

Jet turned then, striding to the bed, seeing Fadiyah lying there, her abaya pushed up to her waist. She moved to pull the robe-like clothing down, as she leaned over Fadiyah. The young woman's eyes were squeezed shut.

"Fadi?" she queried softly.

Fadiyah opened her eyes, shock very clear in them. "Jet?" she queried, as if she were seeing a ghost.

"Hi," Jet said, smiling down at her.

"Jet!" Fadiyah exclaimed, bursting into tears and throwing her arms around Jet's neck.

Jet quickly gathered the girl in her arms, holding her as she lifted her off the bed, the girl weighed almost nothing. Fadiyah buried her face in Jet's neck, crying hysterically.

"It's okay, it's okay, I have you, honey, I have you…" Jet soothed, looking around her. "Fadi, what about Abdul?" she asked, her tone gentle.

Fadiyah shook her head sadly.

Jet closed her eyes, wincing. "I'm so sorry, honey…"

"Jet, we gotta go," Skyler said from the door.

Jet nodded, and holding Fadiyah in her arms, she carried her toward the door. At the door she stopped, turning to whisper to Skyler, nodding toward the small dresser in the room. Skyler nodded and moved past her. Jet carried Fadiyah through the house, purposely keeping her turned away from the body of her father. Sebastian was outside, with the insurgent who'd been intent on assaulting Fadiyah, on his knees. He nodded to Jet, who nodded in response.

She handed Fadiyah to him, then turned to the man who was now sneering up at her. Taking out her Kaybar, she shoved it into his chest without hesitation, and using her booted foot, she kicked him over viciously. She wiped the Kaybar off on his clothing and put it back in its sheath. Sebastian had stood and watched. Even Skyler had emerged to see what Jet had done. Neither of them commented, simply nodding. None of them realized that Fadiyah had watched as well.

Walking back over to Sebastian, Jet took Fadiyah back into her arms, unwilling to let anyone else touch the girl at the moment. They turned, with Sebastian in the rear, and Skyler in the lead. They started back toward the Humvee.

They were a few blocks down and Skyler had peeled off to check the side buildings they were passing when a man jumped out of the shadows with a handgun. He fired and Jet spun to protect Fadiyah. Feeling the burning impact of the bullet striking the outer edge of her vest, she hissed in pain. The man was dead a moment later, shot by Sebastian.

"Jet!" Sebastian exclaimed, as Skyler ran up.

"Jet?" Fadiyah said her tone faint.

"I'm okay, I'm okay," Jet chanted. "Let's go."

They began to run and made it to the Humvee a couple of minutes later. Sebastian took Fadiyah out of Jet's arms, so she could climb into the vehicle. He saw the blood trickling down her arm, but didn't comment. He handed her Fadiyah who was shaking. Jet gathered the girl close, wincing as she moved the arm that had been hit, but refusing to acknowledge the pain.

"Go, go, go," Jet chanted to Sebastian, as he got into the vehicle.

They took off into the night then, headed back to Balad. Jet sat with Fadiyah on her lap. It was obvious that Fadiyah was going into shock, so Jet pulled her abaya around her closer, doing her best to keep her close. Fadiyah had her head against Jet's shoulder, her eyes were closed, but she was shaking and her breathing was shallow.

"Fadi…" Jet said, trying to get the girl to respond. "Honey, I need you to look at me, okay?"

Fadiyah opened her eyes slowly, looking dazed.

"Are you hurt?" Jet asked, her eyes searching.

Fadiyah shook her head, blinking a couple of times. "Are you really here?" she asked, sounding breathless.

"Yes, I'm really here," Jet said. "I'm here."

Fadiyah just looked back at her, like she was seeing a ghost.

Skyler looked back at Jet, their eyes connecting.

"She's going into shock," Skyler told Jet.

Jet nodded, knowing she was right. "Call ahead and see if they can give her a shot or something when we get to Balad. She needs a sedative."

Skyler nodded, getting on the radio.

Chapter 7

When they reached Balad, a medic met them at the helicopter. Jet held Fadiyah as the medic gave her a shot. Fadiyah was asleep minutes later as the Blackhawk lifted off. When they reached Tehran, Skyler landed the Blackhawk at the far end of Mehrabad airport, at the location they'd been given. A lot of strings had been pulled by Jericho to make this particular part of the plan happen. Her father, the former Iranian Ambassador, had called in favors.

They were met by a car that took them to Tehran Grand Hotel. Sebastian climbed out of the vehicle, turning to take the still-sleeping Fadiyah out of Jet's arms. He noticed Jet looked pale.

He leaned over to Skyler. "Get the hotel doctor up to Jet's room, she's losing too much blood."

Skyler nodded, heading into the hotel. Jet climbed out of the vehicle, moving to take Fadiyah from Sebastian.

"I've got her," Sebastian said. "Go." He said it with just enough authority that Jet nodded her head tiredly.

It would have caused a stir walking into the hotel in military uniforms, especially with Jet bleeding and Sebastian carrying an unconscious Iraqi woman. Fortunately, Jericho had arranged for them to use the back entrance and go straight up to their rooms having been met by hotel security.

Ten minutes later, they were shown to their rooms and the hospital doctor met them on their floor. Jet looked over at Skyler her look accusatory. Skyler shrugged, shaking her head refusing to apologize for calling the doctor.

"You need to get checked out, Jet," she said simply.

Jet looked unhappy about the edict, but didn't have the energy to argue. Sebastian carried Fadiyah into the room, taking her to the bedroom area and laying her down on the bed. Skyler marched Jet over to the table in the room, motioning for the doctor to come forward.

"Okay, let's see what we've got," Skyler said, opening Jet's vest and carefully removed it, grimacing at the amount of blood. "Jesus, Jet…." she said.

"I'm fine," Jet said.

"Yeah, that's what you keep saying," Skyler said, giving her a vile look.

The doctor examined Jet's shoulder; the bullet had cut into her shoulder muscle, but hadn't hit bone fortunately. The doctor stitched the wound, cleaning it well and gave Jet some painkillers. Sebastian and Skyler left a little while later. Jet walked into the bedroom and looked around. It was a nice room, once again Jericho's arrangement.

Jet looked at Fadiyah lying on the bed. She was still unable to believe she was actually there, and that at least she'd been able to save Fadiyah. It broke her heart that she hadn't been in time to save Fadiyah's father or brother. Moving her shoulder around and grimacing at the pain, she decided to take a shower to try and soak out some of the soreness. She moved around the room as quietly as possible, pulling out clothes and items from her bags.

A half an hour later, she emerged from the bathroom feeling slightly human. Picking up the bottle of painkillers, she opened it and popped one in her mouth. She picked up her phone, moving to sit in the chair closest to where Fadiyah lay on the bed. Even though there was plenty of room on the king sized bed, she didn't want to make Fadiyah uncomfortable.

Turning on her phone she saw that she had messages from Ashley. She texted Ashley back, and sent Kashena a message telling her how things had gone and that Sebastian and Skyler were both okay. She knew that it was about two in the morning in LA, so she didn't worry about waiting for responses. Jet settled in the chair, curling up and resting her head on the arm. Her eyes settled on Fadiyah sleeping on the bed. She was asleep a few minutes later.

Fadiyah woke slowly some hours later, feeling disoriented. She sighed, thinking that she'd been dreaming the night before. Then she opened her eyes and saw Jet sleeping on the chair about two feet from her. At least she thought it was Jet. This was not the Jet Mathews she remembered. This woman wore black shorts and a black t-shirt, and her hair was longer than Fadiyah remembered. She couldn't believe that she was seeing this. The same woman she'd thought she'd never see again. Still, she wondered if she was dreaming.

Reaching out she touched Jet's leg. Jet woke instantly, groaning as she moved her sore shoulder. Then she looked at Fadiyah and saw that her eyes were open.

Moving to sit forward, Jet dropped her feet to the floor, her eyes looking into Fadiyah's.

"It is really you…" Fadiyah said, her voice sounding surprised.

Jet smiled softly. "Yes, Fadi, it's me," she said.

"Jet…" Fadiyah said, her voice a sigh as tears welled in her eyes.

"Oh, God, please don't do that…" Jet said, moving to sit on the side of the bed.

Fadiyah moved to sit up and Jet took her in her arms holding her as she once again cried. When Fadiyah had exhausted herself crying, she lay against Jet, her head against Jet's shoulder. Jet shifted uncomfortably as Fadiyah was leaning against her injured shoulder, but she didn't want to say anything. Unfortunately, she shifted a little too much and caused a sharp stabbing pain in her shoulder and she hissed.

Fadiyah's head snapped up. "What is it?" she asked, her eyes searching Jet's.

"It's nothing," Jet said. "Just rest."

Fadiyah continued to look at her, wondering what was wrong. Then she shook her head. "You look so different…"

"Well, this is Jet the civilian edition," Jet said, grinning.

"Civilian?" Fadiyah asked, looking confused. "But you were in your uniform…" Then her eyes widened. "You were injured…"

"I'm fine, honey," Jet said, her tone soothing.

"No," Fadiyah said, shaking her head. "You were shot. You were shot… shielding me…"

"Well, I didn't come seventy-five hundred miles to have you die in my arms, Fadi," Jet said reasonably.

Fadiyah stared back at her, her mouth open slightly, her eye reflecting confusion.

"You came from America?" Fadiyah asked.

Jet nodded, looking back at Fadiyah, her look quizzical. "Where did you think?"

"I thought you were still here…" Fadiyah said.

"Fadi, I was discharged shortly after I left Raqqa."

"But then how did you come to be back in Raqqa?" Fadiyah asked.

Jet looked back at her for a long moment, understanding dawning in her mind; she'd realized that Fadiyah really didn't understand. "I came back here for you."

Astonishment swept over Fadiyah's face, she blinked a number of times. "For me?"

"For all of you," Jet said, her voice softer. "I'm sorry I was too late…"

Fadiyah shook her head. "You came all the way back to Iraq from America to save my life, and you are apologizing?"

Jet looked back at her, blowing her breath out, her look circumspect. "Yes?" Jet said.

"No," Fadiyah countered with a narrowed look.

Jet's phone chimed, and she reached for it. Fadiyah watched, fascinated as Jet put in the passcode and read a message, grinning, then tapped out a response. Then she set the phone aside. Fadiyah was still watching her.

"What?" Jet asked.

"So different," Fadiyah said, shaking her head.

Jet looked back at her. "Is that a bad thing?"

"No," Fadiyah said, "I am just surprised."

Jet leaned back against the headboard of the bed, starting to feel the days of travel and action catching up to her again. Fadiyah watched her.

"What is it, Fadi?" Jet asked softly.

Fadiyah looked unsure. Jet reached out, touching her cheek, her eyes searching.

"What?" Jet repeated softly. "Tell me."

Fadiyah clasped her hands in front of her, her eyes downcast, she shook her head.

Jet sat forward, putting her finger under Fadiyah's chin, turning Fadiyah's face up to hers, her light green eyes staring into Fadiyah's silver-gray eyes.

"Tell me what you're worried about, Fadi." Jet said, her tone as gentle as it could possibly be.

Fadiyah grimaced, shaking her head and trying to look away again.

Jet moved closer, putting her head next to Fadiyah's, her hand at Fadiyah's cheek, her lips right next to her ear.

"Please tell me, honey," Jet said whispered.

Fadiyah put her head against Jet's cheek. "I am afraid," she said.

Jet pulled back, looking down at Fadiyah then..

"Of me?" Jet asked, her tone both hurt and sad.

"No!" Fadiyah exclaimed. "No, never of you," she said, her tone earnest. "I am afraid of what I am to become now."

"Become now?" Jet repeated, looking confused. "What do you mean?"

Fadiyah shrugged, looking down. "I have no male relatives now."

Understanding dawned on Jet; women with no male relatives were often outcasts in Iraqi society. Since women were perceived to need men to look out for them, not having any male relatives left women with little or no prospects. Any prospects they did have were far from preferable.

"Oh, honey..." Jet said, taking Fadiyah into her arms again, and holding her, rocking her to try and soothe her.

Pulling back after a couple of minutes, she tilted Fadiyah's chin up again. "You have a couple of options," she said, her tone serious. "First, you have the option of staying here in Tehran to attend the university. You would have an apartment of your own so you wouldn't have to rely on anyone."

Fadiyah looked back at her, shaking her head. "I do not have any money, I would not be able to pay for these things."

"Money is no problem," Jet told her. "It will be taken care of."

"But how?" Fadiyah asked.

"Just trust me on this one, okay?" Jet said. "Your other option would be to come home with me and go to school in LA."

"Home with you?" Fadiyah asked, her voice filled with wonder suddenly. "To America?"

"That's where I live, honey," Jet said, her smile warm.

"But where would I stay? America is so expensive, and—"

"And again, that would be taken care of," Jet said. "And you would stay with me."

"With you?" Fadiyah asked, sounding like a child at Christmas.

"I live in a pretty big house, there's lots of room," Jet said.

Fadiyah simply looked back at her, unable to believe what Jet was saying.

"So," Jet said, her look speculative. "You just need to tell me what you want to do, and I'll make it happen, okay?"

"You can do that?" Fadiyah asked.

"I moved Heaven and Earth to get back here, babe, I can make anything I want happen right now," she said, winking rakishly. "I'm on a roll."

Fadiyah pressed her lips together, her eyes sparkling with suppressed excitement. "I want to stay with you."

Jet smiled fondly and then picked up her phone. Fadiyah watched as she tapped out a message on the phone. A few moments later a message came back. Jet once again tapped out a message and sent it. Again the reply came quickly.

"Okay," Jet said, setting the phone aside. "We should be flying out tomorrow night."

"It is that simple?" Fadiyah asked.

"Friends in high places right now, babe."

"High places?" Fadiyah asked.

"Influential places," Jet explained.

"What influential places?"

"Well, for one, the previous ambassador to Iran. The State of California Attorney General, and the Director of the Division of Law Enforcement for California who also happens to be the daughter of the former Ambassador to Iran."

Fadiyah's eyes widened at the sound of these important people. She didn't know exactly who all of them were, but they sounded important.

"And they can do this?" Fadiyah asked.

"They can do this," Jet confirmed.

They were both silent for a while. Jet felt fatigue starting to push in on her again. She closed her eyes, relief flowing through her, knowing that things were stable now. She was asleep a few minutes later.

She awoke hours later, looking down to see that Fadiyah was asleep against her shoulder. She sat looking down at this woman whose face had been with her for a year. It amazed Jet that she was finally here again, and that she'd found Fadiyah. It still made her ache that she hadn't been in time to save Abdul or Farshad, but she also knew that saving Fadiyah from what had been about to happen to her, was life changing for the girl. She was exceedingly happy that Fadiyah had chosen to come back to America with her.

Jet knew that life for a woman with no male relatives was highly restrictive, to say the least, and could be very dangerous. An unescorted woman could be attacked, raped or killed if any man took offense to anything she did or said. A man could even have her charged if he decided something as simple as being able to see through her veil in a certain light. Things were better in more modern Iran, but the traditions were still very restrictive to women in the Middle East. Without a man to protect her, Fadiyah would always be in danger.

Jet got out of bed, stretching carefully, mindful of her sore shoulder. She walked into the bathroom to check out the wound to the back of her shoulder; it looked red and angry, with black stitches in it, but she knew that she'd been lucky. The man that shot at them only had a handgun, likely a 9 millimeter caliber; it wouldn't have made it through the vest she'd worn. If he'd had an AK like many of the insurgents carried, it would have gone right through the vest, and both she and Fadiyah would likely have been killed. She'd seen that the man had a handgun, so she'd known turning away would protect Fadiyah, at the very least. She'd meant it when she said she hadn't come all that way to save the girl, only to have her die in her arms.

She took a quick shower, making a point of soaking her shoulder for an extra few minutes. Then she got dressed again and walked quietly, gathering her cigarettes, lighter, phone and her portable speaker out of her bags. Down in the kitchen area of the suite, she made herself coffee then stepped out onto the balcony to smoke and drink coffee. She sat and stared out over the city that was just waking up for the morning. She turned on her music, sitting back and relaxing for the moment.

When Fadiyah woke, she was alarmed to find that Jet was not in the room. She got up, walking around the room, looking for the other woman. She was astounded by the room that they were in. It was an entire suite; she'd never been in anything so luxurious before in her life. When she got downstairs she heard music and after a few minutes search she figured out it was coming from the balcony. The sliding door was partially open, she looked out the curtains and was shocked by what she saw.

Jet sat in one of the chairs, her head leaned back on the chair, her eyes closed. She held a coffee cup in one hand and a cigarette in the other. Fadiyah was shocked that Jet smoked, but she was more shocked by the sound coming out of Jet's mouth. She was singing to a rock song playing on the speaker and she had a beautiful voice!

As the song faded, Fadiyah watched fascinated as Jet lifted the coffee up to her lips, holding the cup not by the handle, but with her hand around the cup itself. Then she watched as Jet lifted the cigarette to her lips, inhaling deeply, and blowing smoke out a few moments later as another song started.

The song that began was softer, a single piano. Fadiyah listened to the words as Jet sang them, her sense of wonder only increasing with the way that Jet sang them. They described a "boy" who was alone and had no place to be. It was the story of Peter Pan, although Fadiyah had no way of knowing that. The song talked about Peter Pan coming to talk to the singer of the song and offering to take them to Neverland.

Jet's voice rose on the chorus and Fadiyah felt a shiver go through her at the timber and tone in Jet's voice. It talked about running away from reality and about lost boys "like me." It seemed very poignant to Fadiyah and she could see that Jet felt the words as she sang them.

The song went on to talk about Peter Pan sprinkling the singer with pixie dust and how they flew away to Neverland. Fadiyah found herself holding her breath expectantly as the chorus began again.

The song continued, but Jet lifted her cup to her lips again and took another long drag from her cigarette. Fadiyah opened the slider wider and stepped out onto the balcony. Jet heard the door open and moved to stand immediately. Fadiyah looked at her in surprise. In the Middle East, traditionally men always stood when a woman entered the room, she found it odd but somehow endearing that Jet stood now for her.

"I like that song," Fadiyah said as the song ended.

Jet grinned, gesturing to the chair across from hers and waiting for Fadiyah to sit before she did as well.

"Me too," Jet said.

"You have a beautiful voice, Jet," Fadiyah said, her eyes reflecting her amazement.

"Eh," Jet said, shrugging. "I sing with the radio," she said dismissively.

"And you smoke…" Fadiyah said, gesturing to the cigarette in Jet's hand.

"Yes, I do," Jet said, her light green eyes sparkling in amusement.

"You did not when you were here before," Fadiyah said.

"I couldn't when I was here before, babe," Jet said, her look benign. "Besides the fact that my cigarettes were in the Humvee that went caflooey, I had shrapnel in my lungs, so…"

"So you did smoke then too?" Fadiyah asked.

"I've been a smoker since I was about sixteen," Jet said nodding.

"So young?" Fadiyah askes surprised.

"I was a rebel."

"A rebel?" Fadiyah asked.

"A troublemaker, a rabble rouser, whatever you want to call it." When Fadiyah still looked mystified she said, "A mashaghib," in Arabic.

Fadiyah nodded in understanding then. "You?" she asked, sounding surprised.

Jet grinned unrepentantly. "Yeah," she said.

Fadiyah shook her head, her look scolding. Jet continued to grin.

"You are truly so different than I believed," Fadiyah said, shaking her head in wonder.

Jet gave her a bewildered look. "Fadi, you have to know that the way you met me was far beyond a normal meeting."

"Well, that is true," Fadiyah said. "But still, we talked."

Jet nodded. "Yeah, but I had to be very careful then," she said.

"Careful?" Fadiyah asked.

"Yeah, not to be myself too much," Jet said.

"What do you mean?" Fadiyah asked.

Jet blew her breath out, taking another drag off her cigarette, then pulling one knee up to her chest, wrapping her arm around it before she spoke again.

"Besides the fact that I was an American soldier in an Iraqi home, I was also a gay woman left alone with an Iraqi woman. Add to that the fact that you are Shia, it was a very precarious situation."

Fadiyah blinked a couple of times during Jet's statement. She hadn't realized how much Jet had truly known about the Iraqi culture. She knew that Jet knew that Shia were in a perilous position in Raqqa, but Jet's understanding had gone so much deeper than that. Once again, Fadiyah found herself amazed by this woman. She looked back at Jet for a long moment.

"What?" Jet asked, recognizing that she wanted to ask a question.

"The Daesh…" Fadiyah began, her tone hesitant.

She was referring to ISIS; it was a term that meant both the sowers of discord and also one who crushes underfoot. It was a phrase adopted by many. It was also well known that ISIS had threatened to cut the tongue out of anyone caught referring to them by the name. Because Fadiyah had used it, Jet knew that she was referring to the men who'd killed her father and attacked her.

Jet nodded patiently,, knowing this was hard for Fadiyah, but wanting her to ask what she needed to ask.

"The one that...." Her eyes looked everywhere but at Jet. She made a guttural sound in her throat and said, "Hajam." The Arabic word for attack.

Jet nodded again, grimacing slightly thinking about what the man had been about to do when they'd gotten to the house.

Fadiyah looked directly into Jet's eyes then. "You killed him," she said, her tone strong.

"Yes, I did."

"Shahidat," Fadiyah said, saying in Arabic that she'd watched. It surprised Jet, but she simply nodded, even though the surprise reflected in her eyes. "I was happy to see him die." Fadiyah said, her tone filled with hate, but then she looked at Jet again. "Why did you kill him?"

Jet looked back at Fadiyah looking confused. Finally, she shrugged. "He dishonored you, I couldn't let that stand."

Fadiyah looked back at Jet for a long moment. What she had just said sounded like something that an Iraqi man would say in reference to a woman being disgraced. She shook her head slowly, her eyes reflecting incredulity.

"What?" Jet asked softly.

"You are more honorable than anyone I have ever met," Fadiyah said, her tone reverent.

"You mean for an American?" Jet asked her look expectant, knowing that a lot of Americans were far from honorable, especially when they were in the Middle East.

"Lal eiraqi" Fadiyah responded in Arabic, saying that Jet was more honorable than the Iraqis in her experience.

Jet looked back Fadiyah in shock, drawing in a deep breath, she blew it out, nodding in acceptance for what Fadiyah was saying. She knew that Fadiyah had just paid her an immense compliment; she just had no idea how to respond to it. She was spared having to comment by a voice booming from behind them.

"Were you ever going to answer the door?" Sebastian asked, as he walked out onto the balcony, Skyler behind him.

Jet chuckled, glancing up at them. "Sorry, didn't hear it."

Sebastian kneeled next to the chair Fadiyah sat in, putting out his right hand. "Marhaban," he said, saying hello in Arabic.

Fadiyah looked surprise, but responded by taking his hand in hers, and saying, "Wa'alaykum salaam." Which meant 'upon you be peace.'

Sebastian then put his right hand to his chest, bowing his head slightly and closing his eyes momentarily. Fadiyah blinked in surprise, this man knew traditional Iraqi culture as well.

"Fadiyah, may I present Sebastian Bach," Jet said, beyond happy that Sebastian had remembered Middle East culture so well. He'd immediately put Fadiyah at ease with him.

"And this," Jet said, gesturing to Skyler, "is Skyler Boché."

Skyler put her right hand to her heart, bowing slightly, it was the gesture that indicated respect. Jet loved her friends even more at that moment, as she saw Fadiyah's face light up with appreciation.

"Kayf Halaak?" Skyler queried in perfectly enunciated Arabic, asking how Fadiyah was.

"Bi-khayr, al-Hamdu lillah," Fadiyah responded, saying, 'fine, praise God' in Arabic.

It was a formal response, but in fact held the truth as to how Fadiyah felt at that moment. She was praising God for bringing these people to her when she'd needed them most.

"Your Arabic is excellent," Fadiyah told both Skyler and Sebastian.

"They were both stationed here at one point," Jet said. "Have a seat guys."

"Is that coffee?" Sebastian asked Jet, pointing to her cup.

"Yep, Damascus blend," Jet said, grinning.

Early on she'd discovered that Sebastian liked his coffee as strong as she did, it was one of their common bonds.

"Ohhhh…" Sebastian murmured. "Any left?"

"In the pot inside," Jet said, grinning. "You can refill mine too. Fadiyah do you want coffee? Sky, you want some?"

"I am fine," Fadiyah said.

"Yeah, I'll take mine unleaded please," Skyler said, winking at Sebastian.

"Cream, coming up," Sebastian said, moving to stand, and turning to nod at Fadiyah before stepping back inside the room.

"He certainly understands our culture," Fadiyah said, looking at Jet.

Jet nodded. "He was a Ranger stationed over here for about four years," she said. "He picked up a lot of things in that time."

Fadiyah nodded, agreeing that he seemed to have.

When Sebastian returned, he handed Jet her mug back, now full with steaming coffee. He then handed Skyler hers, and went back inside to get his cup, as well as a pitcher of cream for Skyler.

"You are my new best friend..." Skyler told him as she took the cream, adding it to her coffee.

"Yeah, that's what they all say," Sebastian said, grinning as he sat down.

Skyler, who had already taken a seat in a chair next to Jet's, chuckled.

"You two check in?" Jet asked them.

"I called Devin," Skyler told her. "She's worried about you."

Jet sighed shaking her head. "I'm waiting for my phone to blow up when Ash gets my message about getting shot."

"That's how the little woman gets..." Sebastian said, his tone teasing.

"Bite me, Baz!" Jet said, giving him a dirty look.

"Ash?" Fadiyah queried.

"Ashley," Jet said. "She's a... friend."

Sebastian coughed pointedly. Jet narrowed her eyes at him. He looked back at her trying to look innocent.

"Little woman," Fadiyah said, her tone speculative. "That is an American colloquialism for a wife, is it not?"

Jet looked surprised by her comment, and it made her realize that Fadiyah understood more than she'd imagined.

"I'm not married," Jet said quickly.

"But Ashley is the *little woman*?" Fadiyah asked, confused.

"No," Jet said, her tone patient. "Ashley is a friend, and Sebastian is now going to find his own way home to LA." She said the last with smile at Fadiyah, but with narrowed eyes at him.

Sebastian let out a deep and rumbling laugh.

Fadiyah looked over at Sebastian. "Are you married?" she asked.

Sebastian scowled. "No," he said, with a shake of his head. "But Sky's getting married."

"You are?" Fadiyah asked, smiling happily. "Happy tidings…"

Skyler grinned. "Shukraan," she said, saying thank you in Arabic.

Then Fadiyah looked at Jet again. "But you are not married."

"No," Jet repeated.

Fadiyah nodded, looking like she wasn't sure she believed Jet, but not pursuing the discussion.

Jet's phone chimed and she opened the message.

"Oh!" Jet said, grimacing.

"What?" Skyler asked.

"She's pulling out the middle name now," Jet said, turning the phone to Skyler.

"Oh, yeah, that's not good," Skyler said.

"What did she say?" Sebastian asked, grinning.

"Uh…" Jet uttered, looking at the message. "It says 'Jet Blue Mathews, you send me a picture of that wound right now!' "

"You want me to take a picture of it?" Skyler asked.

"Yeah," Jet said, grinning. "Better or she's really gonna yell…"

Jet pulled her shirt up to expose the wound, and Skyler took the picture for Jet to send.

Jet's phone rang then, and Ashley's picture and name appeared on the display. Fadiyah caught a glimpse of the picture of a beautiful woman with blue eyes before Jet reached over picking up her phone. Jet moved to stand as she answered it, walking to the other side of the balcony farthest from the group.

"Hey…" Jet answered the phone, her tone soft and affectionate.

Skyler and Sebastian exchanged a look as the both saw Fadiyah tense. Skyler and Sebastian did their best to ignore the conversation, but they noted that Fadiyah watched and listened intently to everything Jet said and did while she was talking to Ashley.

Jet stood with her back to the group.

"No, I'm okay, really," Jet was saying. She laughed then, a happy sound bowing her head for a moment. "No, I'm not lying to you, sheesh," she said, then her voice raising slightly, but still smiling as she turned to pace slowly as she talked. "As a matter of fact, I did. Yes it was a real doctor," she said, her tone exasperated, then laughed again, shaking her head. "You are way too suspicious, I'm going to start taking that personally…"

Fadiyah could see that Jet was very close to the person she was talking to on the phone. She also noticed the way she smiled when the other person was talking. She suspected that Ashley was a love interest for Jet.

"No, babe, it's okay," Jet said then, her tone warm. "If you need to head up there, go ahead… The house will be fine… No, just set the alarm, honey." She laughed again, shaking her head. "No, they don't need to be babysat, I promise. If they croak while I'm gone, I'll just replant." After a few more minutes, Fadiyah heard Jet say softly, "I miss you too."

She hung up a few minutes later, and walked back over to where the other three sat.

"Everything okay on the home front?" Sebastian asked, his tone pointed.

Jet narrowed her eyes at him again, but nodded. "Yeah, Ash was just saying she's gotta go up to Seattle tomorrow, she's gotta meet with the editor."

"I think I am going to go try that shower," Fadiyah said, moving to stand.

Jet, Skyler and Sebastian all stood. Fadiyah looked around at all of them surprised yet again, her eyes staying on Jet and Skyler longer.

"It's a butch thing," Jet told Fadiyah.

"A butch thing?" Fadiyah repeated, clearly confused.

Jet grinned. "I'll explain later."

"Okay," Fadiyah said, nodding.

"Let me know if that faucet gives you too much trouble, it's kind of weird," Jet said, knowing that Fadiyah wasn't used to proper plumbing, but not wanting to embarrass her by saying as much.

"I will," Fadiyah said, smiling and nodding to both Skyler and Sebastian before she went back into the hotel room.

"So…" Sebastian said, moving to sit in the chair Fadiyah had just vacated. "How's Ashley?"

Jet gave him a sideways look. "She's fine, thanks for asking," she said, her tone pointedly casual.

"So how's this going to go?" Sebastian asked, obvious ire in his tone.

"How's what going to go?" Jet asked, raising a black eyebrow.

"You bringing Fadiyah home," Sebastian said seriously. "How's Ashley going to take that?"

Jet looked back at him, her eyes saying, *It's none of your business* but she actually said, "She knew it was a possibility that I'd be bringing her back with me."

"Did she?" Sebastian asked, his tone disbelieving.

"Yeah, Baz, she did," Jet said. "What are you trying to get at here?"

Sebastian looked back at her for a long moment. "This girl is going to require a lot of your time," he said, "and I'm just wondering where that'll leave Ash."

Jet heard Skyler clear her throat behind her and glanced over at her.

"You have something to say here too?" Jet asked.

Skyler held up her hands in surrender. "Stayin' out of this," she said simply, as she gave Sebastian a sharp look.

Jet was looking back at Sebastian. "Ashley is free to do whatever she wants, Baz," she told him. "She's a free agent."

Sebastian gave a short sarcastic laugh, nodding his head, his gray-green eyes narrowed slightly.

"I think you underestimate how much Ashley cares about you, Jet," he said.

"And I think you overestimate how much of this is your business, Baz," Jet countered.

"Jet?" Fadiyah said from the door, her voice soft. She'd heard the way they were talking when she'd walked up to the door.

Jet's head snapped around, and she stood. "I'll be right back," she said over her shoulder as she followed Fadiyah inside.

In the bathroom, Fadiyah turned to look at Jet, her abaya swinging around her feet because she'd moved so quickly.

"Why are you fighting with Sebastian?" she asked, her tone worried.

Jet smiled patiently at her. "I'm not," she assured Fadiyah, "he's just voicing his opinion on my love life."

"So Ashley is your love life?" Fadiyah asked, her look furtive.

Jet blew her breath out, moving to lean against the counter in the bathroom, her hands on either side of her on the counter.

"She and I have been together…" she said, her voice trailing off. She sincerely wished she were anywhere else right now, but she didn't want Fadiyah to think she couldn't ask questions.

"Then you are a couple?" Fadiyah asked.

"No," Jet said immediately, "well, yes, but… it's complicated Fadi."

Fadiyah nodded, looking like she was trying to understand.

"And Sebastian does not like that it is *complicated*?" Fadiyah asked.

"Sebastian is way more interested in Ashley than he wants to let on, and he's pissed off that she's with me, and not him," Jet said, her tone sharper than she'd meant it to be.

She blew her breath out in an audible sigh, closing her eyes for a moment. "I'm sorry," she said, "I didn't mean to snap at you. My shoulder is hurting and I'm wishing I had a drink right now. Take your shower. There are clothes here," she said, pointing to the cabinet in the bathroom. "I arranged to have them send up a bunch of things, not knowing what you'd want. There is an abaya, hijab and veil in there too, if you want to do that, okay?"

Fadiyah nodded, knowing that Jet was trying to change the conversation, and willing to let her. Jet moved forward, demonstrating how to turn the shower on and adjust the temperature. She left the room then.

Out on the balcony Skyler was looking over at Sebastian.

"Are you trying to piss her off?" Skyler asked sharply.

"I'm trying to get her to fuckin' think," Sebastian responded.

"And you think she's not?" Skyler asked looking surprised.

"I think she's not worried about Ashley in this."

"And I think you're too worried about Ashley in this."

Sebastian looked back at her, a frown on his lips. "I just want her to do the right thing."

"And what do you think is the right thing, Baz?" Skyler asked.

"Ashley cares about her, Sebastian said.

"And Jet cares about Ashley," Skyler said. "But she hasn't promised that girl a damned thing, I guarantee it."

"And that matters?" Sebastian asked.

"In our world, yes it does." Skyler said, nodding.

"Your world," Sebastian said, his tone annoyed.

"Yeah, Baz, in the lesbian world, butches don't promise anything they don't plan to give."

Sebastian curled his lips, he knew it was true. Kashena was his best friend, and her word was gold. She'd always been completely above board with the women she'd dated before she'd met Sierra. Even then, she'd been agonizingly honest with Sierra. Jet definitely was like Kashena.

"You know," Skyler said, lightening her tone, "if you're interested in Ashley, I say go for it."

"She's into Jet," Sebastian said dismissively.

"Everyone's into Jet."

"Including Fadiyah," Sebastian said, his tone warmer then.

"Yeah…" Skyler said, nodding.

By the time Jet rejoined them, Skyler and Sebastian were both standing to leave.

"We good?" Jet asked Sebastian, her look searching.

"We're good," Sebastian said, nodding.

"Uh… guys…" Skyler said, looking at her phone. "Have you seen your email?"

"No, why?" Sebastian asked, pulling out his phone.

"Read Midnight's email," Skyler said, her look shocked.

Jet and Sebastian both checked their phones, and started laughing.

"Now, that's what I'm talking about…" Sebastian said, grinning.

After Skyler and Sebastian left, Jet sat down in the living area, turning on the TV and lazily flipping channels. She heard a sound behind her and turned, seeing Fadiyah standing in the doorway. She wore black slacks and a cream colored blouse, her hair was uncovered and down, reaching to her waist in a silky black curtain.

Jet moved to stand, turning to look at her again in awe.

"Fadi…" she said. "You look amazing…"

Fadiyah bit her lip, smiling hesitantly.

"How do you feel?" Jet asked, walking over to stand in front of the other woman, her light green eyes searching Fadiyah's.

Fadiyah took a deep breath, blowing it out and nodding. "I feel good," she said.

Jet nodded, smiling at her again. "You look great," she said, her tone sincere.

Fadiyah pressed her lips together. "I was not sure if I should wear at least the hijab," she said, her tone cautious.

"It's up to you," Jet said. "We've now got a private plane home, so you don't have to worry about anyone really seeing you on the flight."

"A private plane?" Fadiyah asked, her eyes wide.

"Friends in high places, babe," Jet said, grinning.

That evening the four of them boarded Joe Sinclair's private Gulf Stream jet for their flight home. Midnight's email had informed them about their upgrade in accommodations. Her words had simply been,

"For American heroes and our newest friend, Joe thought you should travel in style." The email had included a picture of the sleek jet.

Fadiyah looked around her, unable to believe what was happening.

"You know the owner of this plane?" Fadiyah asked Jet.

"Not personally, no," Jet said, nodding at Sebastian. "Baz has met him though."

Sebastian grinned, nodding. "Joe Sinclair is a class act."

Jet and Fadiyah sat together, with Fadiyah sitting next to the window. Fadiyah wound her arms around Jet's right arm, and grasped it tight as the Gulf Stream lifted off. Jet chuckled at her reaction.

"First time flying, huh?" Jet asked her softly.

"Oh, yes," Fadiyah said, her voice filled with wonder.

Jet smiled. Fadiyah spent most of the flight with her arms around Jet's arm, only letting go when they had dinner and later breakfast as they neared Los Angles. When she slept on the flight, it was with her arms around Jet's arm, and her head on Jet's shoulder.

Chapter 8

They made it back to Los Angles in just less than fourteen hours, without stopping for refueling. As they circled for a landing at LAX, Sebastian grinned.

"Helluva a lot better than the thirty hour trip on the way there," he said.

"It took thirty hours to come to Iraq?" Fadiyah asked, looking at Jet.

"Well, we flew into Ashgabat in Iran, but yeah, military flights, unless you're flying a jet, they don't go this fast."

Fadiyah looked shocked, then nodded. Once again she realized how much Jet had gone through to come to rescue her, it was still shocking to her.

"That's what something like sixty-five million will buy you…" Sebastian said.

"I can't see spending that kind of money…" Jet said, shaking her head.

"But you can buy a hundred and eighty thousand dollar car…" Skyler said from behind her.

Jet laughed out loud. "Okay, good point."

"Uh-huh," Skyler said, grinning.

Fadiyah said nothing, shocked at what Skyler had said as well.

An hour later Jet was unlocking the front door to her parents' house and Fadiyah was shocked at the size of the home. Jet showed her around, eventually showing her to the guest bedroom next to her own room.

"I'm going to put you in here," Jet said. "So if you need me I'm right there, okay?"

Fadiyah nodded, looking around the room. It was the most beautiful room she'd ever seen. It was painted with a light blue-green color, and decorated with white and darker shades of the blue green and navy blue. The entire house was beautiful; she could not believe that Jet came from such wealth. Jet seemed so humble, not like the type of rich people Fadiyah had ever had occasion to meet. Jet had made a point of telling her over and over again that this house did not belong to her, but to her parents.

"I'm going to go check on the state of my backyard," Jet said. "Get settled and make yourself at home, okay?"

"Okay," Fadiyah said, nodding, still looking shell-shocked.

A half an hour later, Fadiyah walked out into Jet's backyard, to find her shoveling dirt. She noticed that Jet was sweating, and that she had a cigarette in her mouth. She also noticed that Jet had music on; she remembered that Jet had said it helped with her ADHD.

"Should you be doing that with your shoulder hurt?" she asked.

Jet looked over at her, her look assessing. "Sure," she said, with a grin.

"I do not think so," Fadiyah said, looking around the yard.

The backyard was beautiful, with green trees and flowering bushes. The breeze that blew was cool and nice; the sun was warm, but not the baking sun of the desert. Fadiyah moved to sit in one of the chairs, looking over at Jet as she worked. Jet had changed into shorts from the jeans she'd worn on the plane, and she now had a tank top on. A few times, when Jet would move Fadiyah would catch glimpses of something on her chest, but she could not make out what it was.

After an hour, Fadiyah couldn't stand it anymore.

"Jet, you need to rest," she said, her tone scolding.

Jet looked over at her, quirking a grin.

"I do, do I?" she asked.

"Yes," Fadiyah said, her tone sure. "You work too hard for someone who is injured."

Jet laughed at that, moving to sit down in the chair across from Fadiyah. She reached for another cigarette and lit it. Fadiyah watched her.

"What?" Jet asked, seeing Fadiyah watching her.

"You smoke too much."

Jet grinned. "Yes, yes I do," she said, taking another long drag off of her cigarette. "And you'll find that I drink too much too. Speaking of which…" she said getting up and walking into the house. She came out a few minutes later with a bottle of beer in hand. "I'm sure it's beer-thirty somewhere," she said, grinning.

"It is still morning!" Fadiyah exclaimed, shocked.

Jet looked at her phone. "No, it's like almost noon, I'm good."

Fadiyah shook her head. "You are so mischievous!"

"Well, there's one I haven't heard before…" Jet said, a wicked grin on her lips.

"What does that mean?" Fadiyah asked.

"It means you just called me something no one else has ever called me before," she said.

"I like to be original," Fadiyah said, folding her hands in her lap.

Jet looked back at her smiling fondly.

"Well, I've been taking care of myself for thirty years now, and I think I'm doing okay."

"You are thirty?" Fadiyah asked, looking surprised.

Jet grinned. "Yeah, how old did you think I was?"

"I did not think you were that old," Fadiyah replied.

"Ouch," Jet said, grimacing comically.

"I did not mean any offense," Fadiyah said. "You look younger than that."

"You didn't offend me, honey," Jet said. "But how old are you?"

Fadiyah bit her lip. "I am nineteen."

"Holy shit, really?" Jet exclaimed, then grimaced. "I'm sorry."

"Why?" Fadiyah asked.

"I know that cussing isn't the Shia way," Jet said. "I'm trying to respect that."

"But you are not Shia, so you are allowed to curse."

"Well, trust me, I do a lot…" Jet said, rolling her eyes.

Her phone chimed then, and she reached over to pick it up. She scanned an email and then shook her head.

"Damnit..." She muttered.

"What is wrong?" Fadiyah asked.

Jet sighed, putting down her phone. "It looks like I'm going to have to work tomorrow," she said, looking unhappy about the prospect.

"What do you do?" Fadiyah asked, realizing suddenly she didn't know.

Jet leaned back, taking a drink of her beer and lighting another cigarette. "I'm a cop," she said.

"A cop?" Fadiyah queried.

"A police officer," Jet said.

"Oh," Fadiyah said, nodding. "That is a noble profession."

Jet gave her a lopsided grin. "Not the way I do it."

"I do not believe it," Fadiyah said, her tone very proper.

Jet chuckled. "I work for a task force called LA IMPACT, which stands for Los Angeles Interagency Metropolitan Police Apprehension Crime Task Force... well, here..." she said, picking up her phone, then looking back at Fadiyah. "You can read English too, right?"

"Yes," Fadiyah said, nodding.

"Okay, read this, it'll explain it better than I can," Jet said, handing Fadiyah her phone.

Fadiyah read about the task force and then looked over at Jet. "Which area are you in?" she asked, looking at the different areas of expertise LA IMPACT had.

"I'm COID," Jet said, then shook her head at herself and laughed. "I'm part of the Covert Operations and Informant Development group. I basically do for them what I did for the Army when I was in Military Intelligence."

"And what is happening tomorrow?" Fadiyah asked.

"Well, I need to go in because an operation I've been setting up for about two months now is going tomorrow."

"Going?" Fadiyah asked.

"The sting operation," Jet said, then rolled her eyes at herself again. "I'm sorry, I keep forgetting that I'm not talking shop with another cop. A sting is where we get the bad guy to sell us something illegal so we can arrest him for it."

"Oh, I see," Fadiyah nodded.

"So, want to come see where I work tomorrow?" Jet asked, her tone falsely bright.

"I would love that," Fadiyah said, smiling.

Jet drained the last of the beer and stood up to get another. When she walked back outside with the beer in hand, Fadiyah shook her head. Jet only grinned as she sat down again.

"Don't worry, I rarely get drunk," she told Fadiyah.

"What are you like when you are drunk?" Fadiyah asked, curious.

Jet grinned. "Well, that would be the reason I don't get drunk very often," she said.

"Why?" Fadiyah asked.

"Because I'm a completely open book when I'm drunk," Jet said.

"What does that mean?" Fadiyah asked.

"It means a person could ask me literally anything and I'd answer."

Fadiyah looked back at her for a long moment, her look considering. "Perhaps I should allow you to drink more then."

Jet grinned, looking surprised. "Well, trust me, honey, it takes a lot more than this."

"How much does it take?" Fadiyah asked.

"A lot," Jet said. "And actual hard alcohol, beer isn't that strong, but why do you want me to get drunk? You can ask me anything you want and I'll tell you."

"You will?" Fadiyah asked, surprised.

"Yes," Jet said.

"Okay," Fadiyah said. "I keep seeing part of something there," she said, pointing to the middle of Jet's chest, "What is it?"

Jet lit another cigarette, a grin playing at her lips. "It's a tattoo," she said, with the cigarette dangling from her lips.

"Of what?" Fadiyah asked

Jet reached over, setting her cigarette in the ashtray on the table, and pulled off her tank top, revealing a black exercise bra and the medallion tattoo.

Fadiyah looked at the tattoo and immediately recognized it.

"That is a Shia symbol!" she exclaimed.

"I know, that's why I picked it," Jet said her tone complacent.

"But why?" Fadiyah asked, her eyes looking from the tattoo to Jet's eyes.

"Look closely," Jet said, putting her finger to the Arabic lettering around the edge of the medallion.

Fadiyah's eyes widened. "That is my name!" she exclaimed. "And Abdul's and my father's…" Her voice trailed off as she looked back up at Jet.

Jet's eyes were sad. "It's all I could do when I got back to honor what you did for me."

Fadiyah blinked a few times, tears in her eyes.

"I'm sorry if it seems a little blasphemous," Jet said.

"No…" Fadiyah breathed. "It is incredible."

Jet smiled sadly and stood briefly to put her tank top back on.

Fadiyah moved to take Jet's hands in hers, her eyes staring into Jet's. "You are the most incredible person I have ever met, Jet Mathews."

"I'm glad you think so," Jet said smiling, then she looked at Fadiyah, her look somber. "Fadi, what happened to Abdul?"

"He was killed a year ago," Fadiyah said, her look sad.

"What happened?" Jet asked.

"He was playing in the street when the trucks rolled through the streets, they never even slowed down."

"Oh my God, Fadi, I'm so sorry…" Jet said, grimacing.

Fadiyah nodded, doing her best to control her tears.

That night, Jet ordered pizza for dinner and Fadiyah thoroughly enjoyed the meal. She'd never had anything like pizza before, so it was a treat. After dinner they watched a couple of movies. Jet let Fadiyah pick the movies, so they ended up watching SWAT and Steel Magnolias, neither of which Fadiyah had ever seen, but she had liked the sound of them.

During the second movie Jet began to get tired, so when the movie ended, she suggested they get some sleep. They walked upstairs.

"Do you have anything to sleep in?" Jet asked, realizing that they hadn't managed to go buy anything that day or before they'd left Iran.

Fadiyah shook her head.

"Hold on," Jet said, walking into her room, and opening a couple of drawers.

She came back with an LAPD t-shirt and a pair of sweat pants.

"We can go shopping tomorrow after work to get you some more clothes," Jet said, chagrinned that she hadn't thought about that earlier.

"It is okay," Fadiyah said, smiling.

"Okay, well, goodnight," Jet said smiling.

"Masaa'al-kayhar," Fadiyah replied.

Jet lay in her bed, staring up at the ceiling. Part of her felt relieved that finally she was able to put her past to rest. The other part of her wasn't sure how things were going to go with Fadiyah in America, but she knew that she would protect this girl with her life. The problem was, it was likely to interfere with any woman she dated, not that she really dated women for long enough for it to matter, but it would definitely create a new barrier to relationships.

She was asleep when she heard her name called softly.

Waking up, she turned over and saw that Fadiyah was standing next to her bed.

She moved to sit up, wincing when she once again forgot her shoulder and used her left arm to lever herself up.

"Damnit…" she hissed, looking instantly contrite. "Sorry, what's wrong Fadi?"

Fadiyah shook her head. "I cannot sleep."

Jet gave her a concerned look, then reached her right hand out. "Come here," she said.

Fadiyah took her hand and sat down on the bed, Jet held her arm out, and Fadiyah immediately moved to lie against her, her head against Jet's shoulder.

Jet smiled fondly at the movement. It was becoming almost a habit now. Jet put her arm around Fadiyah's shoulders, her hand smoothing down Fadiyah's back rhythmically. Fadiyah rested her hand on Jet's chest, her thumb brushing over the top of the Shia tattoo that was visible above the tank top Jet had worn to bed.

They fell asleep that way.

The next morning, Jet's alarm went off at six o'clock. Jet groaned, feeling like she'd only just gone to sleep. Fadiyah was already awake, but she still lay with her head on Jet's shoulder, even though Jet had moved them down into a lying position at some point during the night. Fadiyah moved to her elbows looking down at Jet who was reaching for the alarm to turn it off. She saw Jet wince because she was reaching with the arm that had the injured shoulder.

"Are you sure you should be going to work today?" Fadiyah asked.

"I gotta," Jet said tiredly. "If I blow this sting, it'll take months to set up again, if the guy even trusts me again."

Fadiyah nodded, trying to understand Jet's work. They both got up. Jet showed Fadiyah where the extra towels were and also showed her how the shower worked and where toiletries were located. There were a few comical moments where she showed Fadiyah how to use the automatic toothbrush. When Fadiyah couldn't get the hang of it without laughing, Jet pulled out a regular toothbrush and handed it to her.

Jet showered and got dressed, putting on the clothes she usually wore when she was going to work: jeans, combat style black boots, and a black tank top. She wore her silver byzantine-style chain and black obsidian studs in her ears, and a black leather watch.

Fadiyah wore a pair of jeans and a blue cotton button up shirt that Jet had gotten for her. On her feet she wore the same black sandals she'd always worn.

"Wow," Jet said, grinning when she Fadiyah walked into the kitchen.

"What is it?" Fadiyah asked, looking around her.

Jet grinned. "You in jeans. They look good," she said, smiling warmly.

"It is very strange," Fadiyah said, touching the denim at her hips. "I feel much more constricted."

"Yeah, that's progress for you," Jet said, grinning, her eyes sparkling with humor. "Do you want coffee?" she asked, holding up the pot.

Fadiyah looked hesitant.

"It's Arabian, Damascus blend," Jet said.

"That is too strong for me," Fadiyah said, shaking her head.

"Well, what do you usually drink?" Jet asked, as she poured her coffee into a cup.

"Usually tea," Fadiyah said. "It is okay."

Jet walked over to her pantry and pulled out a pouch and a teapot. As Fadiyah stood watching, her mouth slightly agape, Jet put water in the microwave and tea leaves into the steeper inside the glass teapot. A few minutes later, Jet handed Fadiyah a cup with tea in it, and put cream and both a cinnamon stick and a bottle marked as cardamom on the counter in front of her.

Fadiyah sniffed the tea and recognized it, her silver-gray eyes widened.

"This is the kind we used at home," Fadiyah said. "And I see you know how we drink it as well," she said, gesturing to the things Jet had put on the counter.

"Fadi, I was in the Middle East for a long time, I know the traditions," she said, canting her head slightly. "I thought you knew that."

Fadiyah inclined her head. "I did not realize to what extent you knew our traditions."

"You'll learn," Jet said, grinning.

Fadiyah nodded, happy that Jet seemed to be thinking long term with their friendship. It had been thoughts of being in a strange country that had kept her awake the night before. Lying in Jet's arms had been the only thing that stilled those thoughts and fears. She knew that her position was precarious in America. She knew no one other than Jet, and Jet had a life all her own. It was a world that Fadiyah didn't know anything about. Every moment she spent with Jet showed her how little she really knew about Jet Mathews. While she found Jet quite fascinating, she knew that she was an addition to Jet's life, not her priority.

In Iraq she'd known her place. She had her father to look after her, and knew that at some point she would have a husband. Her life was now turned completely upside down. She knew that staying in Iraq or Iran as an unchaperoned woman would be dangerous. She'd been unable to resist the desire to not only stay with the one person left in her world, but also the chance to see America, a place she'd only ever heard of before. Being in America was going to be very different, and Fadiyah was terrified to even try to navigate it. She was eternally grateful to Jet for every little kindness. Silly things like understanding her traditions and having the kind of tea she drank, was a wonderful and very welcome comfort.

Jet noticed the light sheen of tears in Fadiyah's eyes as she prepared her tea, using the cardamom and a small amount of cream.

"We can get some fresh cardamom later today when we go shopping," Jet said, smiling. "I know the dried stuff isn't as good."

"It is wonderful, thank you," Fadiyah said her eyes downcast.

Jet looked back at Fadiyah for a long minute; she knew that Fadiyah was trying desperately to adjust to everything around her. She wanted to help in any way that she could, but her life was non-stop most of the time and it worried her that Fadiyah would get trampled in the process. Blowing her breath out in a sigh, Jet looked at her watch. She needed to get moving.

"Hate to do this," Jet said. "But we need to go."

Fadiyah nodded quickly.

"I can put this in a cup to go if you want," Jet said, reaching for a travel mug.

"Okay," Fadiyah said simply.

Jet put the tea into a cup, handing it to Fadiyah with her right hand, another tradition, and then picked up her gear bag, keys and her own coffee mug.

"Ready?" she asked.

Fadiyah nodded, following Jet out to the garage. When they walked out Fadiyah stood stock still, looking stunned at the vehicles in the garage. Jet noticed that Fadiyah didn't move. She grinned as she hit the button to open the garage, then walked around Fadiyah to put her bag in the trunk of the Maserati.

She held out her hand to Fadiyah as she unlocked the Maserati. Fadiyah walked over to her, and Jet opened the passenger door, holding it open until Fadiyah had gotten into the car. She closed it gently and then got into the car, starting it.

Fadiyah's eyes widened with the low rumble of the engine, she looked over at Jet who looked back at her grinning.

"Is this the one that cost one hundred and eighty thousand dollars or is it that one?" Fadiyah asked, pointing to the Fastback next to the Maserati.

Jet grinned. "I guess you heard that, huh?"

Fadiyah nodded, as Jet put the car into gear and backed out of the garage

"This one," Jet said. "The Stang is a classic, but she's not worth quite that much. She's more of a sentimental thing for me."

Fadiyah looked around the Maserati, noting the expensive looking and feeling leather seats and the trim of the vehicle and all of the gauges. Her eyes were wide, her mouth hanging somewhat open. She had never been inside a vehicle like this one.

Jet grinned as she hit the button to close the garage door. She turned on the stereo, quickly turning the volume down before it blasted them with sound.

The song that came on was in Spanish and Jet sang with it absently as she drove. Fadiyah watched her.

"What language is that?" Fadiyah asked.

"Spanish," Jet said, as she turned her head to look for cars as she pulled out into the intersection.

"You speak Spanish?" Fadiyah asked.

"I speak Spanish, French, German, some Arabic and some Farsi," Jet said, grinning, remembering having a similar conversation with Ashley.

"You speak all of those?" Fadiyah asked sounding surprised.

"Yeah," Jet said, nodding. "It's easier to get someone to work with you in a foreign country if you speak their language. That's why I'm good at what I do."

"I would think you are," Fadiyah said, once again surprised by Jet.

They were both silent for a while and Jet continued to sing with the songs on the stereo.

"What is that song that you were singing at the hotel?" Fadiyah asked after a few minutes.

"Which?" Jet asked.

"The one that talked about Neverland," Fadiyah said.

"Oh," Jet said, and picked up her iPhone. Still watching the road, she scrolled through her phone and found the song Fadiyah was asking about. "This one?" she asked as she hit play.

The first piano chords of the song filled the car.

"Yes!" Fadiyah said, nodding.

They listened to the song, and as Fadiyah had hoped, Jet sang the words. When the song ended, Fadiyah sighed.

"I very much like that song," she said. "Especially when you sing it."

Jet curled her lips in a wry grin. "If you say so," she said, her tone cynical.

"I say so."

"Ma'am, yes ma'am," Jet muttered and got a narrowed look from Fadiyah in response, to which she simply chuckled.

A few minutes later Jet's phone rang, she glanced at the display and saw her parents' picture.

"Oh, lovely," she said, then hit the hands free button. "This is Jet," she answered, as she always answered calls.

Fadiyah looked at the display on the phone and it said T&R Mathews.

"What kind of a way is that to answer a phone?" came a woman's voice.

"The kind where I answer instead of hitting ignore," Jet said, her tone wry.

"Don't be rude, Jet." The woman's tone was chiding.

"What's up, Mom?" Jet asked, her tone impatient.

"Am I interrupting something?" the woman asked, her tone offended.

"Just my life," Jet said, a sarcastic smile on her face.

"That's precisely what we're calling about," the woman said, and Jet grimaced, knowing she'd stepped in it now.

"So what now?" Jet asked.

"We understand you went back to Iraq," the woman said, her tone reproaching.

"It's Iraq, Mom, like your ear, Iraq, not like I-rack," Jet snapped, her tone annoyed.

Jet glanced over at Fadiyah and saw that she was watching her looking shocked. Jet knew that Fadiyah was probably completely appalled by the way she talked to her parents. In Iraq you didn't ever speak to your parents the way that Jet was doing, so Jet knew that it was quite outrageous to Fadiyah.

Jet's mother made an impatient sound at the other end of the phone. "Whatever Jet, just tell me why you would go back to that country when you are no longer in the Army."

Jet chewed on the gum she'd put into her mouth minutes before, her look irritated and her eyes flashing in annoyance.

"Jet?" the woman queried.

"Yeah, I'm here." Jet said.

"Are you going to answer my question?"

"Sure, right after you tell me why you need to know," Jet said, her tone cooler now.

"You are our daughter, Jet, we worry about you," the woman said, her tone upbraiding.

Jet gave a short bark of laughter. "Oh, wait, you were serious about that?" she said then, her lips curled in a sneer.

"Jet, I can't deal with you when you're like this," the woman said, her tone exasperated.

"Sorry, this is the only this I got."

"Are you completely off the Ritalin now?" the woman asked then.

"I was never on Ritalin, Mom, its Adderall," Jet said, rolling her eyes and shaking her head.

"Well, maybe Ritalin would work better."

"Yeah, it's still not going to make me the kid you're looking for, Mom, so get over it already," Jet said, her tone cutting.

"I can't do this…" the woman said, sounding like she was talking to someone else. There was a rustling noise and a muted conversation.

Jet rocked back and forth slightly in her seat, her look impatient, her finger tapping on the steering wheel in agitation.

"Hello? Can we move this happy family experience along please?" Jet asked, losing her patience finally.

"Jet," a man's voice said then, his tone authoritative.

"Oh gee, hi Dad," Jet said, shaking her head and looking up.

"Why are you giving your mother a hard time? We're just trying to check on you. When we called the house your girlfriend told us you were in Iraq. We were just asking why you felt the need to go back there after the last time you were there."

Jet listened to her father's tirade, a calm, nonplussed look on her face.

"She's not my girlfriend," Jet said, answering the only thing she cared to answer at that point.

"So you're letting random strangers stay in our house now?" her father said.

"I don't have to be fucking them to let them stay in the house, do I, Dad?" Jet asked.

Fadiyah gasped at the cuss word Jet had used. Jet shook her head, trying not to laugh at the situation.

"Don't be crass, Jet!" her father's voice boomed through the speakers of the car.

Again, Jet looked completely unaffected by her father's words or his volume.

"Why did you go to Iraq?" her father asked when Jet didn't respond to his order.

"Oh, I dunno, somethin' to do…" Jet said, her tone sarcastic.

"Sarcasm isn't attractive Jet," her father said, his tone caustic.

"Yeah, but it's all I got, so…"

"We're worried about you."

"Uh-huh," Jet muttered, looking unconvinced. "I'm fine."

The man sighed then. "I don't understand why you always have to make things so difficult, Jet…"

"I know," Jet said, her tone not giving an inch.

"Well, we were calling to tell you that we're going to be in LA in two weeks."

"Oh yay," Jet said, without any enthusiasm.

"Stop it, young lady," her father gritted out.

Jet gave a smug smile, she loved that she was getting to her father.

"Are you planning on staying at the house? Should I move out?" Jet asked.

Her father sighed loudly again. "We'll be staying at a hotel, Jet, don't be a smart ass."

"It's the only ass I have, Dad," Jet replied.

"I thought the Army was supposed to teach you respect," her father said then.

"It did," Jet replied. "It also taught me twenty ways to kill a man, so… I'm thinking I probably shouldn't use everything I learned while I was in."

"How about giving the respect thing a shot?" her father asked.

"It's not as fun," Jet replied.

"We'll see you in two weeks, Jet. Try to have a better attitude then."

"Don't hold your breath," Jet replied, before disconnecting the line.

She looked over at Fadiyah then and saw that she was watching her with something akin to horror on her face.

"What?" Jet asked, her tone falsely innocent.

"You speak to your parents that way?" Fadiyah asked.

"All the damned time," Jet replied, her light green eyes sparkling with barely veiled malice.

"Why?" Fadiyah asked, aghast.

Jet looked back at her for a long moment, then shrugged as she looked away. "They never bought me a pony," she said, her tone sarcastic.

"What?" Fadiyah asked, confused by the answer.

Jet shook her head. "Nothing, I'm sorry, I just really don't like talking about them."

"But they are your parents…" Fadiyah said.

"Yeah, well you don't get to pick who gives birth to you, so…" Jet said, her voice trailing off as she reached over to turn the radio up.

Fadiyah realized that she was doing that to avoid talking. It was the first time Jet had shut her out and it stung. A rock song played and Jet sang the words with relish.

The words in the chorus made Fadiyah think that Jet was thinking about her relationship with her parents. It talked about how a person could let things get the way that they were. And how she wasn't going to take any more of this person's denial.

Then there was a bridge to the song that made Fadiyah truly wonder how bad Jet's relationship with them was. Talking about pushing her to the point of an actual fight. Fadiyah wondered if Jet truly meant to fight her parents.

A few minutes later, as they sat in traffic on the freeway, Jet's phone rang again. Glancing at the display Jet narrowed her eyes. Fadiyah saw that it was Ashley.

"This is Jet," Jet answered.

"Hi," came Ashley's voice over the cars speakers.

"Hi…" Jet replied, her tone choleric.

"Uh-oh…" Ashley muttered. "What happened?"

"Did you forget to tell me something?" Jet asked, still irritated.

"Uh…" Ashley stammered.

"Something about my parents?" Jet asked, her finger tapping the steering wheel in agitation.

"Oh, shit, Jet… I'm sorry, I totally forgot in all this Seattle craziness…" Ashley said, clearly cringing.

"Uh-huh," Jet said, her eyes flashing in anger.

"I'm sorry, babe…" Ashley said. "They called right before I left."

"Okay," Jet said. "But why did you tell them I was in Iraq?"

There was silence for a long few moments. "Uh… was I not supposed to tell them that?"

"I don't tell them anything about what I do, Ash," Jet said. "Hell, I didn't even tell them I was in Iraq the first damned time."

"You didn't?" Ashley asked. "But they knew, because when I said you were in Iraq your mom said 'again?'."

Jet chewed at her gum. "That's only because the Army fucked up and told them I was KIA in Iraq."

"KIA?" Ashley queried.

"Killed in action, Ash," Jet said, her tone still sharp.

"Oh," Ashley said. "I'm sorry, but I didn't know all of that…"

Jet sighed, shaking her head. "No, it's my fault I didn't tell you not to tell them anything if they called. I really didn't expect them to call the house. They probably couldn't get through on my cell during the thirty hour flight, so they called the house…"

"I am sorry though," Ashley said.

Jet blew her breath out. "It's okay. So how's it going there?"

"Okay, I should be home the day after tomorrow," Ashley said, sounding relieved that Jet was no longer mad at her.

"Okay," Jet said, nodding. "Do you need a ride from the airport?"

"No, I'm okay, my car is there."

"Okay."

"Hey, are you in the car?" Ashley asked then.

"Yeah," Jet said.

"This early in the morning?"

Jet's lips curled into a grin. "Yeah, I'm on my way in to work."

"Work? Jet, you just got home," Ashley said, her tone rising.

"I know, but my Izadi case is going today," Jet said.

"Oh… damn, that sucks. You be careful please," Ashley said, her tone softening on the last part.

"I will," Jet said. "So you have dinner with Greg yet?" she asked then, grinning mischievously.

"No, that's tonight." Ashley said.

"Oh… I see, well, look out, he might try to knock your socks off."

"Like that's ever gonna happen," Ashley said, her tone cynical.

"It might," Jet said, grinning. "Maybe he'll surprise ya."

"Shut up, Jet," Ashley said, smiling at her end.

"Uh-huh," Jet replied, grinning still. "Just don't let him in your pants," she said then, her tone wicked.

"Jet! Oh my God, you are so bad!" Ashley said, laughing.

Jet chuckled. "You have met me, right?"

"Yes, yes I have…" Ashley said then, her voice dropping an octave becoming sultry.

"Easy now…" Jet said, grinning.

"I will see you day after tomorrow, brat," Ashley said then.

"Okay," Jet said.

They hung up a moment later.

"Your parents didn't know you were in the Army?" Fadiyah asked.

Jet glanced over at her. "They knew I was in the Army, hell they bitched about it long enough, but I never told them where I was stationed."

"How is that possible?" Fadiyah asked.

"Well, honey, I've lived on my own since I was seventeen, and I haven't needed their permission to do anything for longer than that, so…"

"But they are your parents…" Fadiyah said, unable to fathom her father not knowing where she was in her lifetime.

Jet gave Fadiyah a sidelong glance. "Do you really want to get back into this?" she asked, her tone starting to ice over.

Fadiyah looked back at her for a long moment, seeing her light green eyes almost literally frost over. She shook her head.

They were both silent for a bit, then Fadiyah looked over at her.

"Greg?" she queried.

Jet grinned. "Ashley's soon-to-be ex-husband."

"She is getting a divorce?" Fadiyah asked, surprised.

"Yeah," Jet said.

"Why?"

Jet shrugged. "She claims I ruined her for him."

"Ruined her?" Fadiyah asked.

"Well, her perception of her husband," Jet said.

"How?" Fadiyah asked.

"By being me," Jet said her tone completely devoid of ego.

"What does that mean?" Fadiyah asked.

"Well, that's the butch thing."

"And what is the butch thing?" Fadiyah asked.

"Well," Jet said, feeling like she'd had this conversation before too. "In the lesbian community there are women like me who are considered butch, we are the more masculine ones of the group."

Fadiyah nodded. "And your friend Skyler is 'butch' as well?"

"Yeah," Jet said, nodding.

"That is why you both stood when I came out to the balcony, and when I left it as well?"

"Well, yeah," Jet said. "We tend to group ourselves with the more gallant men in cases like that."

"Gallant," Fadiyah repeated the word, nodding. "That is you."

Jet grinned. "Not all the time, honey, trust me."

"I doubt that is true," Fadiyah said. "So how did the 'butch thing' ruin Ashley for her husband?"

"Because I'm more masculine than he is," Jet said simply.

"How?" Fadiyah asked.

"Just things like picking up heavy stuff, opening doors, that kind of thing."

"That does not seem like the type of thing to ruin a marriage."

"Well, I'm not totally sure that their marriage was that great to begin with, but there was another factor."

"What factor?" Fadiyah asked.

"That's the part you probably aren't going to want to hear about," Jet said, chuckling as she did.

"Why?"

Jet screwed her lips around in a grimace. "Because it has to do with sex."

"Sex?" Fadiyah asked.

Jet nodded, her eyes on the road and not looking over at Fadiyah.

"Because she had sex with you?" Fadiyah asked.

"Well, yeah."

"I do not understand."

Jet rolled her eyes, this was not the conversation she wanted to be having right now, and she really couldn't see a way out of it.

"Let's just say I'm better at it than he is," Jet said, trying to end the conversation quickly.

"Better how?" Fadiyah asked.

Jet laughed shaking her head. "You just aren't going to let this one go, are you?"

"I am trying to understand, Jet," Fadiyah said. "Because you are not the type of person to ruin a marriage."

"Well, apparently I am now," Jet said.

"How are you better than Ashley's husband at sex?" Fadiyah asked.

"Well, there's the whole point of sex," Jet said, then grimaced. "I mean, not the reproductive part, although the chances are good I'd be more likely to get Ash pregnant than that guy… But…"

Fadiyah looked completely undone by that comment, so Jet rushed on.

"But the other whole point of sex," she said.

Fadiyah looked confused still.

Jet dropped her chin to her chest, shaking her head as she blew her breath out in a loud sigh.

"Can we please be done with this conversation?" she asked.

"I am making you uncomfortable?" Fadiyah said.

"Oh yeah," Jet said, nodding.

"Okay," Fadiyah said, nodding. "So Ashley is divorcing her husband for you."

"No," Jet said defensively. "She's divorcing him because he's a pussy and she can't deal with that anymore."

"A pussy?" Fadiyah asked.

"Oh for God's sake, please, please, please let us be done with this conversation…" Jet said, shaking her head.

227

Fadiyah chuckled. "Okay, we are done with this conversation."

"Thank Allah!"

"That's blasphemous," Fadiyah said, a barely contained smile on her lips.

Jet saw the smile and shook her head. She was glad that Fadiyah was already learning to tease her. It would make things easier between them. Certain things were bound to be obstacles in their conversations, not the least of which was Fadiyah's complete innocence and upbringing.

In the office, Jet was greeted repeatedly. Once in her cubicle, Jet plugged in her phone, turning the music up and turning on her computer. Fadiyah watched as Jet worked, she was astounded at how many things Jet did in a short span of time. She typed extremely fast, and made phone calls, joking with people on the phone. Fadiyah swore she flirted with people on the phone as well, but couldn't be sure.

At one point a man poked his head around the cubicle wall.

"Uh, aren't you in Iraq picking up a package?" he asked, raising an eyebrow at her.

Jet continued typing the email she was working on, but pointed at Fadiyah.

"John Evans, meet Fadiyah Antar. Fadi, John is a member of my team."

John looked at Fadiyah and smile widely. "Hi there," he said, his tone suave.

"Knock it off…" Jet warned.

John only smiled.

"It is nice to meet you," Fadiyah said, inclining her head to John.

"So, you know you weren't supposed to be back, ya know?" John said, his tone leading.

"Uh-huh," Jet said, nodding her head.

"And you know who is gonna be so thrilled that you're here…" John said sarcastically..

"And he knows this is my op, and he couldn't do it right if his life depended on it," Jet said, her tone even.

John nodded. "Well, trust me, he's going to be pissed."

Jet made a rude sound. "And I care because?"

"You don't," John said. "Just thought I'd warn ya."

"Consider me warned," Jet said, finally glancing at him. "Thanks."

"You got it."

A few minutes later a man walked into the cubicle, looking pretty angry.

"What are you doing here?" he asked without preamble.

He was big man in his mid-forties, with shaggy brown hair and a bit of a belly.

"I work here, Don," Jet said, not sparing him a look.

"You're on vacation," he snapped.

"Actually I was on reserve status, but I'm back now," Jet said, her tone even.

"Well, I'm running this op today, so you should just go home."

Jet froze for a moment. Then she slowly turned her chair around, putting a booted foot up on her desktop, her look could have frozen water.

"This is my case," Jet said calmly, though her eyes challenged him. "And I'll be running the op."

"Kash gave it to me while you were gone," Don said.

"And now I'm back, so…" Jet said, her foot starting to move in reigned in irritation.

"Well, we need to go talk to Kash about this," Don snapped.

"Go talk to her about it," Jet said. "I have an op to plan."

"You can't fucking do that!" he yelled.

Jet dropped her foot to the ground, standing up and getting right into his face. "Do you see the lady sitting here?" she growled. "You watch your mouth."

Don looked back at Jet, his eyes reflecting shock at her action. He mumbled an apology to Fadiyah.

"Now," Jet said, her tone still low and threatening. "Go talk to Kash if that's what you want to do, but I'm done talking to you."

With that Jet turned and sat down again. Don moved out of her cubicle quickly.

"Sorry about that," Jet said to Fadiyah.

"It is alright. Why is that man so angry?" she asked.

"Because he wishes he was me," Jet said, grinning.

A few minutes later, a woman appeared at the cubicle entrance. Fadiyah saw her first, and thought she was very beautiful with long blond hair and dark blue eyes.

Kashena smiled at Fadiyah, as she leaned against the cubicle opening, watching Jet singing, her head moving, her fingers flying over the keys of her keyboard. Kashena had a fond smile on her face; she knew Jet's capabilities, and she also knew that the woman didn't give a shit about being "in charge" like Don had just raged. He'd bordered on insubordination with Kashena, coming close to accusing her of putting her lesbian friends in charge over other officers. She'd waited for that comment as she'd watched him go on and on, pacing back and forth in her office. When he was done she'd told him that it was Jet's operation and that she was in charge of it, period. The fact was, Jet was much more qualified for this job than Don had ever been, with her field experience and abilities with languages, Jet Mathews was invaluable to Kashena. She had no intention of ever letting her go. She'd let the rest of the team go before she'd give Jet back to LAPD.

"So…" Kashena said, when she realized Jet hadn't noticed her.

Jet's head snapped around, and a smile lit her face. Standing up, she moved in to hug Kashena who put her hand to Jet's head, holding her close.

"I'm glad you made it back," Kashena said, her voice low. "And brought back my partner in one piece."

"He brought me back," Jet told Kashena.

"I don't believe that for a second," Kashena replied, winking down at Jet.

Jet turned to Fadiyah then. "Kashena Windwalker-Marshal this is Fadiyah Antar, the woman who saved my life," she said smiling warmly.

Fadiyah stood as Kashena put her right hand to her heart, and inclined her head, then she extended it to Fadiyah.

"You know Iraqi tradition as well?" Fadiyah asked, surprised, as she took Kashena's hand in hers.

"I was in the Middle East for a while," Kashena said nodding.

"You were a soldier too?" Fadiyah asked.

"Yes, I was a Marine," Kashena said, nodding.

Fadiyah nodded, looking impressed. "And your partner is Sebastian?" she asked then.

"Yes," Kashena said. "He and I have been friends for many years now."

Fadiyah nodded again. "He, Skyler and Jet are amazing people."

"Yeah, I agree," Kashena said, nodding and looking at Jet. "And I have to say, I'm very glad to have my best asset back," she said nodding her head at Jet. "Speaking of which, let me see it," she said then, circling her finger to have Jet turn around.

"Geeze, it's no big deal," Jet said as she reluctantly turned around.

"Oh yeah, I can see that," Kashena said, looking the long wound on Jet's shoulder. "You need to get this checked out, Jet, it's not looking happy."

"Well, I kind of pissed it off yesterday," Jet said, grimacing.

"As I said…" Fadiyah muttered.

Jet looked at her, her mouth open. "Was that an Iraqi 'I told you so'? Or am I imagining things?"

"Sounded like an Iraqi 'I told you so to me'," came a voice from behind them.

Kashena turned around and hugged Sebastian. "About time you came to see me!" she said, swatting him on the arm.

"Hey!" Sebastian said, grinning. "I was asleep until about an hour ago."

Moving to Jet, Sebastian hugged her. "What are you doing here?" he asked her, even as he smiled at Fadiyah, inclining his head to her.

"Working," Jet said, her look level.

"Jesus, Kash, you're making the kid work?" Sebastian said, shaking his head at his partner.

"Right, 'cause that's what I do, make people work past their capacity for fun…" Kashena said, narrowing her eyes at Sebastian.

He merely smiled back at her, his look of feigned innocence almost believable, except for the sparkle of mischief in his eyes.

"You," Kashena said, pointing to Sebastian, "in my office we need to talk. You," she said then, pointing a finger at Jet, "I'm going out on this one to keep an eye on you. Be extremely careful, do you hear me?" Her tone was all boss and Marine.

"Ma'am, yes ma'am," Jet said, grinning.

"And don't even *think* about coming in the rest of the week," Kashena told her.

Jet widened her eyes at the edict, but nodded a grin still playing at her lips.

Sebastian and Kashena left the cubicle. Jet moved to sit back down again. She'd turned her music off for a moment to make a phone call. When she hung up, she heard someone on the other side of the cubicle wall.

"Evans?" Jet queried, her voice gravelly.

"And Jet's here…" he said. "And you sound like you've been eating a lot of—"

"Stop!" Jet roared, holding up her hand.

The man's head poked over the cubicle wall at that point.

"Look!" Jet said, pointing over her head at Fadiyah.

The man's eyes flicked over to Fadiyah and widened significantly. He smiled then, looking very guilty.

"Now, come around like your parents taught you manners," Jet said, her tone reproving.

The man walked around the cubicle wall then, smiling at Fadiyah. "Sorry," he said to her.

Fadiyah looked at him trying to figure out what he was apologizing for.

"Nick," Jet said, putting her foot out and kicking him in the butt, "is sorry he was about to be a crude cop-type person, Fadi. Now, Nick Curry this is Fadiyah Antar, and Nick do *not* put out your left hand to shake her hand, use your right… Good…" she said, sounding very motherly.

Nick smiled at Fadiyah. "She's a bossy little thing, isn't she?" he said, his tone amused.

"That is what I hear," Fadiyah said, smiling.

"You can go back to your cubicle now, and don't come out till it's time for the raid," Jet instructed, grinning.

"You're leading it?" Nick asked hopefully.

"Yep," Jet said.

"Thank God!" Nick said. "We'd probably end up at the wrong house if Don was running it."

Jet laughed. "I know, that's why I'm here on my day off."

"You're always here on your days off," John chimed in from the cubicle on the other side, his tone wry.

"Shut up," Jet replied.

Fadiyah laughed at the exchange, it was obvious Jet was well liked by her co-workers, and she liked them as well.

"Okay, we're heading out in…" Jet said, glancing at her watch, "twenty minutes. Gear up."

"Yes, ma'am!" John and Nick said at the same time.

"Assholes…" Jet said, even as she grinned.

She grabbed her gear bag, and also her cigarettes and lighter, nodding for Fadiyah come with her. She walked Fadiyah out to her car, where she opened her trunk and sat against the car, pulling out and lighting a cigarette.

"Okay, you need to listen to me right now," Jet said, looking at Fadiyah, her tone very serious. "When we get to the site of this raid, I'm going to put you in a vehicle. You need to stay there no matter what you see, no matter what you hear, okay?"

Fadiyah nodded. "No matter what I hear or see?" she queried, her look quizzical.

"Yeah, like gunshots, people running, fun stuff like that," Jet said, winking at her.

Fadiyah widened her eyes. "Are you telling me that is possible?" she asked sounding afraid.

"I'm telling you that it happens. This group we're trying to take down have a lot of three strikers, which means they are going to jail for a long time when we arrest them. Bad guys don't like to go to jail, especially when they know they aren't likely to ever get out. So they shoot at us and run."

Fadiyah swallowed convulsively.

"You will be perfectly safe," Jet told her. "I wouldn't take you with me if I didn't think you would be, Fadi, okay?" she said, reaching out to touch Fadiyah's cheek. "Do you trust me?"

"Yes," Fadiyah said unequivocally.

Jet smiled, loving that Fadiyah hadn't hesitated for even a fraction of a second.

Finishing her cigarette, Jet dropped it and stubbed it out with a booted foot. She then opened her gear bag. Fadiyah watched, fascinated as Jet put on her bulletproof vest, then pulled on the jersey with "POLICE" in large yellow letters. Jet then pulled out her holstered weapon setting it aside, and wrapped a gear belt around her waist, securing the holster by tying it around her thigh. She depressed the weapon's magazine release, checking the clip to make sure it was full, then sliding it back into the weapon, pulling back the slide to rechamber the round. She then put the gun in the holster. Next, she reached into the bag and pulled out a shotgun. Taking cartridges out of a box in the bag, she loaded the rifle from the bottom, not chambering a round at that point in time. Then she set the shotgun aside.

Looking over at Fadiyah, she saw that the girl watching her carefully.

"What?" Jet asked, as she reached for another cigarette.

Fadiyah simply shook her head, she didn't think she'd ever see all the sides to Jet Mathews. Jet walked over to the driver's side of the car and started the engine. She hooked her phone up, selecting a song that pumped out of the speakers. Moving to lean on the back of the car again, Jet closed her eyes singing the song between draws on her cigarette. Her head and feet moved in time with the music, her eyes remained closed.

A few minutes later, the rest of the team came out of the office, carrying their gear bags.

"Jet's already started pre-game," Nick called over his shoulder.

"That's 'cause you're late…" Jet said her eyes still closed.

"It's fifteen minutes…" Nick said.

"And pre-game started at ten…" Jet said, grinning.

"Always cheating…" John said as he passed.

"Am not," Jet said.

"She cheats," Nick said.

"And least I'm not always late," Jet said.

"That's what his girlfriends always say," Kashena chimed in and she walked to her vehicle. Their cars were clustered closely together.

Kashena opened the trunk of her newly-replaced black Mercedes SL550.

"Nice boss…" Jet said, grinning.

"Sierra insisted," Kashena said, rolling her eyes. "Like an outrageously expensive house payment wasn't enough."

"Well, it was her ex that crashed your last one…" Jet said.

Kashena laughed. "True," she said, as she put on her bulletproof vest.

When the whole team was ready, Kashena said, "Okay, mount up." Then she looked at Jet. "You told Fadiyah what she needs to do, right?"

"Yep," Jet said, nodding.

"Good," Kashena said, looking at Fadiyah. "You stay where she puts you," she told Fadiyah, her tone serious.

Fadiyah nodded. "I will."

"What is pre-game?" Fadiyah asked in the car on the way to the raid.

"It's what we do to get ready, mentally. For me it's music and smoking. Other cops have other routines."

"Oh," Fadiyah said, nodding.

At the raid site, Jet took Fadiyah over to one of the large police vehicles and introduced her to the staff inside the truck who were monitoring the raid. She showed Fadiyah the cameras and gave her an earpiece so she could hear what was going on.

Fadiyah could see the house from where she sat in the truck. One of the officers wore a camera so they could film the raid. She watched it with fascination.

Jet had the shotgun in her hands; John banged on the door and yelled, "Police search warrant." He stepped back so he could kick the door open. He and Jet moved inside, Jet had the shotgun held at the ready. There was a lot of yelling: "Let me see your hands!" and, "Get on the floor!"

Fadiyah could hear Jet yell, "Don't do it… Son of a bitch!" and the next thing Fadiyah saw was a black woman running out of the house holding a baseball bat, Jet was right behind her. The woman turned suddenly swinging the bat around to try and hit Jet. Jet jumped back, barely missing getting the bat in the ribs. She reached out, snatching the bat out of the woman's hands. The woman went into a low crouch, and Jet stood there looking at her.

"Are you seriously going to make me do this?" Jet asked the woman.

"I can take you bitch," the woman said.

"Many have tried and failed, honey," Jet said, her tone wry.

The woman ran at Jet, who squatted down at the last possible second, and came up under the woman's legs, flipping her over her shoulder.

"Be smart," Jet said, looking down at the woman. "Stay down."

Regardless, the woman scampered to her feet, lunging at Jet, who blocked her by bringing one arm up. She used the other to grab the woman by the back of the neck and started applying pressure.

"I hate this shit," Jet said. "Why did you insist on fighting me?"

"Fuck you!" the woman spat.

"Not likely, honey," Jet said, as she woman dropped to her knees. "Now, you have the right to remain silent, do us all a favor and use that right. But if you don't, anything you say can and will, and I do mean will, be used against you in a court of law. You have a right to an attorney, if you cannot afford an attorney, you're gonna get some kid fresh out of law school trying to get his student loans forgiven by working for the public defender's office… Good fucking luck with that."

Jet cuffed the woman and then hauled her to her feet, walking her over to a waiting uniformed officer. Jet then keyed her radio. "All clear?" she asked.

"Clear," Kashena answered on the radio.

Jet walked over to the truck, opening the door and holding her hand to out to Fadiyah.

"See, how much fun that was?" she asked, grinning.

"I think you are crazy," Fadiyah said, smiling.

"That is highly likely."

That night Fadiyah ended up in Jet's room again.

"This is getting to be a habit," Jet muttered, grinning.

When Fadiyah hesitated, Jet sat up and took her hand pulling her down on the bed gently.

"I was just kidding, Fadi," Jet said softly.

Fadiyah ended up sleeping in her arms once again.

Chapter 9

The next day, Jet took Fadiyah shopping for clothes and necessities. Fadiyah was far too bowled over by the mall. There were so many things to take in and look at that she felt overwhelmed. Jet finally decided they should try someplace more exclusive with less people. That ended up meaning West Hollywood where the shops were boutiques.

They walked in and out of shops trying to find a place that Fadiyah felt comfortable shopping in, but Jet still sensed she was a bit freaked out. At one point she took Fadiyah's hand squeezing it gently.

"We don't have to do this if you don't want to, Fadi," she said, her tone tinged with concern.

Fadiyah squeezed her hand. "It is okay, there is just so much to look at."

"I know," Jet said, grinning.

As they turned to continue walking, Fadiyah held onto Jet's hand, eventually moving to encircle Jet's arm in hers as she had on the plane coming home. Jet smiled fondly, knowing that Fadiyah was trying to assimilate so many things at that point, and it had to be terrifying.

In the end, Jet found a shop that had a private dressing room option. Fadiyah was extremely uncomfortable about strangers seeing her trying on clothes. Jet knew it had to do with the conditioning she'd received growing up that women didn't flaunt themselves. Jet had assured her repeatedly that she was completely within reason to continue to wear a hijab and even an abaya if it made her more comfortable. Fadiyah's response had been that she wanted to wear the kind of clothes that Jet had gotten for her in Iraq; she liked them.

When Jet had finally gotten Fadiyah to try on clothes, she noticed that Fadiyah liked the more feminine styles, and so she started helping Fadiyah select items. Fadiyah kept trying to buy sizes that were far too big for her.

The sales girl that had been helping them, started to get annoyed at Fadiyah's reticence. She began making sharp comments that had Fadiyah shrinking. Jet, who'd been leaning casually against the wall, letting the 'girls' do all the talking, stepped in then. She moved to stand next to the sales girl, lowering her head so her lips were close to the girl's ear.

"If you continue to talk to her that way, I'm going to find it necessary to get rather unpleasant, do you understand me?"

The girl looked shocked, but nodded. Jet turned her head to look the girl in the eyes, her look withering. The girl swallowed convulsively, and stepped sideways. Jet nodded, then looked over at Fadiyah who had watched the scene with a look of concern on her face.

"I like that one," Jet said, smiling.

Fadiyah blinked, surprised by how quickly Jet's mood could shift, but she appreciated Jet looking out for her. The sales girl was much more careful with her words after that and Jet was ever watchful that it stayed that way.

At the register the clothes, shoes and other items rang up to well over $3,000. Jet pulled out her credit card without batting an eyelash. Fadiyah looked over at her.

"How much would that be in dinar?" Fadiyah asked.

Jet simply grinned, shaking her head.

"Jet!" Fadiyah exclaimed. "Tell me."

"It doesn't matter, Fadi."

"It does," Fadiyah said, her look serious.

"I'm not sure," Jet said, hedging as the sales girl handed back her credit card.

Fadiyah looked back at her, knowing she wasn't being honest.

"You can Google it and it'll calculate that for you," the sales girl said, trying to be helpful.

Jet narrowed her eyes at the girl. "Thanks," she said tightly.

When she picked up the bags, and turned, she saw that Fadiyah was standing with her hands on her hips, her look pointed.

"Let's go," Jet said.

Fadiyah shook her head, refusing to move.

"Don't worry about it, okay?" Jet said.

"Look it up," Fadiyah said.

"No."

"Jet!"

"Fadi!"

"Because it is a lot, is it not?" Fadiyah asked.

"To you it will seem like a lot, yes," Jet said, nodding.

"How much?" Fadiyah asked. "Look it up."

"I don't need to look it up, I calculated these numbers in my head for more than four years."

"Then tell me," Fadiyah said.

"About three point five," Jet said, moving around Fadiyah to start walking out of the store.

"Three point five?" Fadiyah repeated, following Jet. "Three point five what?"

"Million," Jet said.

Fadiyah stopped walking, her mouth hanging open. Jet turned around, looking back at her.

"I told you it would seem like a lot to you," Jet said.

"In my lifetime we would never have had so much money, in my father's lifetime…"

Jet sighed, walking back to where Fadiyah stood. She set the bags down, taking Fadiyah into her arms.

"I know that, babe," she said, her voice soft. "But I do make that kind of money, and you need things, okay? So let me do this for you."

Fadiyah buried her face in Jet's shirt. "It is so much…" she said miserably.

"It really isn't, Fadi, not for me," Jet said.

Fadiyah stood in Jet's arms for a few minutes, trying to reconcile her life in Iraq, versus her life in America, and it was mind boggling. Jet stood, holding her, knowing that Fadiyah was trying to make sense of everything, and accept it. She knew that Fadiyah wouldn't like accepting charity; it had been why she'd been hesitant about telling Fadiyah how much it all cost. Fadiyah's family had been extremely poor, with no other relatives to live with to pool resources. To Jet's way of thinking, it was only right that she give back to this girl who saved her life. Though, getting that same girl to accept it was easier said than done.

Later when they shopped for food, Fadiyah asked how much each item was in dinar, shocked at how expensive things were. Regardless, they got through the grocery shopping much easier, since Jet had to eat too. It was an interesting day.

That night Fadiyah once again showed up in Jet's room, and once again fell asleep in Jet's arms. It was definitely becoming a habit. Jet didn't really mind. She was glad that Fadiyah felt that comfortable with her, especially considering the whole "lesbian" thing and the fact that people from the Middle East rarely knew how to handle such an oddity as gay people. In Iraq it was a crime to be gay. As far as Iraqis were concerned, Jet was a criminal in their country. So Fadiyah staying with her, and actually being willing to be around her, even held by her, meant that Fadiyah was either not swayed by what she'd been taught, or she just didn't apply it to Jet. Jet wasn't sure which it was, but certainly didn't ask.

The next day, Jet and Fadiyah were having a movie day. Fadiyah was determined that Jet was going to rest, so she'd insisted on staying home. Jet had suggested that she begin Fadiyah's movie education. They'd taken a break for lunch and Jet was in the kitchen making pasta when Ashley walked in the front door. Fadiyah had gone to the bathroom and didn't see Ashley come in, but she heard the front door close. She came out of the bathroom at the same time Ashley turned into the kitchen.

Ashley walked around the corner into the kitchen and saw Jet standing there leaning casually against the counter.

"Jet!" Ashley exclaimed, practically throwing herself into Jet's arms. Jet happily grabbed her up in a hug. "You're back, you're back…" Ashley said over again, hugging Jet tight, her head against Jet's chest.

"I'm back, honey," Jet said, smiling down at Ashley tenderly.

Ashley lifted her head then, pressing her lips to Jet's. They kissed for a few long moments, Jet's hand cupping Ashley's cheek.

"Okay, let me see it," Ashley said, suddenly pulling away.

Jet grinned. "I sent you a picture…"

"Don't get smart with me," Ashley said, narrowing her eyes at Jet. "Let's see," she said, reaching up to grasp Jet's shoulders to turn her around.

"Okay, okay, hold on, Jesus…" Jet said, grinning. "Always trying to get my clothes off…" Reaching up, Jet pulled her shirt off then turned her back obligingly to Ashley.

"Oh God, baby…" Ashley said, her voice full of sympathy.

"It's just a scratch," Jet said, looking over her shoulder.

"Jet Blue Mathews, scratches don't take five stitches to close!" Ashley practically growled.

Standing on her tip toes, Ashley pressed her lips to the wound, her hands gently touching Jet's back. Jet turned and picked Ashley up to set her on the counter, her light green eyes now staring directly into Ashley's.

"I'm fine," she told Ashley again.

Ashley blew her breath out, shaking her head. "You could have been killed…" she whispered.

"But I wasn't," Jet whispered back.

Ashley touched Jet's cheek, her eyes tearful.

"No crying…" Jet told her firmly. "I'm back, and I'm fine, okay?"

Ashley slid her hand to the back of Jet's neck, pulling her forward and kissing her deeply. Jet tensed, pulling back slightly. "Easy babe, she's here…" she murmured against Ashley's lips.

"Where?" Ashley asked.

Jet looked over Ashley's shoulder, seeing Fadiyah standing in the living room, looking straight at them.

"Uh…" Jet stammered, her grin starting at the inanity of the situation.

Ashley saw where Jet was looking and turned around, still sitting on the counter.

"Oh," Ashley said, looking supremely embarrassed. "Wow, um, hi," she said smiling at Fadiyah.

Jet slid her hands around Ashley's hips, pulling her off the counter gently and setting her on her feet, then she gestured for Ashley to precede her. Ashley walked toward the living room, her eyes meeting Fadiyah's and sensing caution there.

She started to extend her hand to the other woman, but Jet's hand on her shoulder stopped her. Ashley had started to extend her left hand, which was an insult to people from the Middle East. Ashley glanced back at Jet. Jet's eyes were on Fadiyah who had actually backed up a step.

"What?" Ashley asked, seeing Jet's look and Fadiyah's reaction.

"Asif," Jet said to Fadiyah. "'Annaha la taelam."

Fadiyah nodded, her silver-gray eyes on Ashley, still very cautious.

"What did you just say?" Ashley said, having never heard Jet speak Arabic before.

"I apologized and told her that you don't know their traditions," Jet said.

Ashley looked at Fadiyah. "That's true, I don't."

"Ladayk alearabiat w tahsin," Fadiyah said to Jet with a sparkle in her eyes, telling Jet that her Arabic was improving, which had Jet chuckling.

"Shukraan," Jet said, inclining her head.

"It is okay," Fadiyah said to Ashley. "We extend right hands to greet people, as it is believed that the left hand is unclean."

"Oh, I'm so sorry," Ashley said, grimacing. "I didn't mean to offend you."

"It is okay. It is as Jet says, that you do not know our customs," Fadiyah said, a small smile on her face.

"I understand that you are the reason we still have Jet, though," Ashley said, her voice sincere. "Thank you for that."

"It was my honor," Fadiyah said, inclining her head, her eyes on Jet.

Ashley smiled, nodding, then glanced back into the kitchen.

"Uh, Jet…" Ashley said, pointing to the stove where the pasta was attempting to boil over.

"Ah crap!" Jet strode back into the kitchen, turning the fire down just in time to keep the pot from boiling over.

"Score another one for Mathews' culinary skills," Ashley said, grinning and winking over at Fadiyah. "I'm going to go put my stuff away." With that Ashley went upstairs.

Fadiyah and Jet sat down to eat a few minutes later, while Ashley was still upstairs.

"She is very beautiful," Fadiyah said.

Jet nodded, "I'm sorry if you got a little too much of an eyeful when she came in, she didn't see you…"

"It is okay," Fadiyah said. "This is your home, and she is your girlfriend, it is right that she kiss you."

"She's not my girlfriend," Jet said, wondering how many times she was going to have to say that to convince everyone.

"She kissed you like she is," Fadiyah said, her smile knowing.

Jet hesitated, and then blew her breath out, shaking her head. "I'm just going to shut up now, because I know I'm not going to win this conversation."

Fadiyah suppressed a smile and only nodded. "So very wise," she said.

Ashley came back downstairs, having changed into shorts and a loose fitting tank top. To Fadiyah, Ashley was the consummate American beauty with her blue eyes, blond highlights in her hair and her perfect tan and makeup. Fadiyah felt absolutely frumpy next to the girl. It also became very obvious to her that Jet and Ashley were close. Ashley joined them for the movies they were watching. Jet had selected a series of eighties movies.

Jet sat on the chaise lounge end of the sectional, with her legs extending out in front of her. Ashley sat next to Jet and Fadiyah sat on the other side of Ashley. They were watching The Breakfast Club. During the course of the movie, Jet and Ashley exchanged comments about who was like who from their high school.

"No, that's Amber Shelly," Ashley said, indicating the character played by Molly Ringwold, a spoiled rich girl.

"Nah," Jet said, shaking her head, "ore like Amanda."

"Oh my God, you're right," Ashley said, grinning. "She even had red hair like that."

"It was dyed," Jet said.

"How do you know?" Ashley asked, her look pointed.

Jet just looked back at her, a grin on her lips.

"Oh my God, you didn't!" Ashley said.

Jet made a sucking sound through her teeth. "Let's just say the carpet doesn't match the drapes and leave it at that…"

"Jet!" Ashley said, shocked and tossed a pillow at Jet.

"Hey…" Jet said, laughing. "She was into bad girls, what can I say?"

"I thought you didn't do anything like that in high school," Ashley said.

"Who said it was high school?" Jet asked, her look teasing.

Ashley shook her head, looking over at Fadiyah who was watching the conversation with an amused look on her face.

Eventually, Ashley ended up in Jet's arms. Jet had turned so she could sit between her legs, leaning back against Jet's chest. At one intermission, Jet moved to stand, stretching and moving her neck around.

"Gonna go smoke," she said. "The next one should be either Footloose or Flashdance."

"Any preference?" Ashley asked, as Jet walked toward the back door.

"Jennifer Beals is hot…" Jet said, grinning as she walked out of the door.

Ashley looked over at Fadiyah. "And that's a way to grade movies too."

"Which?" Fadiyah asked.

"The hot female factor," Ashley said, grinning. "Jet's kind of a womanizer."

"Womanizer?" Fadiyah asked her look confused.

"Well," Ashley said, trying to think of a nice way to put it, "Jet is kind of popular with women."

"Popular?" Fadiyah queried.

"Yeah, they like her a lot."

"Because of the butch thing?" Fadiyah asked, using Jet's terminology.

Ashley laughed, nodding. "Yeah, that's part of it, but she's really charming too and always says the right thing at the right time."

Fadiyah nodded. "She is very… hateh."

Ashley looked confused. "What does that mean?"

"I am not sure in English."

When Jet came back into the house they asked her.

"Uh," Jet said, shrugging. "As best as I can explain it's for someone that's really attractive, why?"

251

"So kinda like a hottie," Ashley said, grinning.

Jet laughed, nodding. "I suppose. How did hateh come up?" she asked them.

Ashley looked at Fadiyah seeing if the girl was going to tell Jet. When she didn't, Ashley just shrugged and put the movie in.

That night the three of them had dinner and sat out on the patio talking about different things. Jet was smoking, and had a beer, as did Ashley. Fadiyah had opted for tea. Jet sat in one chair, with her feet on the chair Ashley sat on, Ashley's hand frequently touched Jet's leg and feet while she was talking.

Fadiyah noticed again how comfortable the two were together, and she found herself feeling jealous. She knew it was an unreasonable emotion, but it did not stop her from feeling it. She had Jet all to herself for a few days and had thoroughly enjoyed spending time with her. Fadiyah knew that even though Jet denied it vehemently, Ashley was for all intents and purposes her girlfriend.

"Hey, what's happening on that story?" Jet asked Ashley.

"Oh, I forgot to tell you," Ashley said. "They're going to publish it."

Jet smiled. "I knew it!" she said, dropping her foot to the ground and leaning forward to kiss Ashley's lips. Pulling back she looked her in the eyes. "I told you that freelance would work."

"Yes, you did," Ashley said. "And as usual, you were right. Does it ever get exhausting being right so much?" she asked, her tone sly.

"Watch it…" Jet said, grinning.

"They really want the story on Midnight too, so I'm trying to score a meeting with her."

"Did you reach out to Kash?" Jet asked.

"No…" Ashley said. "She's your boss, I didn't want to assume anything."

"Geeze, babe…" Jet said, pulling out her phone. She tapped out a message, then set her phone on the table. "I messaged her."

"You didn't have to do that," Ashley said.

Jet shrugged. "She knows Midnight and you need to get ahold of her."

"Uh-huh," Ashley said, rolling her eyes. Then she looked over at Fadiyah. "Did you get to meet Kashena?"

"Yes," Fadiyah said. "She was very nice."

"Yeah, she's pretty cool," Ashley said, nodding. "Jet, you should take Fadiyah to the club tomorrow night."

"Uh," Jet said, giving Ashley an *are you kidding me?* look. "I'm not sure that's a good idea…"

"Why?" Fadiyah asked.

"Yeah, why?" Ashley asked, looking surprised at Jet's hesitation.

Jet looked between the two women, feeling suddenly like a rat in a trap. She turned to Fadiyah.

"Fadi, it's a gay club," she said.

"Jet she knows you're gay," Ashley pointed out.

"That isn't the point, Ash," Jet said, glancing over at Ashley. "It's one thing for her to be around me, she knows me. Being around strangers is a whole other thing."

"You'd take care of her, just like you took care of me," Ashley said, still not understanding Jet's reticence.

"Ash," Jet said sharply, turning around to look at her, "you don't get it, okay?"

Ashley looked back at Jet surprised by her tone. "So explain it to me so I do get it," she said, her tone even.

"In Iraq being gay will get you hung, shot, your head cut off, whatever they feel like doing to you that day. And being around gay people will also get you killed. So, I'm not putting her through that, okay?"

Ashley looked sickened by what Jet was saying, but nodded. "I didn't know that, I'm sorry."

Jet glanced over at Fadiyah and saw that she was considering what Jet had just said.

"Fadi?" Jet queried, curious as to what the girl was thinking.

"I think that now that I am in America, I should be able to do what I choose," Fadiyah said, her tone strong.

Jet's eyes widened, she put her tongue between her teeth, subconsciously biting her tongue in a figurative sense.

"I'm not sure that's the right venue, Fadi…" Jet said then.

"But you would take care of me, that is what Ashley said," Fadiyah said, glancing at Ashley who was now grinning.

Jet glanced at Ashley and saw the grin, so she narrowed her eyes at the other woman. Ashley merely waggled her eyebrows at Jet.

"I hate you so hard right now…" Jet said to Ashley.

"Love you too, baby…" Ashley said, with a wide smile.

Jet's phone chimed then, and she picked it up, starting to grin.

"Well…" Jet said, her tone smug.

"What?" Ashley asked, knowing she was about to regret her momentary rebellion.

"Oh, nothing," Jet said, moving to put her phone back in her pocket.

"Jet!" Ashley said, moving to grab Jet's phone.

"Oh no…" Jet said, moving her phone away from her grasp.

Ashley got up, moving to sit on Jet's lap, once again reaching for the phone. Jet laughed and stood up, picking Ashley up with one arm and shifting her away. She held her by the shoulder as she held her phone out the opposite way.

"You are such a brat!" Ashley said.

"Yeah, but I'm not the one that needs this contact info, so…"

Fadiyah reached up and grabbed Jet's cell phone from her hand. Jet turned to look at the girl, her mouth hanging open. Fadiyah merely smiled and handed the phone to Ashley.

"Oh, that's it, I'm leaving…" Jet said, shaking her head and turning to walk back into the house.

Ashley moved to stand in her way. Jet started to back up and found that Fadiyah had stood up to block her way as well.

"Ganging up on me now, huh?" Jet asked, grinning.

"Yep," Ashley said, exchanging an amused look with Fadiyah.

"Yes," Fadiyah agreed.

Jet looked between the two women, and sighed with defeat. She sat back down, and then glanced at a very triumphant-looking Ashley.

"Good luck with that passcode," Jet said, winking.

"Brat!" Ashley exclaimed, laughing all the same.

In the end, Jet gave Ashley Midnight's contact information and Ashley went inside to call her. Fadiyah and Jet stayed outside.

"If you do not want to take me to that club, it is okay," Fadiyah told her.

Jet turned to look at her, her look searching. "If you really want to go Fadi, I'll take you. I just don't want you to feel like you have to do things like that to be around me, okay?" She reached out touching Fadiyah's hands, and Fadiyah immediately put her hands in Jet's. "I don't want you to feel like I'm trying to put you in my world, okay?"

"I want to be in your world, Jet," Fadiyah said.

"You are," Jet said, "I just mean the gay part of it."

"You are trying to protect me from something you do not need to," Fadiyah said.

"What does that mean?" Jet asked, trying to understand.

"I do not mind that you are gay, Jet, I never have. It is not a shameful thing to me. No matter what Shia law says; no matter what the Quran says. I know the person that you are and who you are is not shameful."

Jet looked back at Fadiyah, amazed by this girl. She obviously had a great capacity for acceptance, no matter what she'd been taught for years.

Jet took a deep breath, and blew it out slowly, nodding.

"Okay," she said softly. "I will take you tomorrow night, but if you get at all uncomfortable, I want you to promise me you will tell me and we will leave, okay?"

"Okay," Fadiyah said, nodding.

That night they all went to their separate rooms to go to bed. It was a particularly hot and muggy night in Los Angles, so Jet ended up lying on top of her covers, with the fan going full blast. The house's air conditioning was old so it needed to be replaced. She had to remember to do something about it.

"Well, now…" Ashley said, standing to the side of Jet's bed. "That looks like an invitation…" Jet was wearing a black exercise bra and black boy shorts and nothing else. Her leanly-muscled body was on full display. She grinned up at Ashley.

"It is huh?" she asked.

"Mmm hmm," Ashley murmured, moving to sit down on the bed, putting her hand on Jet's stomach and caressing her. "So I wanted to tell you that I'm on the move again," she said.

"Where to now?" Jet asked.

"Down to San Diego," Ashley said. "I'm gonna drive down tomorrow."

"You got a meet with Midnight?" Jet asked, smiling.

"Yeah," Ashley said. "And I have you to thank for that," she said, leaning down to kiss Jet's lips.

Jet's hand reached up to hold her there an extra few moments as she kissed Ashley back. Ashley moaned softly against Jet's lips, the woman never ceased to excite her. She had come into the room to tell

Jet about San Diego, but seeing her lying there the way she was dressed, had sent a visceral reaction through her. She knew the way Jet looked was intimately wrapped up in her head with the incredible sex they had, she'd never been so sexually attracted to someone like she was Jet. She knew it did not a relationship make, but it didn't keep her from wanting the woman, especially not when she kissed her like she was.

Jet deepened the kiss when Ashley moaned, pulling her down against her body. Within minutes Ashley was ready to explode.

"Shhh…" Jet said against her lips as she moaned loudly. "I don't want to freak Fadi out completely."

"Oh, sorry," Ashley said, panting in her need for release.

In the end, Ashley did her best to be quiet, but it had been almost a week since she'd been with Jet and her body was far too primed for her to be able to control herself.

Afterwards, Jet chuckled as she said, "That was your version of quiet?"

"Hey, don't expect miracles," Ashley said, grinning.

"Mmmm…" Jet murmured contentedly, snuggling against Ashley's body.

"How does this always happen?" Ashley asked, gesturing to the fact that she now wore nothing, and Jet still had her bra and shorts on.

"Talent," Jet said, grinning.

Ashley shook her head. Once again, Jet hadn't allowed her to bring her to orgasm.

"Besides," Jet said. "Fadi's been coming in here most nights, and I don't want to be naked if she shows up tonight. Wouldn't look right."

Ashley looked back at Jet still trying to get a handle on why Jet was so protective of Fadiyah, but at the same time accepting that she was.

They talked for a while, and then both fell asleep.

Fadiyah stood in the doorway to Jet's room. She could see Jet and Ashley lying together on the bed, the moonlight illuminating them. Jet was on her stomach half covering Ashley's body with hers. Jet's left arm was over Ashely's stomach and her left leg was thrown over Ashley's leg possessively. Jet's face was turned toward Ashley. Ashley was lying on her back, very obviously naked, her right arm rested over Jet's arm across her stomach, her left arm under Jet's neck, her hand up on Jet's right shoulder.

Fadiyah felt a sharp stab of jealousy and wondered at it. Seeing Jet this way made Fadiyah feel both warm and a little breathless, she didn't understand that feeling at all. What she did understand was that she wanted Jet to be with her the way she was with Ashley at that moment. She wanted to feel as close to Jet as she could be, but she had no idea if Jet would either want that, or would see her that way. She also had no idea how to approach the topic.

She was turning to leave the room when Ashley stirred and opened her eyes, looking right at her. Fadiyah quickly turned and left the room, going back into her room.

Back in Jet's room, Ashley lay in the semi-darkness trying to decide what to do. She had easily seen the envy on Fadiyah's face. Jet had told her that Fadiyah was only nineteen and that led Ashley to wonder about Fadiyah's state of mind. Blowing out her breath in resolute determination, Ashley carefully crawled out from under Jet's body, and put her clothes on.

Walking to the door to Fadiyah's room, Ashley could see that Fadiyah was sitting on the bed, her knees up to her chest. She knocked lightly on the door jam.

Fadiyah's head snapped up, it looked like she'd been crying.

"Is it okay for me to come in?" Ashley asked.

Fadiyah reached up to wipe at her cheeks, nodding slowly, her look cautious.

"I am sorry," Fadiyah said as Ashley stepped close to the bed. "I should not have... I am sorry."

"It's okay," Ashley said, her tone gentle, biting her lip. "Do you want to talk about what you saw?"

Fadiyah looked torn, her eyes everywhere but on Ashley's. Then she finally nodded, looking embarrassed.

"Jet says you are not her girlfriend," Fadiyah said. "But..." Her voice trailed off as she couldn't come up with the words to explain her question.

"But we had sex," Ashley said.

Fadiyah nodded.

"And you figure Jet's either lying to you about me not being her girlfriend or..." Ashley said, letting her voice trail off.

"You are her girlfriend," Fadiyah said, her tone sure.

"No," Ashley said, shaking her head. "I'm not. I wouldn't mind being her girlfriend, but that's not how Jet is."

"But she kisses you, and..." Fadiyah said her look confused.

"Because Jet is a very sexual person," Ashley said. "I'm not saying she doesn't care about me, she does and I know that, but she isn't really into long term commitment."

Fadiyah looked like she was trying to understand.

"Fadiyah, can I ask you a personal question?" Ashley asked.

Fadiyah nodded.

"Are you interested in Jet? I mean, sexually."

Fadiyah looked like a deer in headlights suddenly.

"It's okay if you are," Ashley assured her. "I wouldn't blame you at all if you were. Jet has this animal magnetism for people, she always has."

"Always has?" Fadiyah asked.

"Yeah, I've known Jet since we were in high school together. She was always the center of attention, without ever having to try."

"You love her," Fadiyah said, nodding.

"I do love her," Ashley said. "But it's because she's been a real catalyst for me and if it wasn't for her, I'd have spent my life miserable."

"So you are divorcing your husband to be with Jet," Fadiyah said, as if confirming it to herself.

"No, I'm divorcing my husband because Jet made me realize that there's someone better out there and I deserve it," Ashley said. "I knew that being with Jet wasn't an option."

"Why is it not an option?"

"Because Jet doesn't do commitment," Ashley said.

"Does not do commitment?" Fadiyah repeated, looking like the words were foreign to her.

"She doesn't commit to anyone, stay in a relationship with them. I think Skyler is probably the closest she ever came," Ashley said, furrowing her brow even as she said it.

"Skyler?" Fadiyah asked looking shocked.

"Yeah, she was with Skyler, a long time ago, when they were in the Middle East together."

"I did not know that," Fadiyah said.

"I just found it out not too long ago," Ashley said.

Fadiyah nodded, looking resigned.

"Fadiyah," Ashley said then, her look searching. "Are you in love with Jet?"

Fadiyah looked up at Ashley her eyes wide, her look changing to introspective. After a long moment she said, "I think that I am."

"Oh, God help you then," Ashley said, rolling her eyes and shaking her head.

"What?" Fadiyah queried, her eyes afraid suddenly.

"I'm just saying that it's dangerous to love someone like Jet," Ashley said, she grimaced. "I'm sorry, but it is."

Fadiyah nodded, looking unhappy.

"So, the question becomes what you want from her," Ashley said.

"I do not know," Fadiyah said.

Ashley nodded. "Well, if you just want to test the sexual waters you're in luck," she said, grinning.

"What does that mean?" Fadiyah asked.

"I mean that if you want to have sex with Jet, that won't be hard to achieve," Ashley said.

Fadiyah looked back at Ashley, her look shocked.

"I know, it sounds terrible, but that's the one weakness Jet has."

"And what is that?" Fadiyah asked, still not sure she understood.

"Jet is extremely sexual, and it doesn't take a lot to get her going."

"Going?" Fadiyah asked.

"Excited," Ashley said. "Sexually."

"Oh," Fadiyah said, "I do not think I could do that."

"Oh… you'd be surprised," Ashley said, grinning.

Fadiyah looked back at her, and Ashley decided to drop that direction of the conversation, the last thing she wanted to do was to give another woman instructions on exciting Jet.

"You just need to know how Jet is," Ashley said. "I'd hate to see you get hurt."

"Hurt?" Fadiyah said, looking shocked. "Jet would never hurt me."

"I don't mean physically, Fadiyah, I mean your heart. Jet's very capable of breaking a woman's heart and she doesn't even have to try."

Fadiyah looked like she didn't want to believe that.

"Trust me, Fadiyah, if you don't listen to anything else I tell you, listen to this. If you get your heart too deep into Jet, she will break it, and she won't even know she did."

Chapter 10

The next night, Jet took Fadiyah to the club, against her better judgement. She wore her customary all black. Fadiyah wore a pair of her new jeans and a rich blue blouse and a pair of the new boots she'd picked out. She also wore her hair mostly down. Ashley had been kind enough to give her a few makeup tips that she was able to use to enhance her eyes. Jet had been fairly impressed.

At the club, Jet kept her hand at the small of Fadiyah's back as she escorted her to the group's table. She introduced her to everyone. Fadiyah hugged Skyler and was very happy to meet Devin. Then Jet introduced her to Jericho and Fadiyah became quickly engrossed in a conversation with the director. Jet took that opportunity to grab a drink.

Leaning in she touched Fadiyah on the waist. "What do you want to drink, Fadi?"

"I do not know," Fadiyah replied, looking baffled.

"There's always wine," Zoey said.

"She's nineteen, Zoey," Jet said, shocking both Jericho and Zoey.

"Oh," Zoey said, looking at Jericho.

"Never mind, I'll get you something," Jet said, grinning.

It didn't take long before everyone knew that Fadiyah was only nineteen. Fortunately, the club was eighteen and up, but the fact that Fadiyah had been seventeen when Jet had met her, escaped no one. By the time Jet returned with her beer and a virgin strawberry margarita for Fadiyah, she could see that everyone knew.

"Just shut up…" she muttered to everyone, which caused rounds of grins.

Jet was, as usual, greeted by any number of women, who all happily hugged her and kissed her, especially since Ashley wasn't with her. Many of them asked where Ashley was, but didn't look like they really cared. A few of them hung on Jet a little longer than necessary and Fadiyah longed to have the nerve to say something. She was pleasantly surprised when Jet slid her arm around her, and pulled her closer as she was talking to yet another woman.

The girl looked at Fadiyah, taking in the long dark hair, the petite figure and the silver-gray eyes, then she looked at Jet.

"Oh, Gabby, this is Fadiyah," Jet said, her smile wide.

"Hi," Gabby said to Fadiyah.

"Hello," Fadiyah said, her tone formal.

Jet couldn't help herself, she leaned in, nuzzling Fadiyah's neck. The girl beat a hasty retreat shortly thereafter.

"Sorry," Jet told Fadiyah, not seeing the heated look in Fadiyah's eyes in her rush to apologize. "Gabby is one of those girls that doesn't grasp subtlety."

Fadiyah nodded, turning her head to look away. Skyler, who was sitting next to where Fadiyah stood, saw the look in Fadiyah's eyes, and raised an eyebrow, glancing at Devin and then over at Jet. It was obvious Jet hadn't noticed the reaction.

"Jet!" Skyler said, holding up her lighter. Jet nodded.

"I'm going to go out and smoke, okay?" Jet said, leaning close to Fadiyah to speak in her ear.

Fadiyah shivered, but nodded. She had noted that Jet smelled extremely nice that evening and looked really good in all black. Jet had been very attentive all night and Fadiyah could easily imagine what it would be like to be her girlfriend. She realized then that it was probably that trap that every girl fell into with Jet Mathews. Falling for her gallant ways and her charming smile and those lovely light green eyes; that was how women got their hearts broken by Jet Mathews.

The waitress walked by as Fadiyah set down her empty glass. "Another one, hon?"

"Yes, please," Fadiyah said, nodding.

"That's a lovely accent…" said a woman from behind her.

Fadiyah turned to look at the woman, she had short cropped blond hair and a tattoo on her neck as well as one of five dots on her face near her eye.

"Thank you," Fadiyah said, then turned back around.

"So where are you from?" the woman asked, sliding her finger down Fadiyah's arm.

Outside Jet and Skyler sat across from each other, smoking and drinking. Jet ordered a shot of her favorite tequila, ordering Skyler one too. They drank the shots, and tipped the waitress who was happy to serve these two women.

"So what's going on with Fadiyah?" Skyler asked as she felt the tequila starting to warm her insides nicely.

"What do you mean?" Jet asked, glancing over at Skyler.

"You brought her to a gay club, Jet?" Skyler asked, her look telling Jet she thought she was crazy for doing so.

"It was Ashely's idea," Jet said, shrugging.

"Why would Ashley suggest that?" Skyler asked.

"Like I fuckin' know," Jet snapped.

"Easy…" Skyler said, her tone cautionary as her light blue-green eyes narrowed at Jet.

Jet blew her breath out, shaking her head. "Sorry, Sky," she said, knowing she was on edge at this point. "I don't know why she suggested it, but she did. And for whatever crazy reason, Fadiyah was determined to do it, so…"

"For whatever crazy reason?" Skyler repeated, her look deadpan.

"Yeah…" Jet said, looking at Skyler and seeing the look on her face. "What?"

"Are you telling me you don't see the way that girl looks at you?" Skyler asked her.

"What are you talking about?" Jet asked, looking at Skyler like she was the one that was crazy.

"Jesus, Jet…" Skyler said, shaking her head. "You never fuckin' notice how women look at you, do you?"

Jet shrugged, glancing around her.

Skyler shook her head again. "Well, I can tell you that Fadiyah is looking at you, and you better be careful with that one."

"I'm sorry, Sky, I think you're starting to lose it, maybe too much smoke inhalation from being a fire eater, I dunno."

"And I think you're going blind," Skyler said. "Probably too much pussy," she said, her lips curling.

"Is there such a thing?" Jet asked.

Skyler laughed. "I dunno, Jet, but if anyone is ever gonna find out, it's probably gonna be you."

"Jet," Devin said from the back door to the club.

Jet's head snapped around sensing the warning tone in Devin's voice.

"What?" she said, moving to stand.

"You need to get in here," Devin said.

"What's going on?" Skyler asked.

Devin looked at Skyler, then back at Jet. "Get in here, now."

Jet dropped her cigarette, and walked to the door with Skyler right behind her.

Jet's eyes immediately searched for Fadiyah. She was standing at the end of the table, and there was a very definite butch after her. As Jet walked over, she saw the butch woman put her hand on Fadiyah's shoulder and Fadiyah shrunk away, it was all Jet needed to see.

Striding straight over, Jet got right next to the woman.

"You need to step back…" Jet practically growled.

The woman's head snapped around, her eyes narrowing at Jet.

"You need to fuck off!" the woman said, her tone sharp.

"I'm not going to tell you again," Jet said, her voice dropping an octave.

"Then don't!" the woman said, wielding around and throwing a punch at the same time.

"Jet!" Fadiyah screamed, as Jericho reached out and grabbed the girl, pulling her back from the fight.

Jet easily blocked the punch with her left arm, and punched the woman with her right fist. The woman looked stunned, but stepped forward threateningly. Jet held her ground, glancing over to make sure that Fadiyah was safely out of the way and giving a quick nod to Jericho for the quick thinking.

"She was talking to me, bitch," the woman said.

"No she wasn't," Devin said.

The woman threw a dirty look at Devin and started to step in her direction.

Skyler stepped up then, her arm slightly behind her, her hand held out, to tell Devin to stop. "Don't even think of bringing it here," she said, her voice threatening.

The woman stopped, looking around at the group standing around her. There were varying degrees of threats all around her.

"You'd be wise to walk away right now…" Cat said, her tone a sigh.

"What do you think you can do, honey?" the woman asked, mistaking Cat for a femme and therefore harmless.

"Trust me, sweetheart, you don't want to find out," Cat replied, her look all butch.

"Just leave," Quinn said, moving to stretch her neck as she flexed her hands threateningly.

"Or we'll add to those dots," Jet said, her look pointed.

"What the fuck do you think you can do?" the woman spat.

"Well since I'm a cop, I can arrest you for attempted assault on a peace officer," Jet said.

"A cop?" the woman asked, sounding like she didn't believe Jet.

"Believe it," Cat said.

"And know that we'll be happy to put you back where you obviously belong," Jericho said, her tone dark. She still had her arm around Fadiyah's waist.

"And who the fuck do you think you are?" the woman asked.

"Just the Director of the Division of Law Enforcement for the State of California," Jericho said, grinning.

"Fuck! Fine, I'm leavin'!" the woman finally said, and turned and walked away.

Everyone relaxed, and Jericho released Fadiyah who immediately walked over to Jet.

"Are you okay?" she asked Jet, having seen Jet flinch when she'd blocked the woman's punch.

"I'm fine," Jet said, looking down at Fadiyah. "Are you okay?"

"Yes," Fadiyah said, nodding. "I was not talking to her."

"It's okay, babe, I know. Women like that don't really notice that someone's not interested."

"I was not interested," Fadiyah agreed.

"Okay, honey," Jet said, hugging Fadiyah to her. She caught Skyler raising an eyebrow. "Shut it, Sky," she growled, causing Skyler to chuckle and shake her head.

"Okay, next round is on me," Jet said, motioning to the waitress who had just brought Fadiyah her drink.

The group all had a few shots, laughing and talking as the music started. Natalia immediately grabbed Raine and dragged her to the floor causing a ripple of laughter through the group.

"Okay, so obviously leaving you in here is hazardous to my health," Jet said, her lips close to Fadiyah's ear, so she could be heard over the music. "So come on out with me while I smoke."

"Okay," Fadiyah said, nodding as she finished her drink and was handed the one Jet had just bought.

Outside, Jet held the door for Fadiyah, then stood until Fadiyah was seated. Fadiyah was always surprised by Jet's chivalrous ways, and it never ceased to give her a little thrill.

"Are you sure you are alright?" Fadiyah asked. She noticed that Jet was moving gingerly.

"I'm fine. Not gonna say it didn't hurt," she said, shifting her shoulder slightly, "but I'm okay."

Jet lifted a cigarette to her lips then, lighting it.

"Oh!" Fadiyah said, seeing Jet's right hand.

Jet tipped her hand to look at it, noting the cuts and bruises already starting.

"It's okay, babe," Jet said. "That's what happens when you punch someone in the face."

"I cannot believe you hit that woman," Fadiyah said shaking her head.

"No one puts hands on a woman who's with me," Jet said, her tone serious.

Fadiyah stared back at Jet, trying to decide what she meant by that. Jet gave no clue as she continued to smoke her cigarette. Fadiyah drank more of her drink, she liked the feeling it was giving her, kind of a warm happy feeling.

Jet looked over at Fadiyah and noticed she looked a little bit buzzed.

"Uh…" she said, her look quizzical. "Where'd that drink come from?"

"The waitress lady," Fadiyah said.

"Hand me that," Jet said, putting her hand out.

Fadiyah looked at her like she was crazy for a moment, but then handed her the drink.

Jet smelled it. "Son of a… This has alcohol in it, Fadi!"

"It does?" Fadiyah asked, not looking too concerned.

Jet laughed, shaking her head. "Trying to get my ass fired…" she muttered.

"I am not!" Fadiyah said, reaching over to take the glass back.

"Uh, no," Jet said, holding the glass away from her.

Fadiyah sat back and actually pouted.

"Oh, Jesus," Jet said, handing her back the glass.

Fadiyah smiled and took another drink.

"Hey, Jet…" said a blond walking over. She leaned down and kissed Jet on the lips.

"Hey, Carrie," Jet said, nodding.

"Where's Ashley?" Carrie asked.

"In San Diego," Jet said, not for the first time that night.

"Oh… well, if you get lonely…" Carrie said, sliding her hand seductively down Jet's arm from shoulder to wrist.

"She's with me," Fadiyah said, her tone sharp.

Carrie jumped a little, and looked over at Fadiyah, then walked away.

Jet threw her head back and laughed. "Good God, no more alcohol for you, young lady," she said, grinning.

Fadiyah looked fairly pleased with herself.

"Okay," Jet said, moving to stand and putting her hand out to Fadiyah to help her up out of the chair. "I think for you to have the true club experience, you need to dance."

"Dance?" Fadiyah asked, looking both surprised and scared at the same time.

"You'll be fine," Jet said, leading her back into the bar.

Keeping Fadiyah's hand in hers, she walked over to the DJ. The woman leaned down, kissing Jet hello. Jet put her hand up talking into the woman's ear, trying to be heard over the song that was on. The DJ nodded to Jet, giving her a thumbs up.

The song that was playing started to fade and another song began, Fadiyah recognized it immediately, it was the song she loved that Jet sang. "I Am a Lost Boy from Neverland."

Jet led her out onto the dance floor as people started to dance. She pulled Fadiyah gently into her arms, sliding her arms around Fadiyah's waist.

"What do I do?" Fadiyah asked.

"Put your hands on my shoulders," Jet told her.

Jet moved closer, lowering her head to put her face against Fadiyah's temple, her lips right next to Fadiyah's ear. As the words to the song began, Jet sang them to her. Fadiyah sighed, pressing her face against Jet's shirt and inhaling the scent she wore, a rich musk.

Skyler watched Jet dance with Fadiyah and knew that almost everyone in the club was doing the same. Jet never danced, and yet there she was doing just that, and not only that, but she was singing to the girl.

They'd gone on R and R together, they were in Santorini Greece.

"Oh my God, this place is gorgeous!" Skyler said, looking around her, unable to believe the beauty of the town.

The bright white of the buildings with the rich blue of the domes and the Aegean Sea, were beyond words for Skyler.

Jet grinned. "I knew you'd like it," she said.

Jet had paid for the trip, telling Skyler that it was her treat. Jet had finally admitted that she was a 'trust fund' kid. She was all too happy to spend the money to take Skyler somewhere she'd never been.

The hotel Jet had reserved was insanely luxurious, with its own private infinity pool and views of the ocean from every part of the suite.

"Do I even want to know how much this place cost?" Skyler asked.

"A lot," Jet said, grinning.

They'd already made love in the bed, and in the pool, they were now getting ready to go to dinner. It was a wonderful thing to be able to be completely open with their relationship for once. There were no worries of other servicemen seeing them and reporting them. They were able to completely leave the desert behind and escape.

"I can't believe we're here for an entire week!" Skyler said, shaking her head as they walked through the Japanese restaurant located in the hotel.

They had a wonderful long dinner, drinking wine and talking and sometimes simply looking at the view. Afterwards they found a club where they were able to drink and dance and generally enjoy themselves.

At one point, the DJ played a slow song, and Jet pulled Skyler out onto the floor, taking her in her arms. The song that was playing was a little-known or played Def Leppard song, but naturally Jet knew it. She sang every word to Skyler. The chorus of the song said a lot to Skyler about Jet's state of mind. The song was named Let Me Be the One. The words talked about giving her something to hold on to, and for Skyler to let her be the one.

As the song ended, Skyler kissed Jet's lips, pulling her closer and holding her. It was a time Skyler never forgot.

"You okay?" Devin asked, seeing the way Skyler was watching Jet and Fadiyah.

"Yeah," Skyler said, nodding, lifting her beer to her lips and draining the bottle.

Walking over to the bar she ordered another shot and turned to look back at the dance floor again. She honestly hoped she knew what she was seeing, and it wasn't just Jet trying to be gallant and make the girl happy.

As the song ended Fadiyah looked up at Jet and smiled.

"You know I love that song," Fadiyah said.

"I know," Jet said, grinning.

Jet naturally noticed all the grinning going on as she and Fadiyah walked back to the table. She also saw Skyler give Devin her keys and raised an eyebrow at her.

"Shut it, Jet," Skyler said, scowling at her.

Jet merely grinned, nodding her head.

Later that night as Jet drove them home, Fadiyah looked over at her.

"What were those dots on that woman's face?" she asked.

"Those were prison tatts," Jet said.

"She was in prison?" Fadiyah asked, surprised.

"Yeah, that's what five dots means," Jet said, nodding.

Fadiyah reached over, taking Jet's hand that was resting on the center console. She looked at Jet's knuckles, grimacing at the bruises and cuts. Lifting Jet's hand to her lips, she kissed them softly. Jet looked over at her, smiling.

"Still feeling that alcohol, huh?" she asked.

"Why do you say that?" Fadiyah asked.

"'Cause you're awfully touchy," Jet said.

Fadiyah was silent for a few minutes.

"Jet?" Fadiyah queried then.

"Hmm?" Jet murmured, her mind faraway at that point.

"When did you date Skyler?" Fadiyah asked.

Jet froze, her eyes narrowing slightly. "Who told you that?"

Fadiyah didn't answer.

"Fadi?" Jet queried.

Fadiyah shrugged her shoulders. "You were with her, though, were you not?"

Jet looked over at her again, blowing her breath out. "Yeah, back when I was in the Middle East."

"Before you were hurt," Fadiyah clarified.

"Yes," Jet answered.

"Did you love her?" Fadiyah asked.

"Why are we having this conversation?" Jet asked, her tone sharp.

"I just want to understand."

"Understand what?"

"You."

"There's nothing to understand, Fadi. I'm me."

"But why are you like you are?" Fadiyah asked, knowing that the alcohol was making her brave.

"Why do you think it has anything to do with Skyler?" Jet asked.

"Does it?"

"No," Jet said firmly.

Fadiyah was silent for a few minutes, and Jet hoped that the subject was now done.

"Why do you get women to fall in love with you and then you do not want them to love you?" Fadiyah asked quietly.

Jet's head snapped around looking shocked. Reaching over she cranked the stereo in the car and put her foot down on the pedal. Fadiyah knew she had pushed it too far and that she'd made Jet mad, it wasn't what she'd wanted to do. She wanted to understand why Jet wouldn't stay in a relationship. It made her sad.

When Jet pulled off the freeway on their exit, she reached over and turned down the music. Fadiyah was silent. At the house, she walked in, turned off the alarm and went straight to the liquor cabinet and poured herself a double shot. She drank it and then poured another. She walked into the kitchen and pulled a beer out of the refrigerator, tossing the top on the counter. She then walked out of the kitchen and straight up the stairs, closing her bedroom door behind her.

Fadiyah walked upstairs too, going to her room and changing her clothes. She wanted to cry, and she didn't understand it. For two hours she tried desperately to go to sleep, hoping that when she woke up, Jet wouldn't be mad at her anymore. Finally she gave up and got out of bed. She walked over to Jet's door and just stood there, her hand on the door itself.

In her room, Jet was lying on her bed; she still wore her clothes from the club, she'd just kicked off her boots. She had long since drunk the beer and the shot she'd taken up with her. She was staring up at the ceiling, her left arm up over her head, one knee bent. Her right hand was on her stomach and her index finger was tapping with agitation.

Fadiyah took all of this in when she quietly opened the door. She stood watching Jet for a few minutes, she could see that Jet was rolling something over in her mind, and her finger tapping was a manifestation of whatever she was mentally chewing on.

"Jet?" Fadiyah queried softly.

Jet blinked, but didn't look at her.

"What is it?" Jet asked her tone far from solicitous.

Fadiyah noticed the tone and flinched. Jet was so cold suddenly and it was terrifying. She moved forward to stand beside the bed, her eyes looking down at Jet.

"I am sorry I made you angry, that was not my intent," she said, her voice tearful.

Jet flinched at her tone, she hated where they were at that moment, but her need to protect herself was overriding everything.

"I don't get women to love me," Jet said miserably. "I don't even want that. I'm just me... And I'm always honest with them up front. I don't do love, I don't do commitment, none of that shit... It's just not me. But I'm always honest."

Fadiyah shook her head sadly. "But that does not keep them from loving you, they cannot help but to love you, Jet."

"And what am I supposed to do about that?" Jet asked looking agitated.

"I do not think you can do anything about it," Fadiyah said, her eyes staring down into Jet's. "I did not say it to hurt you. I just want to make sense out of things."

When Jet didn't respond, Fadiyah sat down on the bed next to her, her eyes downcast.

"Please forgive me, Jet," she said then, her voice soft.

Jet closed her eyes, trying to ward off the tone of devastation she heard in Fadiyah's voice. Blowing her breath out, she shook her head, not at Fadiyah but at herself. She was thinking, *You did this to yourself you fucking idiot, this girl depends on you now and you don't get to be a selfish asshole!*

Slowly Jet dropped her left arm, beckoning to Fadiyah with her fingertips. Fadiyah immediately moved to lie next to Jet, putting her head in the hollow of Jet's shoulder. She pressed her face against Jet's shirt, still not sure about Jet's mood, but happy that she hadn't ordered her out of her room.

They were both silent for a long time, Jet's eyes were still on the ceiling, her hand on Fadiyah's back moved constantly in a soothing gesture. Fadiyah snuggled closer to Jet, still feeling some of the effects of the alcohol she had consumed. She was pressed along the entire length of Jet's side, she noticed again how good Jet smelled.

At one point, Jet reached up with her right hand to rub her forehead, she hissed as she felt the pain in her shoulder again. She was fairly sure she'd split a stitch when she'd blocked the woman's punch at the bar but she hadn't bothered to check it.

Fadiyah levered herself up on her elbow, her body pressing closer to Jet as she looked down at Jet in concern.

"You are hurt?" Fadiyah asked, her look searching Jet.

"I'm fine," Jet said, shaking her head, even as she shuddered slightly.

"You always say that, Jet," Fadiyah said, her tone chastising. "Even when you are not fine."

Fadiyah shifted her body up slightly to slide her hand under Jet's shirt to try to reach her shoulder to feel for blood. Jet sucked her breath in sharply, pulling her head back.

"See, you are hurt!" Fadiyah said, even though she hadn't been able to reach the injury on Jet's shoulder.

"I'm... not... hurt," Jet gritted out, even as she closed her eyes, her face contorted in a grimace.

Fadiyah shifted again to look down at Jet. She gasped and put her right hand to Fadiyah's shoulder.

"Please, for God's sake, stop moving," Jet said, her voice ragged.

Fadiyah looked at Jet shocked, she saw that Jet's eyes were squeezed shut.

"I do not understand," Fadiyah said, trying to shift away from Jet because she thought that she was somehow hurting her.

"Jesus, Fadi, please just stop," Jet said, holding her hands out to either side of the girl.

"Jet, what is wrong?" Fadiyah asked, her tone sharp.

Jet blew her breath out slowly, shaking her head, then turning it to look at Fadiyah her eyes heated. Fadiyah's eyes searched Jet's, not understanding the look in them, but feeling her breath catch in her throat. Their eyes locked and Fadiyah felt Jet's breath on her lips, she felt her pulse trip and begin to pound.

"Jet..." Fadiyah whispered, her voice a plea.

Jet was so close to her, Fadiyah could hear Jet's breathing, and she could feel her trembling.

"Jesus, Fadi..." Jet breathed, every nerve in her body was rioting, but she was holding back. Her head was screaming at her to stop and move away, but her body wasn't listening, it wanted this in the worst possible way and wanted it desperately.

"Jet, please…" Fadiyah whispered, her lips brushing Jet's as she did.

Jet yanked her head back away from Fadiyah, shaking it feeling her body scream in protest.

"I can't do this… I can't do this, not with you… I can't, not with you…" Jet said, starting to move away.

Fadiyah pushed closer, not wanting to lose this, her hands reached out to grab Jet's waist, trying to pull her back. Jet's hand grabbed her hand, holding away from her body.

"God, Fadi, don't… please…"

"Jet I want you," Fadiyah said, moving closer to her again.

"No, you can't, no," Jet said, still shaking her head.

"But I do," Fadiyah said, her eyes searching Jet's face. "I very much do."

"Fadiyah, I can't do this, I can't do this to you," Jet said, her voice almost desperate.

"Why?" Fadiyah asked shattered by what she perceived as Jet's rejection.

"Because I can't hurt you," Jet said her voice a rasping whisper. "Not you, please don't make me…"

"You would never hurt me Jet," Fadiyah said.

"Oh, but I would, in this case, I would, Fadi, please…" she said, shaking her head.

"But…" Fadiyah said, her eyes shining with tears now. "I love you, Jet…" she said then.

Jet closed her eyes, wincing in almost physical pain as the implications slammed into her.

"God, Fadi... No..." she said, her tone agonized, her eyes still closed as she shook her head.

"I love you," Fadiyah said again, her voice stronger.

"No," Jet said, opening her eyes and looking at Fadiyah, her tone equally strong.

"But I do," Fadiyah said.

"Well, stop," Jet said, her tone icy. "Because it'll only lead to heartbreak for you."

"You won't hurt me," Fadiyah said, her tone sure.

"I will hurt you," Jet said, her face like stone. "I'll shatter your fucking heart."

With that she got out of bed and walked out of the room. Fadiyah lay on the bed, staring at the door Jet had just gone through, and then the tears started. Moving to get up, Fadiyah went back into her room, closing the door quietly and then lay down on her bed crying.

Jet walked by Fadiyah's room a half an hour later and heard her crying. It took everything Jet had to walk into her room and close the door. She lifted the bottle of Casa Noble tequila she had in her hand and took a long drink. Setting the bottle down she changed into shorts and a tank top and proceeded to get drunk.

Ashley walked into the house the next day. It was eerily quiet. It was just past noon on a Saturday, Jet was usually long up and working in the backyard, her music blasting. Walking quietly upstairs, Ashley saw that both Jet and Fadiyah's doors were closed. Something was definitely wrong. Blowing her breath out, she went to her room and unpacked her overnight case and debated about what she wanted to do. Part of her thought maybe she should just leave and go out for the day and let whatever was going on either blow up or blow over. She knew she couldn't do that. She'd involved herself in Jet and Fadiyah's relationship by talking to Fadiyah the night before she'd left. She had no idea if whatever was going on had to do with that, but she did know that she couldn't ignore the fact that something was going on.

She walked up to Fadiyah's door, and knocked softly. When Fadiyah didn't answer, she cautiously opened the door. She saw Fadiyah lying on her bed, in tears.

"Oh God…" Ashley said, walking in and sitting down on the bed next to Fadiyah. "What happened?"

Fadiyah burst into a fresh set of tears and sat up hugging Ashley.

"She does not want me, I am such a fool…" Fadiyah said through her tears.

Ashley held her for a while, letting her cry. Finally she leaned back, looking down at Fadiyah.

"Tell me exactly what happened," Ashley said.

Fadiyah recounted the evening, including the dance, which shocked Ashley immensely, but she let Fadiyah continue without interruption. When she got to the end Ashley could see exactly why the girl was crying, she felt like crying herself for a completely different reason.

"Okay," Ashley said. "I'm going to go see if I can talk to Jet and see what's going on with her. Are you okay for now?"

Fadiyah nodded miserably.

Ashley got up and as she walked out of Fadiyah's room, steeled herself for what she was going to have to deal with in Jet's room. Knocking lightly on the door, there was predictably no answer. Ashley figured Jet thought it was Fadiyah. Opening the door slowly, she saw that Jet was sitting on the side edge of her bed. Her feet spread wide in front of her, one hand braced on her knee, a bottle of beer in her hand, her head was bowed.

"Okay, what's going on?" Ashley asked, her tone sharp because she was alarmed at Jet's state.

Jet closed her eyes for a moment, then shook her head, staring down at a point on the floor.

"Fadiyah is in her room crying her eyes out, and you're in here getting drunk, Jet," Ashley said, walking over to stand next to where Jet sat. "Don't shake your fucking head at me."

Jet's jaw twitched as she clenched her teeth, her eyes narrowing.

"Why did you tell her about Skyler?" Jet asked, her voice low.

"What?" Ashley asked, surprised by the question.

"Why did you tell her about Skyler?" Jet asked again.

Ashley made an impatient sound. "Because she told me she was in love with you and I was trying to explain that you didn't do relationships. I said that the last one I knew about was Skyler,"

Jet shook her head, like she couldn't fathom what Ashley was talking about.

"Did you hear me, Jet?" Ashley asked. "She loves you."

"It doesn't matter," Jet said her tone even.

"It does," Ashley said.

Jet gave a short soulless laugh. "It really doesn't, Ash."

"Why doesn't it matter?" Ashley asked.

Jet shook her head, lifting the bottle of beer to her lips draining it and setting it next to the empty bottle of tequila. Ashley stepped in front of Jet, her eyes looking down at her.

"Why doesn't it matter?" she asked again.

"Because it doesn't fucking matter Ash, okay!" Jet yelled, her voice strained with emotion. "Because I'm not what she needs."

"And what do you think she needs?" Ashley asked.

Jet shook her head again, her look despondent. "She needs stability, she needs attention, she fucking needs to be loved…" Jet said, her voice trailing off.

Ashley nodded. "Yeah, and you love her, so…"

Jet looked at Ashley her eyes reflecting shock, then she started to shake her head.

"You know, you can fucking tell yourself whatever you want to, Jet," Ashley said, her anger finally flowing out. "But you didn't go back to Iraq to get them, you went back there to get her, because you love her."

Ashley's words seemed to strike Jet physically because she reared back looking up at Ashley, her eyes reflecting actual fear suddenly.

"You love her, Jet…" Ashley told her.

Jet shook her head, her eyes flashing in a combination of anger and panic. "I can't, I can't be…"

"You are," Ashley said, her look sad.

"I'm no good for her," Jet said

"You saved her life, Jet," Ashley said.

"She saved mine," Jet said. "This won't work, this... I can't do this..." she said again, her look almost sick now. "I'm no good for her, I'm no good for anyone..."

"Because of Skyler?" Ashley asked.

Jet's head snapped back then, as if Ashley had just struck her.

"What happened with Skyler wasn't your fault, Jet," Ashley said. "It wasn't you..."

Jet's armor started to crack, even as she tried to hold it together. Ashley saw it and moved in for the kill.

"It wasn't you, Jet. She didn't leave because of you. She left because she was hurt. She left because she was traumatized... She didn't leave you... It wasn't you..." By this point Ashley was in tears because the look on Jet's face was breaking her heart.

She moved forward taking Jet into her arms. Jet wrapped her arms around her, her head against Ashley's stomach. Ashley could feel her shaking and hugged her more tightly. Jet just let go then and finally let out all the hurt that had been there for so long, so close under the surface. At one point, Ashley moved to sit on the bed, pulling Jet with her. Eventually Jet fell into an exhausted sleep, lying on her stomach, her arms around Ashley's waist. Ashley sat stroking Jet's hair, feeling drained herself. She had no idea if she'd just made things better or if she'd made them worse.

She found out later that afternoon. She'd fallen asleep with Jet lying against her but woke alone. Jet was gone, she'd left the house. Ashley found out that she hadn't said a word to Fadiyah. By that evening Ashley was getting worried. Fortunately she got a text from Skyler saying that Jet was at her and Devin's house.

Jet had showed up at their house looking like hell. Devin had immediately put her in a bedroom and told her to get some sleep, exchanging a look of concern with Skyler. That had been when Skyler had sent Ashley a text. After sleeping fitfully for the afternoon and into the night, Jet had finally given up and wandered out to the backyard in the middle of the night. Skyler was alerted by Benny. Skyler had walked out to see Jet smoking, sitting on the retaining wall that looked out over the ocean.

"Hey," Skyler said, walking up.

Jet looked over at her, but her eyes didn't seem to see her, then she looked back out over the ocean.

"Ever miss it?" Jet asked.

"Miss what?" Skyler asked.

"People shooting at you," Jet asked.

"I can say a definite no to that one," Skyler said, her look quizzical. "What's goin' on Jet?"

Jet looked over at her again, her look vacant as she shook her head.

Skyler stayed in the backyard with her for two hours. Jet didn't say anything else, and it worried Skyler no end.

When she crawled back into bed with Devin, Devin looked at her. "What's going on?"

"I have no idea…" Skyler said, shaking her head.

The next day Jet spent the entire day on the beach alone. Skyler had tried to join her, but Jet had simply said she needed space. Skyler knew better than to push Jet, the girl could push back harder than anyone she'd ever met, so she backed off. By the end of the day on Sunday, the entire group knew that something was going on with Jet, and Skyler was getting endless texts about it.

Skyler finally called Ashley and talked to her about what was going on. When she hung up she walked over to the cupboard where she and Devin kept the alcohol, taking out a bottle of tequila and downing a couple of shots. Devin watched from the couch.

"What did she say?" Devin asked.

Skyler closed her eyes for a minute, then opened them again and poured a third shot.

"Sky!" Devin said, her tone worried.

Skyler held up her hand, it immediately scared Devin. It had been the way Skyler had acted when she'd suffered a minor breakdown over the crash. Standing, Devin walked over to Skyler, taking the bottle gently out of her hands, and taking her hand to walk her over to the couch.

"Tell me what's happening," Devin said, her voice calm.

"It's my fault," Skyler said. "It's my fault Jet is so fucked up."

"How is she fucked up?" Devin asked. "She seems pretty set in her life."

Skyler shook her head. "You mean set in the way that she's with a different woman every night? That she doesn't stick around with any woman for too long? Set like that?"

"Maybe that's how she wants to live her life, Sky," Devin pointed out.

"And maybe it's my fault she won't commit to anyone."

"How is it your fault?" Devin asked.

Skyler shook her head. "I left her, Devin. I left her there without a fucking word…"

"Skyler you were hurt. Jesus, you can't have been expected to wrap everything up nicely," Devin said her concern for Skyler overriding the need to be nice about this.

"I could have contacted her later though, at least tried to explain."

"You can't control everything in life, Skyler. You were doing the best you could."

"Yeah, well, my best sucked," Skyler said her look tormented.

Devin's eyes searched Skyler's face then. "Sky…" she said, her tone taking on a cautionary sound.

Skyler heard it, and felt her heart lurch. "Devin…" she said, shaking her head.

"No, wait," Devin said, holding up her hand. "I need you to think about this."

"I don't need to think about anything," Skyler said, her voice strong.

"Maybe we shouldn't do this next month," Devin said, her voice as even as she could make it, even though her heart was threatening to beat right out of her chest.

"Devin, God… No, that isn't what this is about, babe, please…" Skyler said, having known what was coming from the second Devin's voice had changed.

"I love you," Skyler told Devin.

"You love her too," Devin said.

"I did love her," Skyler admitted. "I did, and that's why I feel so shitty now, because I never even told her. But you're who I love now, and nothing is going to change that. I feel like hell because in my rush to forget everything about my time in the Middle East, I forgot the person that meant so much to me for a time. And now I'm seeing the fallout from that. That's hard for me, yes, but that doesn't mean I don't love you."

Devin looked back at her, trying to understand what Skyler was saying. It did make sense. She'd never even heard about Jet Mathews until she'd shown up in LA at Kashena's party one afternoon. Skyler had been honest with her all along about who Jet was, at least for the most part.

"Why didn't you tell me that you loved her?" Devin asked then.

Skyler shook her head. "I guess I really didn't think it mattered now. And I figured it was all water under the bridge with her too, so…"

"Did she tell you she loved you?" Devin asked.

"Not in so many words, no, but looking back now I can see that she was telling me she loved me in lots of other ways. I was just too blind to see it, or maybe I didn't want to see it, I don't know."

Devin nodded. "And you are sure you don't want to at least postpone the wedding."

"Devin, I love you," Skyler said, her eyes staring straight into Devin's. "I want to spend the rest of my life with you, nothing is going to change that."

Devin nodded. "Okay, I guess I needed to hear that."

"I'm sorry, babe," Skyler said, shaking her head. "I really didn't know how badly this was backing up on me until Ashley told me what's going on."

"So what is going on?" Devin asked.

Skyler told her about what Ashley had said.

"So do you think Ashley is right?" Devin asked.

"Yeah, I do," Skyler said. "I think she's been in love with that girl from the start."

Devin nodded. "Is there anything we can do to help?"

"I think there's something I need to do," Skyler said, her look resolved.

Devin nodded, worried, but knowing that, like going to Iraq with Jet, it was something she needed to do to make amends.

Later that day, Skyler walked outside, finding Jet once again sitting on the retaining wall. She lit a cigarette and walked over to where Jet sat. Jet was on top of the thick wall, her knees up to her chest, her arms resting over them. She was smoking.

"Hey," Skyler said, walking up and leaning on the wall, looking out over the ocean.

Jet glanced over at Skyler, blowing out smoke as she did.

"Hey," Jet said, turning her head back to the view.

They were both silent for a few minutes.

"So we need to talk," Skyler said.

Jet gave a short laugh, shaking her head. "No, we really don't."

"Yeah, Jet, we really do," Skyler said, her tone serious. "We have needed to for years now."

"Years?" Jet repeated, raising an eyebrow.

Skyler nodded, her look telling Jet that she knew what she meant.

Jet blew her breath out, shaking her head. "You don't need to say anything, Sky? Okay? It's done, over."

"Right…" Skyler said. "But I've never apologized."

"You apologized," Jet said.

"I apologized for not being there, Jet, but not for the way I left things."

"You got medevac'd home, Sky, what do think you needed to do, huh? Send me flowers?" Jet asked her tone sarcastic.

Skyler narrowed her eyes at Jet, knowing she was being defensive because she didn't want to talk about the subject. *Too bad*, Skyler thought.

"I could have contacted you after that," Skyler said.

Jet said nothing, simply looking out over the ocean, and taking a deep drag on her cigarette. Skyler noted the silence, and knew it was because Jet had thought the same thing.

"And I didn't, and that's where I fucked up," Skyler said.

"You didn't fuck up, Sky," Jet said, her tone sad.

Skyler turned around, hopping up on the wall, sitting facing the house, her eyes looking into Jet's.

"I fucked up, Jet because I never told you that I loved you," she said, her tone strong. "And God I loved you…"

Jet gritted her teeth, shaking her head. "Doesn't matter."

"It does," Skyler said, "because that stupid mistake broke something in you, and I want to help fix it."

Jet gave a short sarcastic laugh, looking at Skyler with her eyes flashing angrily.

"Why does everyone think I'm fucking broken?"

"Why?" Skyler asked her tone sharp. "Because you're in love with that girl and she's in love with you, and you're not going to get involved with her because you think something is wrong with you."

Jet shook her head, looking away.

"You love her, Jet…" Skyler said.

Jet shrugged.

"That doesn't happen all the time," Skyler said.

"It's happened before," Jet said, her tone wry.

"Why didn't you ever tell me you loved me?" Skyler asked then.

Jet gave her a sarcastic grin. "I thought I did."

"You never said the words, Jet," Skyler said.

"I just figured it was easier that way," Jet said.

"You were afraid I wouldn't say them back," Skyler said, pinning Jet with a look.

"Maybe," Jet said her tone non-committal.

"I loved you," Skyler told her.

Jet blew her breath out, shaking her head sadly.

"You were my life line over there Jet," Skyler told her. "I don't even know if I ever realized how much I loved you for that... But please let me help you now."

"Help me what, Sky?" Jet asked.

"Help you find your way back," Skyler said.

"The way back isn't the hard part," Jet said, grinning wryly. "It's the being here that's hard."

"Fadiyah loves you," Skyler said. "And I think you have loved her since you were hurt and she saved your life. Let her save your life again."

Jet blew her breath out in a rush. "I don't know how to do this..." she said.

"Yeah you do," Skyler said, smiling fondly.

Fadiyah was standing in the backyard, but she wasn't seeing the backyard. She was trying to imagine what her life would be like back in Iraq. Would she even have the option to go back to Iran as she originally had? Or would they just send her back to Iraq? She realized she had no idea what would happen and it scared her. It was bad enough that she would suddenly be without this woman who she'd come to realize she loved desperately, but she would also be without all of the people she'd met. Ashley had been so kind, trying so hard to help her. Skyler and Sebastian who'd come all the way to Iraq to try to save her with Jet. Jericho who had done so much behind the scenes to make the mission to save Fadiyah go smoothly. The list went on and on and Fadiyah felt like she was losing everything. The tears she thought she had run out of began again.

Jet walked into the house, looking around, and seeing Fadiyah standing outside. Drawing in a deep breath she set down her keys and walked to the back door, opening it and stepping outside.

Fadiyah turned at the sound of the door opening. Jet took one look at her tear-streaked face and completely broke. Striding to her, Jet cupped her face in her hands, her lips moved to kiss Fadiyah, her hands gentle, her lips tender. Pulling back she looked down into Fadiyah's eyes.

"I'm sorry," Jet said, "I love you."

Fadiyah let out a cry and wrapped her arms around Jet's neck, kissing her. Jet picked her up in her arms, her lips still on Fadiyah's. She carried the girl inside and up to her bedroom. Laying her down she continued to kiss her and lay down on the bed next to her, pulling her into her arms again. Jet took her time, kissing her and caressing gently. As they kissed Fadiyah pressed close, her need making her tremble.

"God, babe…" Jet said, her voice ragged. "Wait, please… wait…" she said, pulling her head back away from Fadiyah.

"What did I do wrong?" Fadiyah asked, her look afraid.

"No, honey, you didn't…." Jet said, blowing her breath out. "I just need to calm down a bit…" she said, looking like she was having a rather difficult time doing so.

"Calm down?" Fadiyah asked, looking confused.

Jet blew her breath out, nodding. "You're killin' me right now," she said.

"What?" Fadiyah asked, sounding alarmed.

"No, babe, not literally," Jet said, laughing at the ridiculousness of her situation. Blowing her breath out, she knew she needed to explain. "This," she said, motioning to Fadiyah's body pressed her hers, "is getting me really keyed up right now…"

"Keyed up?" Fadiyah queried.

Jet dropped her head back, thinking if nothing else this conversation was helping to cool her off a bit. She grinned, because she had never in a million years imagined herself in this kind of situation.

"You are exciting the hell out of me," Jet told her. "And honestly, I'm afraid if I don't calm down, I'll ravish you and scare the crap out of you."

Fadiyah stared back at Jet, her mouth slightly open, but Jet could see when it clicked in her head that she had power here. *Oh shit,* was the thought that ran through her mind as Fadiyah moved to slide her body over Jet's, making Jet groan loudly.

"And I so shouldn't have told you that…" Jet said, her voice reflecting the desire now coursing through her again.

After that, there were no more words. Jet did everything she could to control her desire but in the end they cried out in their release together. They then spent the next few hours exploring each other.

When they lay completely sated, Fadiyah moved to look down at Jet, who lay on her back with one arm behind her neck.

"What does this mean?" she asked Jet.

Jet looked back at her, her eyes searching. "I'm not sure," she said honestly. "What I am sure about is that I love you and I will do everything I can to make this work… I just can't make you any promises right now."

Fadiyah nodded, already getting more than she ever expected to get from Jet. "I want you to promise me one thing," she said then.

"What's that?" Jet asked her voice soft.

"That while we are together, whether that's for a day, a week or a month, you will not be with any other woman."

Jet looked back at her for a long moment, wondering if she should tell her that she was usually only with one woman at a time.

"How do you know I keep my promises?" Jet asked.

"I know you do," Fadiyah said. "You are too honorable not to."

Jet had to give her that one. Finally she touched her lips to Fadiyah's, then pulling back to look into her eyes as she said, "I promise."

Later as the sun started to go down, Jet walked out into the backyard. She found Ashley sitting there. Jet turned the stereo on with her phone, and music began to play.

"Hey," Jet said moving to sit down a light a cigarette.

"Hi," Ashley said, her smile wide, a knowing look in her eyes.

"I take it you *heard*?" Jet asked, grinning.

"I think half the neighborhood heard," Ashley said, still grinning.

Jet pressed her lips together, her eyes twinkling.

"You look happy," Ashley said.

Jet drew in a deep breath, and blew it out slowly. Moving to lean forward, Jet kissed Ashley on the lips sweetly.

"And I know I owe you," Jet told her as she moved to sit back down. "Thank you for that."

Ashley shook her head. "I just wanted to help."

"Yeah, a lot of women in your position wouldn't have," Jet said.

"Well, I kinda love ya, so I want you to be happy," Ashley said.

"Love me?" Jet asked, her look quizzical.

"Not in that boil your bunny kind of way," Ashley replied. "But I know that Fadiyah is the woman you love, and that is what I want for you, my friend. After everything you've done for me."

Jet smiled over at her, her eyes indicating that she understood what Ashley was saying and appreciating that Ashley wasn't going to make her feel bad about how things happened. She wasn't sure she could take anymore guilt right now.

"Where's Fadiyah?" Ashley asked after a few minutes.

"She'll be down in a few," Jet said, moving to put her foot on Ashley's chair companionably.

When Fadiyah walked out, Ashley couldn't believe the change in the girl. She looked beyond happy, she looked absolutely blissful. It almost hurt to see it.

Fadiyah moved to sit on the arm of the chair that Jet sat in. Jet slid her free hand around Fadiyah's waist and Fadiyah leaned down to kiss Jet on the head.

They all talked for a few minutes, then Fadiyah picked up Jet's phone.

"How do I find that song?" she asked, looking at the phone.

Jet reached up, bringing Fadiyah's hand that was holding the phone down so she could see the screen. "Touch there," she instructed, "here, and here…"

Ashley watched them with a smile on her face, they were an awfully cute couple.

The song, "I Am a Lost Boy from Neverland" that Fadiyah loved so much, flowed out of the speakers.

She watched enchanted as Jet sang the song. When the song ended Ashley grinned, looking at Jet.

"Are you the lost boy?" she asked Jet.

"No," Fadiyah said, her smile warm. "Jet is Peter Pan. I am the lost boy that she came to bring home to Neverland."

Epilogue

Jet walked into the house at four in the morning. She dropped her gear bag on the entryway bench and climbed the stairs tiredly. Entering the bedroom as quietly as possible, she glanced over at the form sleeping in the bed and smiled fondly. It had been a month since she and Fadiyah had officially become a couple. Jet had found that being with Fadiyah much easier than trying not to be with her. So far things had been good between them. Jet sincerely hoped it stayed that way, but there was always a small part of her that watched and waited for things to go wrong. She tried to squelch that part of her as often as possible.

Taking off her clothes, she went into the master bathroom and showered. Finally crawling into bed behind Fadiyah at four thirty, she slid her arm around her and gently pulled her back against her chest. She was asleep a minute later. At six her phone started ringing. Groaning she had to resist the urge to throw the device across the room. Fadiyah turned over in her arms, reaching past her to pick up the phone and look at the display.

"It is your parents," Fadiyah told her.

"Oh, good, I can ignore it then."

"Jet!" Fadiyah said, handing her the phone and giving her a pointed look.

Jet made an annoyed sound in the back of her throat, but answered the call anyway.

"This is Jet," she said, knowing it would annoy her mother.

Fadiyah could only hear Jet's side of the conversation, but watched her face as she talked to her mother.

"Okay," Jet said, her look mild. "I'm tired, I just went to bed an hour and a half ago." She rolled her eyes. "I was at work, Mom, not partying." She took a deep breath, blowing it out slowly. "Yes, I actually do work that late sometimes…" Again she rolled her eyes. "Uh-huh, I know." Her eyes flicked over to Fadiyah's, seeing that the girl was watching her closely, she winked, making Fadiyah smile. "Right, okay, got it," Jet said, her tone short. "Yep."

She hung up a few moments later.

"What did she say?" Fadiyah asked.

"They are postponing their trip down here again," Jet said, sounding relieved.

"And?" Fadiyah asked, knowing Jet's mother had said more.

"She told me how I should stop partying so much and grow up," Jet said, blinking, with a sarcastic smile on her face.

Fadiyah looked back at her surprised.

"Why would she say that to you?" Fadiyah asked, her tone reflecting her surprise.

Jet sighed, settling back on the bed and tossing her phone on the nightstand. "Because babe, my parents don't like me much, and frankly I don't like them either, so at least it's mutual."

"Your parents love you, Jet," Fadiyah said.

Jet gave a short sarcastic laugh. "No, babe, your parents loved you, my parents see me as a disappointment."

"How could they see you that way? That is not possible," Fadiyah said, shaking her head.

Jet smiled at her. "Unfortunately, babe, it is highly possible and believe me, they let me know it regularly. I'm their biggest failure in life."

Fadiyah shook her head, unable to fathom how Jet's parents could see her as any kind of failure.

"It bothers you," Fadiyah said quietly.

"No," Jet said, shaking her head.

"It bothers you," Fadiyah said again, her eyes searching Jet's. "That is why you talk to them the way you do."

Jet looked back at her, her look amused. "Are you sure you don't want to go into psychology instead?"

Fadiyah laughed softly. "No, I need to be a nurse to keep up with this kind of thing," she said, touching the dark bruise and one inch gash on Jet's upper arm.

"It's fine," Jet said.

"You always say that," Fadiyah said. "Even when you were shot, you said you were fine."

Jet grinned. "It's my go to. But this doesn't even hurt."

Fadiyah pressed her finger against the wound making Jet jump.

"Hey!" Jet said, laughing despite the pain.

"I thought it did not hurt," Fadiyah said, her look narrowed.

"Well, as long as you don't friggin' poke it, it doesn't hurt, sheesh!"

Fadiyah just grinned at her.

"Always going to call me on my bullshit, aren't you?" Jet asked, not looking unpleased by the prospect.

"I am," Fadiyah said, nodding affirmation.

"Probably a good thing," Jet said, smiling.

"I believe so."

Skyler woke to the feeling of a tongue on her face. Groaning, she pushed Benny's muzzle away.

"It would be okay, dude, if you were an insanely beautiful woman..." she muttered tiredly. "But you have dog breath..."

"Will this insanely beautiful woman do?" Devin asked, standing beside the bed, looking down at Skyler, her emerald-green eyes sparkling in the morning sunlight.

"Yes, you'll do nicely." Skyler grinned, taking Devin's hand and pulling her down on the bed.

Devin laughed as she moved to lie over Skyler.

"Is it time to get up?" Skyler asked, glancing at the clock.

"No," Devin said, smiling. "Benny just wanted to say good morning."

"How about you?" Skyler asked. "Do you want to say good morning?"

"Definitely," Devin said, lowering her head to kiss Skyler's lips.

Skyler's arm encircled her, pulling aside the covers and pulling Devin closer to her. They made love, exciting each other as they always did; they had always had incredible sexual chemistry.

Afterwards they lay together, Devin still over Skyler, her face pressed against Skyler's neck, trying to catch their breath.

"Is it bad luck to have sex before the wedding?" Skyler asked, still slightly breathless.

"It's bad luck to have sex with someone else before the wedding," Devin replied, grinning.

"You mean other than the person you're marrying?" Skyler asked, grinning as well.

"That's deadly, yeah," Devin said, moving to look down at Skyler, her eyes narrowed. "Especially for you."

Skyler grinned. "Why especially for me?" she asked, already knowing the answer.

"Because I'd kill ya," Devin said, her look pointed.

"Mmm…" Skyler murmured her light blue-green eyes looking amused.

"I'm mean," Devin said.

"Uh-huh…" Skyler said, nodding.

"I can be."

"You can, huh?" Skyler said, her grin widening.

"Skyler Boché!" Devin exclaimed. "Stop doing that."

"Doing what?" Skyler asked.

"Giving me that look like you are so amused by me."

"But I am amused by you, babe," Skyler said.

"You know what I mean…" Devin said, attempting to be angry, but failing miserably.

"Yes, I know," Skyler said. "And I'd never do that, so its moot point."

"Okay then," Devin said, her grin in place again.

"And you're really okay with leaving on Tuesday for the honeymoon?" Skyler asked then.

"Yes," Devin assured her. "I know you need to be there for that meeting and I want you to be, so it's totally okay."

Skyler looked like she wanted to ask something else, but then changed her mind.

"What?" Devin asked, seeing the look and knowing better than to let Skyler avoid addressing something.

Skyler looked at her, her eyes searching. "And you're really okay with the idea that I'm going to be working around Jet again?"

Devin smiled softly, having thought that might be Skyler's question.

"Sky," she said, her tone sure and her look direct. "I love you, and I trust you, okay?"

Skyler nodded. "I just don't want you to think that Jet is the reason I'm changing jobs," she said then. "Things have gone to shit at LAFD since our captain retired and—"

"Babe, I know that," Devin said. "I've heard what you and Jams have been talking about for months. And I know you're both unhappy there now. This is a great opportunity for both of you, and I want you to grab it."

Skyler drew in a deep breath, blowing it out, shaking her head. "I don't know how I got so lucky," she said, smiling. "Of all the women I could have found, how did I find you?"

"You didn't, I found you," Devin told her. "And I chased after you mercilessly until I got to keep you."

Skyler smiled, what Devin was saying was partially true. Devin had definitely chased her and pushed her to accept her affection. Skyler hadn't been willing to accept anything from anyone at that point in her life, other than sex. Devin had changed her mind about that, by being there and not giving up on her. It was for that reason that Skyler loved her so much.

"Well, you need to know that I know how lucky I am that you did," Skyler told her.

"You can show me for the rest of our lives, babe," Devin told her.

"I plan to."

"Good," Devin responded, smiling.

Later that evening, Jet stood in the backyard, smoking and waiting on Fadiyah. She looked extremely debonair in black slacks, a crisp white long sleeved shirt with starched cuffs with obsidian cuff links. The shirt was open at the throat exposing a fair amount of chest, and her dog tags; the Army star on one tag, and the two silver bars of the rank of Captain on the other. In her ears she wore black obsidian studs. Her black Dolce & Gabbana silk suit jacket with satin accents on the collar and pockets hung over the chair she sat in. On her feet she wore very expensive looking Italian leather boots with a two inch heel.

She made a very striking picture that took Fadiyah's breath away when she walked up to the back door looking for Jet. She was nervous because Ashley had helped her with her outfit and makeup, and she had no idea how Jet would react.

She wore a dress that Jet had paid for but hadn't seen yet. Jet had handed Ashley her credit card and told her to help Fadiyah find a dress for Skyler's wedding. Fadiyah had wanted to surprise Jet.

Holding her breath, she opened the back sliding door and stepped carefully outside.

Jet turned at the sound of the back door, and literally froze, her mouth agape, her eyes sweeping from Fadiyah's head down to her toes and back up again. Then she moved to stand.

Fadiyah wore a long gown that was black lace over a beige silk under-gown. The neckline was a sweetheart shape and the dress nipped in sharply at the waist, hugging down past Fadiyah's mid-thigh, then flared at the bottom. The dress itself was strapless, but Fadiyah wore a sheer black and lace shrug to cover her shoulders and arms. Her silky black hair fell in long graceful curls, with the top held back with black jeweled combs. The makeup that Ashley had helped her apply was just enough to enhance her beautiful skin and bone structure, and to show off her silver-gray eyes.

It took Jet a few long moments to find her breath.

"My God you are so beautiful…" Jet said reverently.

Fadiyah smiled shyly. "You look very handsome," she said, biting her lower lip.

Jet stepped over to her, touching her cheek with her hand, leaning in to kiss her lips softly. She pulled back and just looked down at the girl in amazement.

"You look absolutely amazing, baby girl," Jet said, her tone awed.

Fadiyah couldn't stop smiling. Jet always made her feel like she was the most incredible woman she'd ever seen. Fadiyah knew from watching Jet at the club, and from talking to Ashley, that Jet had been with a lot of women. It made her feel extremely special and lucky to have captured Jet, even if it was only for the time being. She never completely believed that she could keep Jet forever, but she promised herself not to worry about such things. She enjoyed the time with Jet now.

Sebastian opened his front door, and was stunned. Ashley stood at the door with a navy blue gown on that hugged her in all the right places. She'd asked Sebastian to be her date at the last minute, not wanting to be the third wheel to Jet and Fadiyah. She loved them to death, and was slowly but surely getting over Jet, but sometimes she just wanted to get away and breathe. Calling Sebastian had taken a serious amount of courage building, but she'd been secretly thrilled when he'd been more than happy to take her up on her offer.

"Wow," Sebastian said simply, his eyes taking her in.

"Wow yourself," Ashley said, taking in his attire.

Sebastian was dressed in black slacks, with a rich green shirt that came fairly close to matching the color of his eyes. He also wore a black alligator skin belt and dress boots that matched. His blond hair was still damp from his shower, and he hadn't buttoned his shirt yet, which exposed a very nice expanse of well-muscled golden skin, marred only by a scar on his left pectoral muscle.

"Obviously I'm running late," he told her as he opened his door wider to let her walk in.

Ashley smiled. "I think I'm a little early too, so we'll call it even," she said, smiling, proud of herself for not stammering.

The man definitely had sex appeal in spades.

"I'll be ready in just a minute, okay?" Sebastian said, winking at her. "Make yourself at home."

Ashely looked around his apartment, noting that he definitely wasn't a slob. He had good taste in furnishings, rich woods with just enough style to keep them from being plain, but not fussy at all. It was 'manly' furniture, Ashley thought, grinning to herself.

Jet had told her that Sebastian was the kind of man she thought she should date. Ashley tried not to let it bother her that Jet was trying to push her to dating other people. She knew that Jet was with Fadiyah and had accepted that it was the way things were meant to be. But it didn't hurt any less when Jet very obviously wanted her to move on; it wasn't that easy. She did love Jet, she'd come to realize she probably always had. The emotions were mixed up in nostalgia and some sort of hero worship. Ashley knew it was something she needed to deal with to move on, and she knew that Jet would do whatever she could to help. It just wasn't easy and would take some time.

It took Ashley a couple of minutes to notice that Sebastian had music on in his apartment. Walking over to where the iHome sat on a sofa table, she looked at the song displayed on the iPod. The words were so incredibly apt for her situation she had to know who sang it. The song was a rock/rap type of song by Linkin Park called "In the End." She found herself closing her eyes and moving her head to the beat, the words so fitting it was like the song had been written for her. The last verse and chorus said it all. It talked about putting her trust in someone and that for all she'd done, she still ended up with nothing.

Sebastian watched Ashley from the doorway to his bedroom. He saw the way she closed her eyes listening to the song. He knew the song and he could see that she felt every word it said. Something inside him twisted. For whatever reason, this girl had gotten under his skin, and he knew she hadn't even tried. He could tell that she wasn't the kind of woman that knew how to get to a man, nothing about Ashley was contrived. She was wide open, and even when she was trying her best to be brave, he could see right through her. For a man like him, who was very used to women throwing themselves at him, using every weapon in their arsenal to catch him, someone like Ashley was an anomaly.

He knew damned good and well that she was in love with Jet, and he could only imagine what Jet's eventual rejection had done to her. He saw a big difference in her from when he'd first met her, to the woman that stood listening to his music now. She had more confidence now, extending to calling him to ask him to be her date for the wedding. He'd been very surprised, but also very pleased that she seemed to be pulling herself away from Jet finally.

The cynical part of him wondered if this was some kind of ploy to make Jet jealous, he knew if that was the case it was bound to fail miserably. It was obvious to everyone who'd seen Jet with Fadiyah now that she was deeply in love with the girl. It had broken his heart a bit for Ashley, and he knew it was that broken heart that ached for her now, as he watched her listening to a song that talked about losing something you'd tried so hard to get.

Moving from the door jamb he was leaning against, he walked over to Ashley, touching her gently on the arm. She jumped slightly, and then grimaced.

"I'm sorry, I was kind of..." she began, then shook her head. "Never mind."

"It's a good song," Sebastian said, his look understanding.

"Yeah..." Ashley said, doing everything she could to keep the sadness out of her voice. She succeeded in keeping it out of her voice, but nothing would erase it from her eyes.

Once again, something in Sebastian clenched, he wanted to see her smile without that shadow in her blue eyes.

"Are you like Jet in the listening to music constantly thing?" she asked then.

Sebastian grinned. "Yeah, I guess I am," he said, nodding.

"She says it's because of her ADHD, is that you too?" Ashley asked, cringing inwardly thinking she was talking way too much about Jet!

Sebastian looked pensive. "I don't know. I've never thought about that. I just need the chaos."

Ashley smiled. "That's an interesting way to put it," she said.

"You ready to go?" he asked her, pulling on his jacket.

"Yes," she said. "Oh, wait." she said then, reaching up to straighten his collar for him.

He stood, patiently waiting for her to finish, a grin on his lips. *Classic romantic moment, Bach. Are you brave enough?* his brain asked him. For once in his life he didn't grab the easy opportunity. He didn't want to push her, or make her think that he was after her because he figured she was easy.

"There," Ashley said, smiling up at him.

"Let's go," he said, smiling at her.

She was happily reminded that Sebastian Bach was every bit the gentleman. He opened doors for her and helped her up into his vehicle. Driving to the venue, Ashley found that she was very happy that she'd been brave enough to ask him to be her date. The last thing she'd wanted to do was to show up to this wedding where literally every one of her friends was in a couple, either alone or with Jet and

Fadiyah. It just reminded her too much of high school, and that was just not a memory she wanted.

The venue for Skyler and Devin's wedding was beyond amazing. It was called Vibiana and was located in the historic part of downtown Los Angeles. Since the wedding was small, the ceremony itself was held outside on a beautifully decorated veranda. The colors for the wedding were a rich deep purple and black. Everything about the decorations reflected those colors. The chairs for the guests were covered in black silk with a long purple satin runner down the center. The flowers were all shades of purple, with various styles and textures. It was an early evening wedding, so it was already getting dark and on the veranda was up lit with purple hues.

As the wedding guests walked in, they all exclaimed at the incredible beauty of everything.

Jet escorted Fadiyah to a seat, then leaning down to kiss her lips softly, she said, "I'll be right back."

Walking over to a side area, Jet located Skyler.

"So how ya doin'?" Jet asked, grinning.

"Shut it, Jet," Skyler said, grinning too.

Jet took in Skyler's suit; she looked damned good in all black with a purple tie and pocket square.

"You look nervous," Jet said.

"I look scared out of my fucking mind, Jet," Skyler shot back.

Jet chuckled. "Nah, you'll be okay," she said, smiling.

Skyler took a deep breath and nodded. "I need a damned cigarette."

"Well, see... That's what your troublemaking friends are good for," Jet said, pulling her pack out of her jacket and shaking out one to offer to Skyler.

"If I mess this jacket up, Devin will kill me..." Skyler said, still tempted by the need to smoke.

"So take it off and hang it over there," Jet said, pointing to a tall arrangement of flowers.

"Got it," Skyler said, unbuttoning her jacket and doing as Jet had suggested.

Skyler put the cigarette between her lips and Jet lit it for her. Skyler took a deep drag and closed her eyes in near ecstasy.

"You are the best friend I've ever had..." Skyler told her.

"What does that make me?" Jams asked, coming up behind the two.

Skyler laughed. "My copilot."

"Is that better or worse?" Jet asked.

"Neither," Skyler said, grinning.

"So you're really gonna put off your honeymoon to be there on Monday?" Jams asked. "You know I can meet this liaison and give you a full report."

"I know," Skyler said. "But I just want to get the full lay of the land..."

Jet and Jams nodded. LA IMPACT as a whole was adding an aviation group to their arsenal. They'd gotten lucky and received an offer of assistance from a local military operation. They were meeting with the liaison that Monday to go over what options they had and how the liaison would work with them. Skyler and Jams were making the move into law enforcement in as much as helicopter use would allow. It was taking a big change for them, but they felt it was time.

"Better get this show on the road," Skyler said when she finished the cigarette.

Jet extended her hand to Skyler, who pushed it aside and hugged Jet tight.

"You'll do fine," Jet said, smiling as she hugged Skyler back.

"I know," Skyler said. "I'm glad you're happy, Jet."

Jet pulled back, looking at Skyler. "I am, and I owe you for that too."

"Nah, just be happy," Skyler said.

"Working on it," Jet said, nodding.

Jet went back to her seat and a few minutes later the wedding began. Jams was standing up for Skyler and Devin hadn't bothered with bridesmaids. Devin's father was walking her down the aisle to give her away to Skyler.

When Devin appeared at the end of the aisle, Skyler felt her heart flutter. Devin wore a Pnina Tornai wedding gown that was shorter in the front, and long in the back. It was a strapless gown that was covered in appliques that sparkled and winked as she walked toward Skyler. Her hair was done in a loose up-do that left curled tendrils loose around her face and shoulders. Her makeup was dramatic and done in a way that made Skyler think that she was definitely the luckiest woman on the planet. Devin's eyes shined brightly as she looked at Skyler, her smile pure love.

The vows were exchanged, bringing tears and a little bit of laughter to everyone. The reception was held in a two-story room with vaulted ceilings and an incredible amount of flowers and crystals and purple lighting. The evening went far too fast and before long there were only a few people left. Mostly their core group that always hung out together, including Sebastian.

They were all sitting around one table, drinking and smoking and talking.

"This was an amazing wedding," Zoey said, sitting next to Jericho who nodded in agreement.

"Yeah, you did a great job," Xandy told Devin.

"Thanks," Devin said, smiling, her bare feet on Skyler's lap, while Skyler rubbed them where Devin's wedding shoes had caused red spots. "But a very expensive wedding planner handled most of it."

"Pays to pay someone sometimes," Kashena said, grinning.

"Be quiet, you made me keep it to a minimum," Sierra said, swatting Kashena on the arm.

Kashena only laughed.

"You both looked so gorgeous!" Cat said, smiling.

"And I love that dress Devin! I think I need one like that..." Jovina said, letting her voice trail off as she looked up.

"Ohhhhh...." Quinn said, grimacing.

"Quiet you," Xandy said, poking her girlfriend.

"Damn..." Jericho said, shaking her head at Quinn.

"I think you should be careful here too, Jerich," Quinn said, nodding toward Zoey.

Jericho turned to look at Zoey. "Hi," she said, smiling with a faked kind of innocence.

"Don't *hi* me," Zoey said, her look pointed.

"Ouch," Jet said, grinning, her hand in Fadiyah's.

"Well, I think it was a wonderful wedding," Ashley put in.

"It's one of the best I've ever been to," Natalia said.

"This is my first," Raine said, grinning.

"Hmmm…" Natalia said, her look mischievous.

"Ohhhh…" said a few of the group together.

Raine looked pensive. "What did I say?"

"Hablaremos más tarde," Natalia said to Raine.

Raine nodded.

"Wow…" Jet said.

"What did she say?" Ashley asked Jet.

"That they'll talk later," Jet said.

"Run, Raine, just run," Sebastian told the girl.

"Hey! Callete gringo!" Natalia exclaimed, grinning all the while.

Sebastian laughed, leaning back in his chair and putting his arm around the back of Ashley's chair.

Jet had noticed that Sebastian had been especially attentive to Ashley all evening. He hadn't been pawing her or anything, which relieved Jet greatly. In pushing Ashley at Sebastian, she had been just a little concerned that she'd misjudged Sebastian, thinking he was a complete gentleman. Part of her had worried that she'd need to rescue Ashley from him at some point, and she wasn't sure how that would go over with Sebastian, Ashley or Fadiyah. It was a very odd situation to be in, and she knew it. She was happy to see that she'd been right about Sebastian. She also thought they looked damned good together.

It was a great night for everyone.

***

She smoothed back her hair, and checked her makeup again in the car mirror, just to be sure it wasn't overdone or smudged. Everything looked fine. She couldn't believe how frigging nervous she was! Her phone rang then and grinning she picked up the call on the car's Bluetooth.

"Hi!" she said, knowing exactly who it was without even looking at the display, she always knew when to call…

"Hi," came the response. "How are you doing over there?" asked a warm voice.

"I'm nervous as hell!" she responded, shaking her head.

"You are going to do fine, honey, you know that."

She took a deep breath, blowing it out, glancing in the rearview mirror again. "I know, I know."

"Then get in there," was the warm response.

"I love you," She said.

"I love you, too, babe," came the reply.

Taking a deep breath she climbed out of the car and settled her cap on her head, making sure the brim was right at her brow level. Her uniform was pressed, her boots were shined and she looked as sharp as she possibly could. Walking a few steps she stopped and reached inside her gear bag for the cigarettes waiting there. She'd been smoking since her last deployment, it calmed her nerves. She knew she needed to quit, but hadn't managed it so far.

Lighting the cigarette she leaned against her car and did her best to let the smoke calm her. She had no idea she was being observed.

"Think that's her?" Skyler asked, as she and Jet walked past the parking lot.

"Gotta be, how many military personnel you think show up here?" Jet replied.

"When did they start letting Playboy bunnies into the military?" Skyler asked, grinning.

"I dunno," Jet said, her tone sly. "But she's definitely hot…"

"Let's get in there," Skyler said, shaking her head.

She walked inside the building and signed in. The security guard directed her to the room where her meeting was being held. Outside the room, she shifted her neck around, hearing it pop. Glancing through the door window she saw there were a lot of people seated in the room, so she imagined that she was one of the last to arrive. She took a deep breath and blew it out slowly, then reached for the door.

Walking in, she was the picture of military precision and efficiency. She walked to the podium and when everyone quieted down she smiled.

"Good morning. I'm Captain Shenin Devereaux-Hancock, most people just call me Dev, and I'm your new Air Force Aviation Liaison."

Printed in Poland
by Amazon Fulfillment
Poland Sp. z o.o., Wrocław